Through the Wilderness

Through
the
Wilderness

Janice Cole Hopkins

AMBASSADOR INTERNATIONAL
GREENVILLE, SOUTH CAROLINA & BELFAST, NORTHERN IRELAND
www.ambassador-international.com

Through the Wilderness

ISBN: 978-1-62020-850-2
eISBN: 978-1-62020-882-3

Cover Design & Typesetting by Hannah Nichols

AMBASSADOR INTERNATIONAL
Emerald House
411 University Ridge, Suite B14
Greenville, SC 29601, USA
www.ambassador-international.com

AMBASSADOR BOOKS
The Mount
2 Woodstock Link
Belfast, BT6 8DD, Northern Ireland, UK
www.ambassadormedia.co.uk

The colophon is a trademark of Ambassador, a Christian publishing company.

I will make a pathway through the wilderness.

- Isaiah 43:19c -

Chapter One

CHANGES

FAITH ALLEN LUGGED THE HEAVY crate from the cabin and hoisted it into the back of the wagon. Uncle Jed had helped with the carrying through the morning, but, at lunch, he said his back had started to give him fits, and he hadn't moved from the rocker since then. Faith put her hand on her back to brace it as she walked back to the cabin for another load. She knew how he felt. Pain shot through her back as if a logger had taken an ax to it, but she knew better than to slow or complain.

"You're a young'un," Aunt Mabel would say, "and you're plenty able to tote and work. Not like us old folks who're about plumb wore out."

She glanced up at her uncle rocking on the porch. Since he'd slowed down, he hadn't remained quite as skinny as he'd been at one time, but he still looked muscular and fit. His hair had turned white, and his skin had a wrinkled leathery look. His expression never changed much. Faith wouldn't call it a scowl, but she'd rarely seen the man smile. He usually showed very little emotion at all.

"Are we goin' to git this done today?" Aunt Mabel asked as she poked her head from the cabin. Her dull gray hair almost glowed in the rays of the setting sun. She didn't have as many wrinkles as her husband, but she had gained weight in recent years, and that seemed to stretch out her skin. "Robust" would describe her better than "fat," though. Aunt Mabel had a perpetual frown, as if she expected life to be hard, and it had yet to disappoint her. Faith had never seen the woman act loving toward anyone. She didn't act cruel, but she never showed affection either.

Faith shook her head. What had come over her? She should count her blessings that she had a home at all. Her aunt and uncle had taken her in after her parents died, and she could have had it worse. Life had been hard in the Kentucky mountains, but they'd managed to keep enough to eat most of the time and a roof over their heads. Sometimes Faith wondered what would happen to her after the McCraes died, but she'd tackle that problem when it came. *Forgive me, Lord, for unkind thoughts, and put into me a thankful heart, I pray.*

"Reckon if we don't, we'll just finish up in the morning," Uncle Jed finally answered. "Don't guess hit makes a hill of beans difference. Hit'll still be a mighty long road to Californy."

"You said we'd have a long layover in Missouri, though, didn't you?" Aunt Mabel wanted clarification.

"Yeah. I didn't see no ways around hit and not have to travel through the harsh of winter. We'll have to wait in Independence 'til the sprang grasses come in, so we'll winter thar."

Aunt Mabel gave a nod. "I'm glad our son had that friend whose mama said we could have rooms in her boarding house if Faith would help with the work. That shore will make thangs a whole lot easier."

Faith wanted to ask when they were supposed to meet up with the other travelers headed for Independence, but she held her tongue. Her aunt and uncle wanted her to be seen and not heard, as they'd told her often enough.

She had mixed feelings about this trip. The McCraes' son had gone to California when he first heard about the gold found there. He'd written that he had struck it rich and asked his parents to come out and join him. He hadn't wanted Faith to come along, but when his folks refused to come unless she did, he'd reluctantly agreed.

Faith couldn't help but be excited about the adventure of it all, but she dreaded leaving the safety of what she knew. It had surprised her that her aunt and uncle had agreed to move, because they'd always been pretty set in their ways.

"Let that be the last load for tonight," Uncle Jed told her, as he eased up from the rocking chair. "Go ahead and start gettin' supper on the table. I'm a mite hungry."

"Yes, sir."

Faith looked over the stuffed wagon as she set her last load in it. Only the last minute things that they'd need tonight or in the morning remained in the cabin. They'd be able to leave in the morning.

She turned and stared at the little log cabin in order to memorize the image. Her throat clogged up at the thought this would be her last night here. It didn't look like much, but it and the surrounding garden, field, and woods had been her home since she'd come here at ten years of age, almost a decade ago. She'd done a lot of her growing up in this place.

Well, no time for loitering with work to be done. She'd walked her trails through the forest last Sunday and said most of her good-byes then, but she decided to go to her favorite spot one more time in the morning. She would get up early, before anyone else stirred, take the lantern, and slip away for some quiet time.

How many times had she done that in the past, especially on Sundays? The spot beside the creek had become her favorite church.

The next morning, she sat beside the creek before the sun showed its face. Not far from the house, it remained hidden, and she felt secluded. She didn't give dangers but a passing thought. The fire in the lantern should keep the wildlife away. This felt like home to her.

Thoughts of worry about this trip and the future wanted to push in, but she held the door shut and refused to let them. Only God knew what the future held, and He'd see her through. He always had.

She voiced some of the Bible verses she'd memorized over the years. They always helped her stay positive, even after her parents had died. It's what they'd taught her to do.

Some would deem her life here with her aunt and uncle hard, but she'd learned to be thankful for it. Even though they weren't nurturing, neither were they abusive, and they'd kept her from worse situations. If she'd had a meager existence, she'd learned to make do and improvise. If she had to work diligently, then she'd learned to do all the tasks she would need in taking care of her own family someday. She bowed her head, thanked her Lord and asked for His continued care and guidance as she journeyed into the unknown.

———

"Well, there you are, Jakey. I've been looking for you. I'm afraid you've quite caught my fancy."

Jacob Parker hated the name "Jakey," but when he looked at the gorgeous woman in front of him, his irritation dissipated into the crisp September air of evening. At the age of twenty, Lucille had everything a man looked for in beauty. She had light strawberry blonde hair, creamy white skin, and eyes as green as grass, which blazed according to her moods. Surprised she had noticed him at all, he stood a little taller.

Jacob had always felt he stayed on the fringes of the high society around Richmond. He'd grown up the youngest son of a wealthy planter, but his older brother, Charles, would inherit the plantation. Occasionally, he'd been invited to some affairs, like this harvest ball, but he'd been away to college and had rarely been home lately.

"I'm flattered, Miss Staten."

"Lucille. You must call me Lucille. Would you like to stroll in the garden with me?" Her hand came out to rest upon his arm. The gentleness of it sent warmth up his arm like hot molasses. "I know it's cooling off this evening, but I need a turn of fresh air after all the dancing I've done."

"I would be honored, and afterwards, perhaps you would also save a dance for me."

"That sounds delightful."

Lucille looked around the back area of the house. "Where's that girl of mine? She's supposed to stay close, but, when I need her, she's nowhere to be seen. Would you be a dear and fetch my stole? Mother will be furious with me if I go into the night air heated as I am. She'll declare I'll catch my death from cooling off too quickly."

"Of course, where is it?"

"It's in my room, the closest door to the top of the stairs. It should be lying across my bed. I distinctly recall telling Mavis to put it out in case I should require it."

"Your bedroom?"

"Yes. I'd go myself, but I am quite spent after the last Virginia reel. Why, I do think I must have danced every dance, and my limbs feel quite wobbly. Oh, pardon my forwardness. I spoke before I thought."

"Think nothing of it. I'll be right back. Why don't you step inside, while you wait?"

"How considerate of you. You're just the sweetest thing."

Her batting eyelashes made the entire scene seem too theatrical and a bit overdone, but Jacob felt too stunned to let it bother him. He'd rarely given the female gender any concerted effort, but he'd now finished his studies, and courting had become more feasible. He couldn't help feeling a sense of pride in Lucille's sugary attention.

Jacob quickly climbed the steps and entered Lucille's room without a problem. This all seemed strange to him. Lucille had never noticed him before, and, although he didn't know all the social graces as well as Charles, he knew he shouldn't be in a woman's bedroom.

Thankfully, the wrap lay on the bed right where Lucille had said it would be. He picked it up and turned to leave when she came in and shut the door.

"I got to thinking and didn't know if Mavis actually pulled the stole from my bureau, but I see she did. Here let me take that now." She stepped close and reached for the shawl.

The door burst open and Mrs. Staten let out a blood-curdling scream. "What are you doing here with my daughter?" she screeched.

"Jacob just came up here to help me out, Mother," Lucille answered for him. "We were going down for a stroll in the garden, and I needed my wrap. We haven't been here long."

"I know why a man goes to a woman's bedroom, Lucille. Even if what you said is true, which I doubt, your reputation is quite ruined now."

"No one needs to know." Lucille smiled.

"I'm afraid that's not true," Mr. Staten said, as he entered the room. "Look." He indicated a group of people standing at the bottom of the stairs and staring up through the door Mrs. Staten had left open. "They all heard my wife scream. I think I'd better have a word with you in my office, young man."

"The only recourse I see here is for you to wed my daughter. I hope you can see that."

Jacob sat silently. Marry Lucille? Jacob had never thought such a thing to be possible. Why, Lucille had become the most favored woman in Virginia and probably in the entire country. Men from as far away as Maine had courted her.

"I've made plans to leave for Oregon before spring, sir. I'm the youngest son, and this seems the best way to obtain a place of my own."

"I thought you'd just graduated college."

"I have, because that's what my parents wanted, but I like farming, and would like to start a place to hand down to my children someday."

"I think that might actually work out for the best. To be honest with you, I'm afraid we've spoiled Lucy terribly. We had her late in life, fifteen years after her brother had been born, and we've catered to her every whim. I think she still needs to learn responsibility and do some growing up. Pioneering may be just the thing for her. Marrying her is the only honorable thing for you to do under the circumstance, and the sooner, the better. Rumors are going to be flying after today."

Jacob felt hooked and pulled in like a bass. He didn't know if he was ready for marriage, didn't want to be caught like this, but he seemed to have little choice in the matter now and still be an honorable man. Perhaps marrying Lucille wouldn't be such a bad idea. He'd need a wife when he got to Oregon, and he'd heard women were in short supply in the West.

"Of course, I'll finance your trip as the biggest part of Lucy's dowry. I even have a friend in St. Louis who's helped outfit some emigrants. I'll wire him to start purchasing the things you'll need."

"That's very generous, sir."

"Good. It's all settled then. We'll plan for the wedding in about a month, and you and Lucy can spend the holidays here and then have a delayed honeymoon in St. Louis. I'll take care of all the details. Welcome to the family, son."

Jacob took the hand extended to him. He felt conflicting emotions of elation and dread. What was he doing? Well, he might be forced into matrimony, but it would be to the prettiest woman he'd ever seen.

———

"Here, let me help you, Miss Faith," Dexter hurried to take the two pails of water she'd been carrying up from the river. "You work way too hard."

"Well, that's just the way it is. There's a lot of work to be done." Faith didn't know why it bothered her for Dexter to call her "Miss Faith" instead of "Miss Allen," but it did. She'd been trying to hold him at arm's length, but it didn't always work.

"You need a man to take care of you." He gave her a grin that seemed to stretch from ear to ear. Dexter didn't look that bad. When he got over his gangly youthfulness, he'd probably be a handsome man, but he seemed so immature and carefree now. However, she'd have to admit she liked his smiles and his cheerfulness, and he did seem to lift her spirits.

"What you doin' over here again, pup?" Uncle Jed bellowed. "Haven't we had to shoo you off enough already?"

"I'm just carrying the water buckets up." To Dexter's credit, he didn't cower.

"And what makes you thank Faith ain't able of carrying her own buckets?"

"I wanted to be a gentleman, Mr. McCrae."

"Go grow into a man first."

Dexter set the buckets down, tipped his hat to Faith, and gave her a hidden wink. "I'll be going, then. Good day to you, Miss Faith, Mr. McCrae." He nodded to each, turned, and left at a normal pace.

"You don't need to be encouragin' that young feller."

"I try to dissuade him, but he doesn't seem to pay my attempts any mind."

"Well, try harder. You're both too young, especially him. How old is he, anyhow? About fifteen?"

"He says he's sixteen but will be turning seventeen soon."

"Humph. Too young to be sniffin' 'round here. Maybe I'll commence to gettin' up the water myself, and you can get an earlier start on fixin' our vittles. If he don't stay out from around this wagon, I'm a gonna take my shotgun after him. You understand me?"

"Yes, sir. Perhaps you should have a talk with his father, too."

"That's not a bad idee. I thank I might do just that."

Chapter Two

MISSOURI

"PLEASE SAY WE CAN STAY here instead of leaving for Independence tomorrow," Lucille begged. "You know I'm not going to be suited to life on the trail. Why, I've never even boiled water before."

She moved close to Jacob, put her arms around his neck, and looked up at him with big, pleading eyes. She only acted interested in him when she wanted to get her way.

"I plan to farm in Oregon Territory, Lucille. You knew that when we married." They'd had this argument over and over again, since arriving in St. Louis, and Jacob had grown tired of it.

She stomped her foot as if she were killing a spider and backed off. Her pretty face twisted into a grimace. "You just don't love me."

Jacob could have said the same thing to her, but he didn't. His marriage certainly hadn't worked out the way he'd hoped.

Lucille had been very cordial until they were married, but, from their wedding night on, she'd turned cold and unresponsive. Had Lucille wanted to marry someone else, perhaps someone her parents didn't approve of? Well, he'd agreed to marry her and made his vows before God, and he intended to live up to them. It would be futile to speculate about the past. He just didn't want her to regret marrying him and hoped she still wanted him as her husband. The way things had been going, however, that didn't look promising.

He turned his back to Lucille and looked out the window. If he were honest with himself, he'd been willing enough to marry her. In fact, he'd been flattered and proud to marry the belle of Virginia. The wedding had certainly been the most lavish affair he'd ever attended, and Lucille had taken his breath away. Now, she only used her wiles on him when she wanted something.

He turned around and looked at her sitting on the edge of the bed pouting. No doubt she had always used her beauty to get what she wanted. If she'd been a more willing partner, he would have probably spoiled her rotten, too. He tried to tell himself she had been a victim of circumstance just like him, but the longer they were married, the less amicable she became. He feared the arduous trip to Oregon would fast make them enemies, for, as things looked now, he expected Lucille would fight him all the way.

"Well, can we at least go to the opera tonight? I hear the touring group is quite good for a backwoods village." She spit the words out like the venom of a snake.

"I'd hardly call St. Louis 'a backwoods village,' and we'll need to get an early start in the morning."

"But this is the last chance for culture, perhaps in my whole life." Her voice sounded resigned and didn't carry her usual whiny tone.

"Very well, if it would make you happy, we'll go, but you know I don't enjoy opera." Sometimes giving in took more valor than refusing to concede.

"Thank you for your generosity." Now the words dripped with sarcasm and made him regret agreeing to go.

He sighed and hurried to dress, as she began to choose a gown. That could take a long time depending on her mood. He would get dressed, while Lucille kept her eyes averted—her choice not his. Then, he'd go downstairs to the hotel lobby and wait, because Lucille would have a hotel maid help her dress, and she wouldn't want him there.

The wagon trip across Missouri to Independence had been as strained as Jacob had feared. Lucille remained upset the whole time and rarely spoke. If Jacob thought she'd been cold before, she now seemed frozen through and through. He'd done all the cooking and chores, because Lucille had refused to lift a finger to help.

He looked over at her. "Honey, let's make the best of things. It'll be easier on both of us if we choose to be positive."

"Be easier for you, you mean. What do you expect me to feel when you lead me across Misery, and things are sure to get worse?"

She'd almost made a joke by twisting the state's name. He looked at her hopefully, but her face still frowned in displeasure.

"I can't eat this stuff." Lucille dropped her plate of ham and beans on the ground and stomped to the wagon.

"I know I'm not the best cook," Jacob told her, "but you're welcome to do the cooking if you can do better."

"I've never done menial tasks, and you know it. You could have at least taken the slave Father offered to send with us. I have no intention of being your servant on this trip."

"You know how I feel about slavery." Jacob actually almost regretted not bringing the Negro. For her help along the way, he could have freed her when they got to Oregon. That would have only delayed things, however, because Lucille would still need to work on the farm when they got there, and he wouldn't be able to hire anyone to help her until they got well-established.

"I don't understand you," she continued. "You were born into a family who depends on slaves, just like mine. You grew up with slavery. What's wrong with it?"

"I think everyone should be treated with respect and not be some-one's property. Besides, there's to be no slavery in Oregon Territory."

"Pooh, all the more reason not to go there. Don't think I'm going to do the housework for you. Be smart, and turn back now. We don't even have to go back to Virginia. I'd be happy to build our life in St. Louis. Why, there's plenty of opportunities there for an intelligent young man like you. With me by your side, it's no telling how far you could go. I could probably make you governor eventually."

"I'm not interested in politics, Lucille. I want to farm. Charles will inherit our plantation, but I want to own a farm of my own."

"I hope you'll reconsider. We could go on to Independence, sell our outfit for a profit, come back on a packet, and begin anew in St. Louis. I'd be ever so grateful." She looked at him pleadingly and batted her lashes. Didn't she know how obvious her ploys were?

If he thought she'd be a loving wife in St. Louis, then he'd take her back there, but he knew better. She had shown him over and over again that when he gave into her wishes her pleasure wouldn't last long. If he had to resign himself to a loveless marriage, he might as well do what he thought best. "I'll re-examine the situation when we get to Independence."

"That's better than nothing," but she looked skeptical. She was learning him, too. "Why didn't we plan to take the packet from St. Louis to Independence? It's still too cold to be camping out."

"Your father's friend would only outfit us in St. Louis, and I thought it would be good to get familiar with a wagon and camping before we left for the West. You know, it's been mild for the last few days. Perhaps we'll have an early spring. In addition, your father approved of me taking you to Oregon."

"I can't understand that at all. It's almost as if he were trying to get rid of me, punish me or something. I'd like to give him a piece of my mind." Lucille pursed her lips as if she felt she'd said too much. She had become such a complicated puzzle to try to figure out.

"Perhaps he thought a change would be good for you."

"He just knew if I stayed there, I'd come running to him when you were unreasonable, which is most of the time. Really, Jake, you're so selfish."

She only called him Jake when she became upset. She knew he preferred Jacob. Come to think of it, she always called him Jake, except when she wanted to cajole him, and then he became Jakey. He hated that one even more.

He cleaned up from supper and spread out his bedroll underneath the wagon. He would have preferred to share the warmth of his wife, but he certainly wouldn't be welcome inside tonight, if ever again.

Before morning he would probably regret not pitching the tent, but he felt too tired and frustrated to worry with it now.

———————————

"What in tarnation? Have you ever seed the likes of this?" Uncle Jed looked out at the sprawling city of Independence, Missouri, and the bustling people.

"I've never seed so many people in all my born days," Aunt Mabel declared. "Have you, girl?"

Faith didn't answer because her aunt didn't expect her to. Salisbury might have been about this size, but that had been a long time ago, when her parents were alive, and she didn't remember the town clearly. Besides, she felt sure it never had this much activity.

"This ain't nothing," a boy of about twelve said as he ran along beside the wagon. "Just you wait. The closer it gets to spring, the more people'll come. Why, by April, it's sometimes impossible to even walk down the streets."

"You don't say?" Uncle Jed seemed almost flabbergasted.

"Thar." Aunt Mabel pointed up ahead. "Thar's Lullamay's Boarding House. Ain't it big and purty?"

The boarding house might have been big from the outside, but the rooms they'd been given seemed small, even after being used to a cramped cabin. Faith's looked more the size of a roomy outhouse with only a tiny cot as furniture. A little shelf beside the bed held a candle, and pegs on the wall would hold her clothes. Uncle Jed and Aunt Mabel's might be a bit bigger, but it didn't have any extra room for two people.

"Well, I guess it beats staying in the wagon and camping out over the winter," Aunt Mabel said, although her voice sounded uncertain.

By March, Faith knew what the boy had been talking about. The population of Independence had swelled to at least three times what it had been when they'd first arrived.

Faith had spent all of her time working in the boarding house, however, so she'd had no time to fight the crowds anyway. Changing beds, doing laundry, cooking—the tasks never ended. Faith dreaded the laundry most of all. Her hands seemed as rough and dry as those dusty ears of last year's corn. Sometimes they cracked open and became sore.

There hadn't even been a day of rest on Sunday here. They'd lived too far from a church to attend one in Kentucky, but at least she'd been able to read her Bible and have a day with few chores, other than the necessary ones. Now she worked from sunup to sundown seven days a week with no break. She had to admit Lulamay worked just about as hard, but the rooms usually stayed filled, so the work never ceased.

As much as she'd tried to discourage Dexter, she would have loved to see his smiling face and have a minute to talk with him. She wondered where his family had wintered and how they'd fared. Well, it wouldn't be much longer now. Soon they'd leave the boarding house, take their wagon, and camp with the rest of their group. Faith looked forward to that day. Surely it wouldn't be as demanding as this, or, if so, it would have some changing scenery along the way.

━━━━━━━━━━━━━━

Independence was mayhem, the wildest place Jacob had ever seen. The town bulged with people of every sort and station in life. Some were selling, some were buying, and many were trying to get ready to travel to Santa Fe, California, or Oregon.

The throng even included pickpockets, thieves, and swindlers. With so many people milling around, it became almost impossible to make one's way down the streets. Lucille didn't try to venture far from the wagon because she ended up being bumped, shoved, and bruised every time she did. Jacob guessed some of it came from men taking advantage of the situation to touch such a beauty.

Even when dusk fell, they could still hear the wagon builders hammering, horses whinnying, and oxen bellowing. Sleep didn't come easily, and Lucille became even more irritable.

They were camped outside of town with a large group of other emigrants. In the middle of March, all the travelers waited for the grass on the prairie to green up enough to support the grazing of the livestock. The men were hoping it would be soon, because they were anxious to be underway.

Jacob quickly realized Lucille wasn't the only woman reluctant to make this journey. Several of the wives were not speaking to their husbands. Most of the men were confident this would be a temporary state of affairs. "Once we get on the road, the women will adjust," they assured him.

Jacob wondered if they were trying to convince him or themselves. It looked as if many of the men were pulled to a new western horizon by some invisible rope. Their ancestors must have felt much the same when they came to America. Would Oregon Territory be enough to hold them, or would they always want to move on, to find something better? Jacob knew he wanted to settle down.

He feared Lucille would only grow more dissatisfied, however, as they traveled farther away from civilization. A vast chasm existed between some of the women, who saw the possible dangers all too clearly, and their men, whose sense of danger often failed them as they sought adventure.

He couldn't help but wonder why Lucille had married him in the first place. She'd seemed enthralled with him at first, but maybe it had just been a temporary infatuation. As the wedding approached, she'd seemed to have a strong case of nerves. She even became upset enough to be vomiting, but it had passed. Jacob had assumed most women were frightened of their wedding night, but he may have been wrong in this case. *Lord, please help us to work all this out. Help us to have a good marriage, one that honors Thee.*

As he looked around and talked with others, Jacob realized that Mr. Black, the man in St. Louis that Lucille's father had chosen to outfit them, had done an excellent job. He had packed the wagon with all the necessary items in a compact and practical manner. He'd even left Jacob an inventory of everything and how some of it should be used.

In addition to the wagon and supplies, he had six oxen to pull his wagon, and six more to use to keep the first team from becoming tired and worn. They had a milk cow and three chicken coops with four hens and a rooster. Jacob also had a sturdy riding horse, which would be especially needed when the men hunted buffalo. Yes, everything, looked promising, except for his wife and her attitude.

"You're right smart to choose oxen over mules or horses," an old scout told Jacob. "Horses jist can't hold out pullin' a load that fer, 'cross the prairie, through the desert, and o'er mountains. Mules might be faster, but the oxen are sturdier, able to graze better, and more suited fer the long haul. Yes siree, you got hit right. I've never seed a wagon packed any better. You should do jist fine. Some of these folks'll be lucky to make hit. Their food's liable to give out afore they're halfway thar."

"I thought there would be outposts where we could buy supplies if needed."

"Thar's some forts where you might do that, but hit'll cost you an arm and a leg, that is if'n they're not outa supplies from folks who've already passed through. No, you're better off tryin' to carry enough with you, 'cept for some fresh meat you might kill on the way. With jist you and the missus, I'd say you've got plenty, though."

That was good to know. Although he couldn't hide his excitement about the adventure, a grain of trepidation over the dangers involved still nagged at him. It wouldn't be so bad if he only had himself to consider, but he had Lucille also. Their marriage might have a rocky start, but he certainly didn't want any harm to come to her.

Jacob had been praying things would get better between them. He realized he'd agreed to the wedding before giving it much thought, and he definitely hadn't consulted God. His mother had taught him better than that. But, this involved extenuating circumstances, he told himself.

After they'd been caught together in her bedroom, what else could he have done and still be honorable? Lucille had been willing enough during their brief courtship. Why had she become so unwilling after the wedding? He'd tried to treat her special and show his love, and he had loved her at first. It may not have been the deep-rooted, all-consuming love he'd hoped for, but it could have been the beginning of that. Now, he found himself becoming more and more disillusioned, as she became increasingly difficult. *Lord, help us both.*

Chapter Three

WAGON TRAIN

THE PARKERS HAD STAYED IN Independence until the first of April. It had rained much of the time, and most of the talk revolved around starting the journey. At least the rains had finally brought green grass to the area, and their boring wait would finally be over.

The rain made it harder to cook, so Jacob had humored his wife and ordered some of their suppers from a restaurant. It made things easier on him, too.

Jacob had met with the other men. They'd hired Wayland Marshall as the wagon master of the train and Obadiah Wilson, the seasoned mountain man who'd given Jacob advice, as their scout. They'd asked Jacob to run in the election for the council, but he'd refused at first. "I'm just a tenderfoot at this," he told them.

"But, you've got a good head on your shoulders, son," John Brenner had said.

Jacob appreciated the vote of confidence, but he didn't know that he wanted the responsibility. He agreed to run in the end, however, and the people elected him. He hadn't realized he'd made such a favorable impression on his fellow travelers. He'd be the youngest man on the council.

"You're going to regret this," Rex Caulder said, as he stomped off. He'd lost in the election for the council.

The forty-seven wagons started off at a slow, plodding pace. Jacob rubbed his forehead and glanced at his wife in the wagon seat beside him. Lucille sat straight and rigid with the look of a stone sculpture. She wore a pretty brown traveling suit and a straw bonnet. She'd refused to wear a sunbonnet, like the other women, and said this straw monstrosity was concession enough.

Jacob had secretly bought enough cotton fabric for her to make some things she might need and hadn't packed. He could hire a lady to sew them if need be. He'd also purchased her a sturdy pair of shoes and three aprons, but he planned to give them to her as they were needed. Mr. Staten had bestowed five hundred dollars on him to help them on the trip and make sure they stayed somewhere suitable for his daughter, while they waited in St. Louis. Jacob knew that meant somewhere luxurious, but he still thought his father-in-law had been more than generous, especially since the cash came on top of the outfitted wagon. And, Jacob had a small sum he'd saved over the years, as well as some money his father had contributed. It should be enough for a solid start if he were careful.

He knew Lucille had packed three large trunks of her personal things, but they were filled with too many silks and ball gowns that she'd never be able to use, either on the trip or in Oregon. He hadn't said anything, however. There'd be time enough to dispose of them later. Perhaps they could even trade some of her shiny things along the way, but it would be easier to fight that battle when the necessity arose than to reason with her now.

The group departed with plenty of fanfare. Not only did many of the men give a shout of joy, but cattle lowed, chickens clucked in their coops, horses neighed, dogs barked, wagons clanked and jingled, and tar or grease buckets jostled from underneath.

Some of the wagons were overloaded and their sides hung with chairs, stools, tools, and swinging pails. Almost all of them bound for Oregon had a plow strapped on somewhere. Most of those headed to California had no need of a plow since they'd be looking for gold.

"Oregon here we come," Jacob whispered. He'd been eager to get underway.

"Whoopee," Lucille said sarcastically.

The wagons alternated right and left as they fell in line to form two columns. The permanent residents had to be glad to see the mob go, all except the merchants and businessmen, but there were others coming to town to take their place. Independence had quadrupled its population in the last thirty days, as spring travelers came to town.

Friendly Indians, the Otos, Kaws, and Osage, had come in to trade before they left. Jacob had traded all the tobacco he'd brought from home for a deerskin jacket. He didn't like the stuff anyway and had only brought the package at his father's insistence. It would be worth much more here than in Virginia.

He'd had a restaurant pack them a picnic lunch, hoping to placate Lucille, but she only nibbled at it during the nooning and never said a word to Jacob. He decided right then she would either learn to cook, or she'd go hungry. He'd put some beans in a covered pot to soak last night. She could begin her first cooking lesson at supper.

When they stopped for the night, they'd made fifteen miles their first day, despite the fact they'd gotten a later start than they normally would. The grass had turned green, but it hadn't gotten tall yet. Flowers dotted the backdrop of green with white blooms, pink verbena, wild indigo, larkspur, and wild geraniums. Jacob knew this because he heard the other women and girls exclaiming over them. Lucille had gazed straight ahead, never looking at anything.

"You can't be serious," Lucille scowled when Jacob informed her she would cook the beans and fry the bacon. She pulled back like a coil ready to snap.

"I have the fire going, and I'll be here to help you," he said. "I'll try to make some cornbread tonight, and you can learn to bake it another time."

They were getting a late start on supper, since he'd already un-hitched the oxen and led them to water, before turning them out with the others.

Jacob would have to stand guard soon, but his turn wouldn't be for two more nights. Each guard would be on duty for a four-hour stint, but no one would be required to serve consecutive nights. There would be two shifts each night. Every man over fourteen would be required to have his turn at guard duty in the rotation.

Lucille slammed the pots and utensils around, but she followed his directions without comment. He mixed up some cornmeal, eggs, butter, milk, and baking powder to help it rise. Then he poured the batter into a greased spider, a covered skillet with legs. He set the spider at the edge of the fire and heaped coals onto the lid.

When Lucille had the beans rinsed and boiling, he showed her how to fry the bacon. He cautioned her to keep it out of the hottest part of the fire to prevent the grease from popping out on her hands as she turned it. The bacon would be cooked before the beans and cornbread, but that would work to her advantage. She could pour the grease into the beans to season them.

They were hungry by the time supper was done. The beans were still a little chewy, but they were edible. The cornbread stuck to the pan, but it tasted fine. He bragged about the bacon, hoping to encourage Lucille, but she gave him an angry scowl.

"Should I pitch the tent for me, or shall I sleep in the wagon with you?" he asked after he'd finished cleaning up.

The glare she gave him could have frozen a cup of water in the midday desert. "Pitch the tent," she hissed.

He didn't know why he even bothered to ask because deep down, he'd known the answer. He shouldn't feel the sharp stab of rejection, but he did. He walked away looking down at his boots and told himself to be patient with her. Things would get better. But a sinking feeling within warned him that would be unlikely.

He'd just finished with the tent when Lester and Morton Agner came by. Lester was younger, shorter than his brother, and somewhat thin. Morton was slightly older, taller, and fatter. They nodded in unison like marionettes with their strings twisted together.

He smiled to himself as he realized their names suited them. Less and More.

"Hello," Jacob greeted them.

"Evening," they responded. "The folks are getting together to celebrate the completion of our first day on the road," Morton said. "It'll be a good chance for folks to meet, sing, and dance. Hope you and the missus can join us."

"Thank you for letting us know. I'll ask Lucille."

They nodded again and left. Jacob took a deep breath and went to the back of the wagon.

Lucille wanted to go, but she insisted on changing dresses. She appeared in about thirty minutes in a pretty yellow dress, only a little wrinkled from the packing.

"I'll never get used to these conditions," she grumbled.

"You look lovely, as always."

"Not as attractive as I do at home."

"You'll be prettier than anyone else here."

"Well, that's not saying much, is it?"

"Be nice, Lucy. Let's make some friends here."

"Don't call me Lucy. You know I want you to call me Lucille."

"As I want you to call me Jacob, but you rarely do."

They walked toward the music with her in a pout again. No matter how much he promised himself only to say nice things, they somehow managed to end up quarreling. It would be better if he could keep his lips sealed, but that could be hard to do.

The small band played "Oh, Susannah," as they walked up. The people were talking, singing, watching, or dancing. Benches, stools, and chairs had been set around, so Jacob led Lucille to a chair and stood beside her to watch.

"Would you like to dance, Miz Parker?" Lester asked, grinning widely. He looked to Jacob for approval. Jacob nodded slightly. Maybe someone else could coax her into a better mood.

Once the men saw Lucille might dance with them, her partners never ceased. Jacob sat down in the chair she had vacated and watched. Lucille seemed to enjoy the dancing, but, to her credit, she never gave any one man much attention, and she didn't appear to flirt, something she'd done incessantly in Virginia before they were engaged.

"You sure do have a beautiful wife."

He looked to his side to see a thin, wiry woman with gray hair pulled back in a bun. A few wrinkles lined her face, but she gave a friendly smile. He smiled back.

"Yes, I do."

"Been married long?"

"A few months. We were married in October."

"Newlyweds, huh? I'd never have guessed it. I'm Lena Haywood, by the way."

"I'm Jacob Parker and that's my wife, Lucille."

"You folks from the South?"

"From Virginia, and you?"

"We're from Kentucky."

"Why did you say you didn't think Lucille and I were recently married?"

"She's not looking at you with moon-eyes like I'd expect. You're just as handsome in your own way as she is pretty, you know. I guess all that's none of my business really, and I shouldn't have said anything." She looked abashed.

He looked at the woman again. She seemed genuinely concerned, and Jacob needed someone with whom he could talk.

"Things haven't turned out as I'd hoped. Lucille is not keen on making this trip. She's used to having slaves to wait on her, and she doesn't want to become a farmer's wife in Oregon."

"But she knew you planned this before you were married?"

"Oh, yes. She knew. She also seemed quite taken with me before we wed, but, since then, things have become more strained all the time. Perhaps she thought she'd change my mind about going to Oregon."

Lena reached out with a feathery touch and patted his arm. "It's always a bad idea to try to change a person after you marry them. Maybe things will get better when she gets used to it all. I'll be praying for that."

"Thank you. I'd appreciate your prayers, and I hope you'll keep what I've said confidential. I'd hate for word to get back to Lucille that I've been talking about her."

"Oh, I know when to keep my mouth closed. Everyone needs someone to confide in though. If you ever need to talk or want some advice, you know where to come. My Harlan says I'm just full of all kinds of advice." She laughed.

Jacob liked someone who could laugh at themselves, and he found himself liking Lena Haywood more and more. He looked out at Lucille. He'd be happy if he could get her to even smile. That didn't happen often anymore, and, when she did, it looked as if it had been painted on by an inexperienced artist, because the smile never reached her eyes or lit her face.

He got up. "Well, it's time I danced with my wife."

The musicians started a slow song, and he pulled Lucille into a waltz. She started to tense up and move stiffly, but she soon relaxed and moved closer. She sure knew how to dance and matched his moves without effort. She felt so good in his arms he didn't want the dance to end.

"Thank you, darling, that was wonderful," he whispered as the dance ended.

"Yes, it was nice," she replied.

Maybe there was hope for them after all. Perhaps he should have never taken her away from all she knew—the servants, the dances, the social engagements. But her father had thought it best. Were Mrs. Haywood's prayers already starting to work? He sure hoped so.

The celebration began to break up, so he led Lucille back to the wagon. Afraid he might say the wrong thing and bring up more disagreements, Jacob said nothing. But he walked with his arm around her waist, and she didn't pull away.

She hesitated for a moment at the back of the wagon. "Give me about ten minutes to undress and then come to bed in the wagon, if you'd like," she said.

"All right."

He helped her into the wagon and sat down on the wagon seat to take off his boots and give her some time. He couldn't recall the last time she'd invited him to share the night with her, and he smiled into the darkness. Things were looking up.

Faith sat beside the dying embers of their campfire and listened to the music. It had been a long time since she'd heard any more than her own voice singing in the woods of Kentucky. The music touched her, and she almost wished she could go to the dance.

Did she still remember how? Her father used to dance around the parlor and kitchen with her and her mom some evenings. They'd laugh and have a good time as they sang or hummed their own music. She sighed. Those times were long gone.

But maybe there would be new opportunities. Maybe next time Uncle Jed wouldn't forbid her to go to the gathering.

"I won't have you goin' out there and gallivantin' with inny men," he'd said. "That boy who kept hangin' 'round on the trip to Independence wuz bad enough, but I'll not have you steppin' out here."

Faith didn't understand what the problem could be. Didn't they want her to ever marry? Marriage would solve the problem of their son not wanting her in California. Marriage would give her a place to feel at home and a true family. She hadn't had that, not since her parents had died.

She gave another sigh but then smiled. God would work things out. She just needed to be patient. Besides, she'd likely feel out of place with all those people around, especially if someone asked her to dance. Would someone ask her to dance?

Well, that was a moot question right now. She went back to reading her Bible. The Psalms always comforted her.

Chapter Four

KAW AND BIG BLUE

THE NEXT MORNING DIDN'T GO smoothly. Jacob got up, started the fire, and put on the coffee and biscuits. He left Lucille with instructions to fry some bacon and then three eggs, while he went for the team and brought up the cow to milk. She'd allowed the bacon grease to get too hot and it popped out on her hand. She had fried the eggs too early, and they were cold before he got back. In the meantime, the biscuits had overcooked and were hard on the bottom, but they ate it all anyway. He had planned to have Lucille wash the dishes while he hitched the team, but since she'd burned her hand, he did them. He barely finished in time to pull his wagon into line.

They were in the middle of the first division of wagons today. Each day the last wagon from the day before would move to the head of the train. In that way, everyone would eventually take every position. Since the back of the line got much more dust, everyone preferred to be near the front.

The trail had begun to get rough, as the wagons rolled and jolted over rocks and ruts, but at least they had a semblance of a road if you could call it that. Jacob didn't think it would last much longer, though. Many of the women and children were already walking to keep from being bounced and bruised.

"If you'd rather walk, it might be easier," Jacob told Lucille.

"If you think I'm going to walk two thousand miles, you're crazy. Besides, my shoes would be gone in a day."

"I bought you a practical pair of shoes in Independence. They're in the back of the wagon under your cot if you want to get them. I knew you'd need some before we got to Oregon."

She thought a minute, rose without saying a word, and went into the wagon. She returned wearing the new shoes. He stopped the wagon and helped her down. She trod along beside the wagon. Jacob wanted to talk with her, but the noise from the wagons and the distance made a conversation impractical, if not impossible.

He liked watching her, though. He liked her walking beside him, and he wished it signified her willingness to walk beside him and support him through everything life brought their way.

She looked up at him, and he smiled at her. She turned her face away.

He let his thoughts drift. Last night had not been the reconciliation for which he'd longed. Once he settled in beside her on the cot and pulled her into his arms, she stiffened up again and grew unresponsive. His kisses met unyielding, cold lips. She didn't refuse him, but she didn't give anything. Was it him? Was he doing something wrong? Were they always going to be mismatched? He kept trying to give his best, but she didn't seem to reciprocate. She didn't even appear to put forth any effort to make their marriage work. *Lord, help me. I can't do this without some cooperation from her. Show me what to do. Help us to communicate better.*

"I can't walk another step," Lucille said at the nooning. She did look exhausted. "It's going to take a while to get these new shoes broke in."

"Maybe you can try lying on the cot for a while. It may still be way too bumpy, but the padding may make it less bruising. You could give it a try."

"I guess." She swatted a strand of hair that had come loose.

Lucille stayed in the wagon for about three hours. She got down and walked again for a couple of hours before they stopped for the night. She looked tired, but she stood ready to help with supper. They ate beans left over from the night before, and Jacob cut two slices from the ham and Lucille fried them, and he made biscuits again. He placed them farther out from the flames and told Lucille to turn the spider half-a turn in about fifteen minutes. They came out better than before.

They ate, cleaned up, and went to bed. Jacob slept under the wagon. He felt too tired to pitch the tent, and he'd have guard duty tomorrow. Driving the team and doing most of the chores had worn him down. He would have to come up with another way to get everything done. He fell asleep before he had time to think about it.

The next day went pretty much the same, except Jacob walked beside the wagon, too, while he drove the team of oxen. He saw that most of the men with oxen walked beside their animals, and Jacob's were docile animals and easy to drive. They didn't require reins like the mules, but they were directed with a whip. Jacob found he didn't need to use the whip on his. They'd been well trained and only needed a touch, but usually, they didn't even require that. They seemed to know their job and followed the wagon ahead of them.

He found walking to be smoother than being on the swaying, bumping, jolting wagon seat. He would also be one less thing the team would have to pull.

They ate a cold meal of leftover ham and biscuits at the nooning, and Jacob asked around about getting some help. He learned the Agner brothers were traveling by themselves to California. He asked them, and they agreed to milk his cow mornings and evenings and to take his oxen to water before turning them out to pasture for the night. In return, they would take half the milk. They seemed happy with the arrangement since they didn't have a cow.

The days continued in a monotonous routine. They rose early, just as the light began to nudge out the darkness. Jacob continued to help Lucille fix breakfast, but she had learned to make some things. She could now cook pancakes or make porridge. Biscuits would come later.

They usually ate leftovers from either breakfast or supper the night before at the noon stop. Lucille could now make beans or a meat stew for supper, and she'd just learned to make cornbread.

He would have liked to have one of the women show Lucille how to cook. They would have known more than he did, but Lucille had refused. She hadn't made any friends, and it embarrassed her to let the other women see her ineptness. So, they struggled along as best they could, more like the blind leading the blind. He'd never done much cooking himself, but he planned to teach her as much as he could. By the time he taught her what little he knew, he hoped she would feel competent enough to allow one of the women, maybe Lena, to show her more. That way, she'd be proficient by the time they got their land in Oregon.

If Lucille hadn't wanted them to keep mostly to themselves, they could have joined with some of the others after supper. Several of the families told endless stories, almost as if they tried to fill the emptiness of the prairie with their tales.

He sent Lucille with the women to the stream Saturday afternoon to do their laundry. He stayed at the campsite to take care of the cooking. The women decided to wash the bulk of their dirty clothes every Saturday evening, so they could dry on Sunday, the lay-by day. Of course, they might wash a few pieces along in between if they needed them.

The council had decided to rest most Sundays, the Lord's Day. The teams and the people could use a day of rest. A preacher moving his family to Oregon would hold services mid-morning for those who wanted to attend.

"I don't know how to do laundry," Lucille protested.

"Just take some soap and our dirty clothes, and do what the others do. It can't be that difficult to learn."

She stomped off mad, but she went. Jacob knew she didn't want the others to think he had to do everything. They both knew some of the women had been whispering about her. People ought to learn to take care of their own households and not meddle in the affairs of others.

"How did it go?" he asked Lucille when she came back from washing clothes.

"Fine, I guess. I talked with a newly widowed woman at the creek. Her husband died not long after we left Independence. I told her about my family and your plantation. She seemed impressed with our backgrounds."

"Oh, who was it?"

Jacob wanted to tell her to keep their money situation to herself. He didn't want anyone to guess that he had a good amount with him, but, since she had tried to make a friend, he didn't want to squelch Lucille's efforts, so he kept his thoughts to himself.

"Her name's Iris Bates. She's rather attractive in a flashy sort of way, but she's older than I am."

"Is she traveling alone now?"

"I think she has some fifteen-year-old boy driving her wagon for her. She seems flattered that he appears infatuated with her." Lucille gave a look of disapproval.

Jacob raised his eyebrows but said nothing. At least she had carried on a conversation with him for a change, and he didn't want to be discouraging in any way.

"Jacob, I have something I need to tell you," Lucille said to him after breakfast on Sunday.

"Certainly. What is it?" She didn't normally begin a conversation. Perhaps things were gradually improving.

"We're expecting a baby, probably in July." Lucille lowered her eyes as she told him.

Jacob froze. This came as a total surprise, but perhaps a baby would bring them closer together. Although they weren't arguing as much, their relationship remained strained and fragile.

"That's wonderful, darling. How long have you known?"

"I've suspected since February. I'm about five months along now."

"Why didn't you tell me earlier?" Or, more pointedly, why didn't she use this to keep them in St. Louis and off the Oregon Trail?

"I didn't know how you'd take it, and I didn't want to use the baby as a means to have my way. I was afraid you'd resent us both if I did." She looked up at him now.

He'd never seen this side of Lucille before, and he didn't know how to react. His thoughts became so jumbled he had to pause and sort them out before he could say anything.

"I'd never resent our baby," he reassured her. "Why aren't you showing more? Is everything all right?"

"I've been binding myself, so I wouldn't show, but that's getting harder to do, and I need to stop. Everything's fine. The baby's been moving, and I feel good."

Jacob moved closer to her and pulled her into a gentle embrace. "I wish you'd told me sooner, so I could share this with you. We should be close to Oregon before the birth, but I hope the trip won't be too hard on you. I'll continue to do as much as I can to help you, and the other women will help if you need them."

She put her head on his shoulder and sniffed back the tears. He held her closer.

"Don't worry. I'll take care of you. We can even turn back if you want. We're not all that far out of Independence now. We can sell our rig like you wanted and take a packet back to St. Louis. I'm sure I can find some sort of work there."

"I'm not worried, Jacob. I'm just amazed at how supportive and caring you are. I know I've put you through a lot, and I want you to know I appreciate all you've done. I hope I can make you the wife you need."

"I do care about you, Lucille. Don't you know I love you and the baby? I'll always try to do what I think is best for you both. You can depend on me."

He didn't know what path his love had taken. It often felt as if he navigated uncharted trails through a wilderness.

This hadn't turned out to be the love he wanted or expected to have for his wife. Lucille still remained an enigma in many ways and acted so bad-tempered she'd made it hard for his love to grow. He did care for her, however, and he wanted their love to strengthen. Maybe it would, even if it only came from their feelings for their child. That would be a strong and deep love they both could share.

She looked up at him and stroked her hand down his cheek. "I know I can depend on you, Jacob, and I do appreciate you."

She raised her head higher and brushed a kiss on his lips, the first intimate gesture she'd ever initiated. He wanted to hold her and thoroughly kiss her, but he didn't. From past experience, he felt she'd freeze up again if he did. Instead, he softly returned her kiss with only his lips. She pulled back and smiled. He saw some new emotion flicker across her soft, green eyes. Was it regret?

He noticed she hadn't said she loved him, but he would take what tenderness she offered. It sure beat her stiff coldness or the arguments and anger.

Lucille went into the wagon to get ready to go to the services, and he sat thinking about what he'd just learned. It made no sense to him that she would bind her body to keep him from knowing she was expecting. He couldn't believe she'd thought he might be displeased. And, after she'd begged and pleaded for them to not go to Oregon, why hadn't she used this to get her way? None of this seemed rational to him. The baby was the best grounds she could have found for not coming on this trip, and yet she'd failed to use it. Why? He'd never understand this woman.

The wild game became more plentiful, but Jacob only went hunting a few times. He would have liked to go out more, but Lucille seemed to depend on him. She didn't fare well when he rode off for long. How ironical that she wanted him near but not too near. He guessed he liked her wanting him in any way, but it seemed a mixed blessing. Fresh meat would sure taste good.

The area held wild turkeys, deer, and an occasional elk. There were also panthers and giant gray wolves, but Jacob never mentioned those to Lucille.

They came to the Kaw River, a muddy mess that brought fear to many of the women and children because they would have to cross it.

Some hearty-looking Indians stood on the banks operating a ferry of sorts. They'd strapped some logs together and added some supports on the front and sides.

Only one wagon at a time could be transported. The ferry operators locked the wagon wheels by placing long poles through them. They also looped ropes through the hooks on the sides of the wagons and attached the lines to the edges of the logs on the ferry to keep the load stable.

Some of the men from the train mounted horses to drive the livestock across the most fordable location. They'd made sure the animals had plenty to drink before crossing, so they wouldn't stop to drink. Jacob would have liked to join the drivers, but he could feel Lucille's fear, and he knew he needed to stay with her on the ferry.

They were the third load to cross, and Jacob sighed in satisfaction. He had wanted to get this crossing over with. It must have been raining upstream, because the waters of the Kaw continued to rise, and the current continued to rush faster. The river moved rapidly, like a herd of school children pushing out to go home.

When the water splashed as their wagon entered the river, Lucille winced and drew back. She gripped his upper arm and closed her eyes when they reached the middle of the river. At least she seemed to think he offered her some security. The fact she would turn to him to keep her safe in troubled waters gave him a small measure of hope. His load made it across with no problems.

Toward the end of the train, however, the fast-rising river threatened to sweep away the ferry and its cargo, but the Indian men were strong and knew what they were doing. With straining muscles, they managed to get each load across, until they came to the last wagon.

With some hand signs and their broken English, the ferrymen indicated the last emigrants should wait until morning to join the group on the other side because the waters had become too treacherous. The wagon train planned to make camp on the north side of the Kaw since it would soon grow dark.

This wagon held an older couple. Their younger son, the only family member with them, rode with the drovers. They insisted on crossing now, so the Indians finally obliged. They were halfway across when a heavy current washed down upon them, and the entire ferry, wagon, and load, flipped over and went down.

The men on horseback tried desperately to save the couple, but the waters raged and the rapids swirled. The river held the elderly couple under, bubbling them up for only a few seconds at a time like a great throat gargling its water.

No sound could be heard from the startled crowd, except for an occasional gasp. The shock of the scene rendered everyone speechless at first.

The rescuers managed to pull the Indians out, for they were strong swimmers and knew the river. The braves were able to catch hold of some of the debris or ferry logs, which had now broken apart. The couple's son and some friends took lanterns and searched all night, but they couldn't find the victims.

They held a memorial service the next morning before they resumed their journey. The watery grave had been a stern reminder of how fragile life could be, especially on the Oregon Trail.

After the drowning, Lucille became quieter and looked more depressed. She loosened her wraps gradually until Jacob couldn't believe how rounded her belly had become. How had he not noticed it the night he'd slept beside her in the wagon?

He guessed it had been dark, he hadn't suspected anything then, and she'd had her nightgown bunched over her midsection. Besides, Lucille had never liked a lot of touching. They got together so seldom that the thought of her pregnant had never entered his mind. He worried about her now, however. She needed to keep her spirits up. He knew some women believed a woman's disposition during the nine months determined the health of her child.

He tried his best to pull her out of her doldrums. He talked to some cute little girls and had them pick bunches of wildflowers for Lucille. He asked Lena to help him, and he cooked some special dishes for supper to coax her to eat better. Lena even brought by a pie and stayed to talk with his wife, but nothing seemed to help.

Becoming desperate, he located Iris Bates, the woman Lucille had talked with while doing laundry. Perhaps she could encourage Lucille.

Iris looked him over, batted her eyelashes, and gave him a seductive smile. Maybe this hadn't been such a good idea. The woman looked more like a barmaid with her flaming red, unruly hair, low-cut bodice, and lightly painted face.

"Sure, dear. I'll be glad to come by your wagon anytime you want me."

He left as quickly as possible. He was committed to his wife, but, even if he wasn't, he still wouldn't want a woman like Iris Bates.

Chapter Five

BETWEEN

"COME GO FOR A SHORT walk with me," Jacob told Lucille one evening after supper.

The day's sun had almost died a glorious death wrapped in a shroud of blazing colors. The scenery on the plains often held a special beauty all its own if one took the time to notice.

"Talk to me," he continued when he realized she didn't intend to say anything. "Tell me what you're thinking."

"I'm going to die out here, you know." Her voice sounded resigned and so quiet he had to strain to hear her.

"You shouldn't think that. Only God knows the future. We're young and healthy, and I'm sure we'll be fine. Many others have made the trip, so there's no reason to think we won't, too."

"We've already lost two people, and there will be more before we get to Oregon."

"There're always some risks to life, sweetheart. The couple we lost should've never tried to cross the river with it raging like that. They should have taken the advice of the Indian guides. I would never take such a risk with our lives. I'll always choose the safest course."

"Was going to Oregon the safest choice?"

"Your father thought it for the best, and so did I. There are dangers in any place on this earth. Safety is never guaranteed, not even in St. Louis or Virginia. People die there too, but if you want to turn back, we will. Just give me the word, and we'll go anyplace you want."

"It's no use. Life anywhere is just too hard."

"I've tried to make it easier for you. What else can I do to help?"

She gave a strange, eerie laugh that would have sounded deranged if it'd been louder. "It's not your fault, Jacob. It's my fault and the life I lived before I found you."

What did she mean by that? "Let the past go; leave it behind. We all have regrets in the past, but we can build a new life, a better life."

"Do you think that's possible?"

"I wouldn't be going to Oregon if I didn't. I know it is. God says it is. If you have regrets in the past, ask for forgiveness and begin new and fresh. You know I'll do anything I can to make life better for you."

She turned to him, and he embraced her. She melted into his arms with her head on his chest. He put his head on top of hers and reveled in the moment. This was only the third time in their married life she had physically turned to him. It had been such a rarity that he'd been able to keep count without trying.

"You're too good for me," she mumbled.

"I want to be good to you and for you," he told her. "I want us to have a good marriage, but I need you to want that too."

She pulled back. "You don't understand."

"Then, help me to understand. Explain things to me. Trust me, Lucille."

"Not now, but talking with you has made me feel better. Thank you, Jacob. The only thing I ask of you is to be patient with me. Give me until after the baby comes. I think things will be better then."

"Okay, darling, but remember, any time you want to talk, I'm here. I want you to come to me no matter what it is. I want us to share everything, and I promise to be a good listener. I won't hold anything in the past, before you met me, against you."

"You're a good man, Jacob. I'm lucky to have you for a husband. You've been very understanding."

He wanted to be understanding. He wanted to understand her and their situation, but he didn't. He didn't understand at all. Why had she stayed so cold and distant most of the time? In the five months they'd been married, he could remember only three times she'd been tender with him, and she'd never really been loving. He knew in his heart she didn't love him, so he wondered again why she'd married him. He guessed being caught in her bedroom had forced her to. Would she ever love him?

Please, God, help us to fulfill the promises we made to each other in Thy presence. Help us to love each other and become one, as the Bible says. Guide and touch us both, so we'll become the man and wife we should be. I pray in Jesus' name. Amen.

Would the baby be the force that pulled them into a loving relationship? He hoped and prayed something would.

It seemed to Jacob his relationship with his wife would take a baby step forward and then a few giant steps backward. Today, she remained silent and sulking, as if she regretted confiding any of her feelings or thoughts. He had to make a concerted effort not to let himself get discouraged and depressed. If both of them gave in to despair, all would be lost.

As Jacob went about the day's routine, he fell back on the faith his mother had planted in him early on. He had done the best he knew how, so he needed to leave the situation in God's hands. He trusted those hands without reservation.

He could remember his mother saying, "As Christians, the task ahead of us is never as enormous as the Power within us."

When he took his team of oxen to the river for water, some of the men had tried to tease him about being hen-pecked. "You're supposed to get the little woman to look after you, not the other way around," one man laughed.

"He's so hen-pecked, he probably molts twice a year," another quipped.

"Listen," Jacob told them. "You have no idea what's going on with us, so it's best you just stay out of our business and mind your own."

No one said another thing to Jacob, but he felt sure they said plenty when he couldn't hear. But even Jacob didn't understand his relationship with Lucille. Not much of anything seemed to be going on, except for the baby. She kept growing bigger, and Jacob wondered what she would look like at nine months. Perhaps it would be twins. If everyone would be healthy, Jacob wouldn't mind twins.

"Do you want a son, like most men do?" Lucille asked him after supper one night.

She surprised him, because she rarely said anything, much less started a conversation. He glanced at her, and she looked him in the eyes for a change.

"I wouldn't be disappointed if it's a girl, but, yes, I'd like a son," he said honestly. "As a farmer, it would be good if we had a son, who could help me on the farm when he grew up some." She nodded.

"Are you feeling okay? Is there anything else I can do to help you out more?"

"I'm okay. I've just been feeling tired lately, but, from what Lena tells me, that's normal. You do plenty—more than most husbands."

"I wish I could take away all your worries or at least carry some of your burdens for you."

"I wish you could, too, but these are totally my problems. They really don't involve you."

"Of course they involve me. I'm your husband. Whatever involves you, involves me. I wish you'd confide in me. I know it would help you; it would help us."

"I can't do that, and I can't tell you why, but, believe me, it wouldn't help if I talked about it. What will help is when I can forget the past hurts and get on with my life. I'm hoping that will happen after this baby comes. I'm hoping, at some point, I can turn to you, Jacob. You've been very patient and caring with me, and you deserve more than I've given you. Right now, however, I can only ask you again to be patient with me. Wait until I heal after the baby, and I think I can be a better wife to you."

"I wish you would trust me more, but I'll try to be patient, as you ask."

What other choice did he have? He would never mistreat her, and he wouldn't leave her, either. She had given him a seed of hope, so he'd be patient and wait for that seed to germinate, grow, and produce fruit he hoped. In the meantime, he would pray.

Jacob sat on horseback looking at Big Blue. He sucked in a deep breath. This river stretched much wider and traveled even faster than the Kaw, and this time there'd be no ferry. They planned to ford the hundred yards of raging river.

First, he'd help the men drive the loose stock across. Then he'd come back and drive Lucille and their wagon to the other side. She couldn't see the river now, because their wagon came toward the last of the line today, and Jacob felt thankful for that. His wife had turned into a pessimist and just knew some tragedy would befall her before they got to Oregon Territory.

At first, he thought the animals were going to refuse to go into the current, and he didn't blame them. With some prodding, however, they plunged in. Then the task became keeping them on the path the scout had picked out as the shallowest and easiest to navigate.

The oxen seemed to set their eyes on the far banks and wade across, as if determined to get there. A few of the cows, however, were almost washed downstream. Jacob watched as some of the other men roped the wayward beasts and pulled them back on track. Jacob didn't try to help because his skill with roping left much to be desired. Eventually, however, the animals were across, and the wagons moved into place to cross.

The wagons crossed one at a time to enable others to help if need be and to keep one mishap from also taking down others. The second wagon to cross hit a hole and almost flipped but somehow managed to stay upright and get back on the right path. They lost only a crate of chickens and a sack of flour. Those would be missed, but not like the entire wagon or their lives.

With all the extra livestock across, Jacob crossed the river again to get ready to drive his wagon through. He stood near the bank and watched the wagons struggle one by one against the water's force. Sitting in their wagon beside Lucille, who already gritted her teeth and wrung her hands, made him tense and nervous.

He waited until their turn neared and he needed to pull his team up before he heaved himself up into the wagon seat. Most of the other men had done the same thing, so he hadn't held up anything.

His wagon would be near the last to cross, but he felt blessed. By the time his turn came, the river depth actually seemed to be receding and the current slowing. He guessed water from overnight rains had swelled the water at first, but the effects were beginning to wane. He managed to drive his team across without mishap, even if Lucille's fingers did turn white from her tight grip on the wagon seat. The floor of their wagon hadn't even flooded like some.

Now they would follow the Little Blue for a while. The wagon trains followed rivers as much as possible because they needed to stay close to water. It seemed like their very lives on the trail were directed by these winding, crooked rivers.

Chapter Six

THE PLATTE

THE TRIP HAD BEEN TRYING from the very beginning, but it got worse. A plague of green-headed flies and large, flying gnats hit. By day, they were relentless, and hordes of mosquitoes took over at night. The insects attacked Lucille more than they did Jacob, but no one had immunity. They made sleeping nearly impossible, and even some of the livestock whimpered with them.

Some of the people applied mud to their faces and exposed skin to help keep the bugs away, but Lucille refused to do so. Personally, Jacob thought the mud she could wash off would have been better than the red welts she couldn't, but he knew better than to voice his opinion.

One morning Lucille mixed some pancake batter. She went to the back of the wagon to get the molasses and when she got back, the batter had become black with mosquitoes. She skimmed as many as she could off the top, and cooked the rest. She knew if she made more, the pests would just cover the new batter before she could get the pancakes fried.

"I'm going to cook eggs from now on, as long as the insects are this bad," she told Jacob. "I hope the chickens keep laying."

"Don't worry," Jacob said as he gobbled his breakfast down before more landed, "they taste pretty good with a little extra meat added in."

Lucille gave him a cutting look. She didn't take it as the joke he'd meant it to be.

If insects didn't cause enough problems, the sun either baked everything within sight, or the storms the heat brought in bellowed with thunder, lightning, rain, and hail. Then, the trail turned into mud-ways, which were nearly impassible until the sun baked them dry again. When wagons did go, they made ruts in the rain-softened soil deep enough to be canals for the next rain.

In fact, the furrows in the road were so deep, the wagons swayed and tilted until they almost toppled on their sides. Some of the wagons tried to detour around the worst of them, but, by this time, the grasses were getting high, which made it difficult to see what lay beneath them.

One particularly bad hail storm struck them one night not long after Jacob had crawled into his tent. There would be no sleep until this blew over. It sounded as if artillery shelled the encampment. Jacob sat back from the opening and watched the hail bounce off the ground, some for more than a foot.

"Jacob, Jacob!" he heard Lucille call.

He threw a folded piece of canvas over his head and ran for the wagon. He didn't take time to pull on his boots, but he still had all his clothes on. Despite the canvas, he felt the hard knocks of the ice balls.

He jumped into the wagon as quickly as he could. "What's wrong?"

Lucille pointed upward. The hail had torn apart the covering on the wagon, and it had two layers. Rain poured into the wagon and drenched everything.

"Come with me. The tent seems to be holding up, so far." He guessed the daily sun had weakened the wagon canvas.

He helped Lucille down from the wagon, shared the tarpaulin with her, and they ran for the tent. It seemed awkward with one arm around Lucille's back, the other hand trying to clutch the canvas, and their sides bumping as they ran. So far, there were no leaks in the tent, but the rain had begun to run underneath it.

He snatched up the bedding before it became soaked and had Lucille spread the piece of canvas on the high corner of the tent before he spread the bedroll back out. By now, the tent seemed to be swaying from the gusts of wind. He hoped it held.

"Here you go. Rest here." He indicated for Lucille to use the bedding, but he realized she couldn't get down that low without great difficulty, so he helped ease her down.

"Thank you. I'm getting quite unsightly, I know," she said.

"Honey, you couldn't be unsightly if you tried, and you're still beautiful." However, he didn't know how she'd make it until July if she kept getting bigger. This was only May.

The storm finally played out. Lucille had been lying back, listening to the sounds.

"Go on to sleep here," Jacob told her. "I'll have a look at the wagon and try to find some dry bedding, while the tent drains out some more. If I can't find anything dry, is it all right if I lie down beside you until morning?"

"Yes, if you need to."

All the linens in the wagon seemed drenched, but he couldn't do much about it tonight, so Jacob went back to the tent and scooted in beside Lucille. She seemed to be asleep, although she could have been pretending.

After feeling so tired, Jacob felt sure he would drop off immediately, but sleep wouldn't come. His wife's warm body beside him toyed mercilessly with his thoughts, and he found himself mulling over what else he might do to bridge the gulf between them.

Everyone had damage, and much of their cargo needed drying out, so the council voted to stay where they were for another day. The women began by laying out the things that had just gotten wet and not dirty. Then they washed the dirty clothes and muddy things. It helped, although everything came out more dingy than usual from the muddy river.

Since Lucille had a hard time bending over to do the washing, Jacob gathered up their laundry and headed toward the stream. Pride wouldn't keep him from helping out and doing their laundry.

"Here, give those things to me," Lena said when she saw him. "You go on back to your wagon and start unpacking the things that need drying out."

"I don't want you to have to double your washing. I can do ours."

"Now, I know you can, and it's to your credit that you want to, but I don't have all that much. Besides, I'm sure Faith Allen will lend me a hand. She seems to like helping others, and she's a worker, that one is. You probably haven't met her, because her aunt and uncle keep her on a tight tether, if you know what I mean."

"All right, if you're sure. I do appreciate it. Lucille's already so big that it's hard for her to stoop over."

"Never you mind, now. I'm tickled to do it."

Jacob walked back to the wagon and began sorting out their wet things, which needed sunning, and Lucille walked over and spread them out on the tall, thick grass. The grass grew so high now, that she didn't have to bend much.

"Just leave my trunks," she said, "and I'll do them after we eat. I can sort through them, while you take care of your personal things and the tent. I checked in the trunks earlier, and all seemed dry, except for a few damp things on the very bottom. I'll unpack them and let you carry the trunks out to sun."

After Jacob carried Lucille's trunks out to dry, he stripped the canvas off the wagon. Someone needed to repair the rips.

"I don't suppose you sew, do you?" he asked Lucille.

"I can do crewel work, but I've never made or repaired clothing." She must have seen the puzzled look on his face, because she added, "Crewel work is embroidery, decorative needlework. Why'd you ask?"

"We need to repair the wagon covering."

"I can try and see what I can do. At least I can thread a needle, and I do have needles, thread, and a thimble."

Jacob smiled. Lucille had made progress. At one time she'd have refused to lift a finger, and now she was willing to try.

He put her in a chair beside the wagon and brought the second cover to her. Since it had been underneath the other, it hadn't torn as much. Mr. Staton's man in St. Louis had outfitted the wagon with double coverings. The wagons with just one had not fared as well.

Lucille worked slowly, but she'd managed to finish half of the repairs on one canvas when Lena came up. She handed him the basket with their laundry all washed, dried, folded, and stacked.

"The sun is out so strong today, it didn't take the clothes but a couple of hours to dry," she said.

"Harlan helped me with the drying out, so I've got all my things taken care of for now. I thought I'd return these and come lend you a hand."

"You've already repaired your wagon cover?" Jacob asked after he'd taken the laundry and thanked her.

"Sure did. I just took it over to Faith's wagon, and she and I worked together. She and her aunt had already sewed theirs up. That Faith sure is a worker, but her aunt and uncle won't let her out of their sight if they can help it. I worry about that girl; I sure do. Do you know they made her stay at their wagon during the celebration our first night? Her aunt fixed her a plate and took her." Lena shook her head in disgust.

Lena took a look at the top cover Jacob brought up. "You got any heavy cloth or lightweight canvas we can use to patch some of these biggest holes?"

"If it's in too bad a shape to repair, we can just use the one cover," Jacob told her. "Lucille has it almost fixed." He looked at his wife and gave her a smile he hoped conveyed how proud he was of her.

"Land's sake, no," Lena said. "This one's not nearly as torn up as Faith's. I expect theirs had some age on it to start with. No, Lucille and I'll have this one put back together in no time."

While the women sewed, Jacob gathered up their things, which were now dry, and put them back in their place. He placed Lucille's trunks in the wagon, but he'd let her repack them. He got the idea she didn't want him to touch her things.

"You got you a real good man there, young lady," he heard Lena say to Lucille. "He's mighty nice to look at, too."

"He is a good man," Lucille replied. "He's handsome, too, but I've never been partial to dark hair. I do like his blue eyes, though. So many men, with hair as dark as his have brown eyes."

"Well, I think you two make a striking couple. Now, when's this baby due?"

"Sometime in July, I think."

"You sure are showing to be no farther along. Do you think it could be twins?"

"I've wondered as much myself. I think maybe with all this walking, I've lost some weight, which makes my belly appear larger. Twins would be okay, though, a boy and a girl."

"Well, when your time comes, you have Jacob fetch me. I've delivered many a baby back in Kentucky."

"Thank you, I will. It worried me when I heard no doctor came on this wagon train, so I'd appreciate your help."

Another storm hit the next night, but this one didn't contain the ice pellets. The rain came down in torrents, however, and, although the thunder and lightning moved off, a steady rain lasted most of the night.

Jacob slid his bedroll into a high corner again, although the ground lay pretty level on the plains. He was glad they'd repaired the wagon cover, but, considering the way the rain came down, it might still leak. Lucille didn't call for him this time, however.

Lord, give me the patience I need. I find myself wanting things to be right between Lucille and me now. I'm finding it hard to wait. Help me to be patient and wait on Thy timing. Show me Thy will and direct my paths, I pray. Amen.

The next morning, the road had turned extremely muddy. Some of the wagons got stuck in the mud that oozed up the wheels. They cut tall grass and lay it in front of the wheels, while someone urged the team forward to pull the wagon from the muddy grasp intent on holding it. The wagon train only inched forward, if it moved at all, but they'd already been delayed by the hail storm, and they needed to continue.

Jacob felt sorry for Lucille. Her heaviness and awkwardness made it hard for her to trudge along beside the wagon with him, and she tired quickly. Yet, the jolting wagon made it almost unbearable for her. She did take a break from walking by lying on her cot in the back, but she never stayed for more than an hour. Even that jarred her too much.

"If I stay in that moving wagon, it's going to shake the baby from me," she said.

Some of the women sewed pebbles into the hems of their dresses to prevent the wind from blowing their dress tails up. At first, Lucille refused, but, after struggling all day to push her skirt down, she gave in and added the weight to her two plainest frocks.

The other emigrants had started getting up and down from moving wagons long ago. The oxen moved so slowly, it wasn't difficult, but Jacob always stopped his wagon for Lucille. In her unwieldy condition, she needed his assistance. He hurried to get back to moving, so no one would be held up, and he soon had the gap between his wagon and the next one narrowed again.

Some of the children had been injured by falling and being run over by the wagon. One little boy, just six years old, had fallen beneath the wheels and died when the wagon ran over his head. He had been an only son, and his family was devastated—another tragedy of the trail. Jacob was glad he hadn't witnessed that scene.

The wagon train entered the Platte Valley. The river still lay to the north, but, since it ran northeast until it hit the Missouri, they would come to it soon enough and have to cross it several times.

Trees became scarce in this part of the prairie. They would likely go buffalo hunting soon, but that would mean the possibility of hostile

Indians. They'd probably see Pawnees first, because they roamed farther east in the valley. Jacob dreaded any encounters.

The days were so endlessly tiring and monotonous, everyone became more irritable and tempers flared. One family had had enough, and they turned their wagon around and headed back. In the council meeting, Wayland Marshall said they probably wouldn't be the last of the "turnarounds."

Since the man in the turnaround family had been on the council, the travelers elected Rex Caulder to fill his place. Jacob hoped the man didn't still hold a grudge, but by the look on his face, he did.

"We'll be at the Platte River tonight." Marshall rode by and hollered the news.

"That's good," Jacob said to Lucille, although he didn't think she heard because she gave no indication. "Our water barrel needs filling."

The Platte didn't look anything like Jacob expected. Sometimes this muddy river would be wide enough to have islands dotting its middle as it cut a vertical brown line across the prairie. A few spindly willows or cottonwoods often grew along the banks. Here, high, green grass surrounded the wide, muddy river. Silt and debris churned in its waters, and they were supposed to drink this? It barely looked fit for the animals, much less human consumption.

He met Lena going to the river with her buckets. "I guess we'd better let this stuff set overnight, so some of the dirt settles out. How's Lucille doing?" she asked.

"I'm worried about her. She's so uncomfortable, whether she's walking or riding. She's started staying in the wagon more, but that's hard on her, too."

"Are you raising the bottom of the cover to give her some air?"

"I am, but she still stays miserable."

"Don't worry. Many a woman has given birth on the trail. It'll all be over soon enough."

"Not soon enough for me, and she's still got about two months."

Lena nodded with sympathy. "Is your marriage getting any easier, if you don't mind me asking?"

Jacob looked at the woman beside him. He needed to talk to someone, and she'd kept his secrets so far.

"Not really. Things are not as contentious as they were at one time, and Lucille seems more resigned to going to Oregon, but we're no closer than we were. She has asked me to be patient and said she hoped things would get better after the baby comes."

"Well, maybe that means her intentions are good. That's a start, don't you think? I'll just keep praying for you both. God always answers prayers in one way or the other—either yes, no, or wait."

"I've been praying, too, but it doesn't seem to be doing much good."

"Are you asking or telling God what to do? Many Christians want to serve God but only in the role of advisors."

Jacob couldn't help but smile at the caustic comment. It held a lot of truth, though.

When Jacob went for the team the next morning, they were grazing near the river. Flocks of geese took to the sky from the banks. Their wings cut through the air and beat against their sides making a loud, rushing noise. He would bring his gun to the river the next morning. A goose roasted on a spit sounded mighty good. He needed to be carrying his gun anyway in case Indians appeared.

They nooned beside a prairie dog town. The critters looked cute as they darted in and out of their holes and stared at the travelers, as if they were as curious about the people as most of the people were about them.

Jacob had guard duty that night. Obadiah told them to be especially vigilant, because the Pawnee could appear at anytime, and they loved to steal horses or mules. During his watch, he noticed more lanterns and movement in the camp than usual. When his replacement came to relieve him, the man said that sickness had broken out, and, with the symptoms of vomiting and diarrhea, they were afraid it might be cholera.

Cholera, a dreaded word and a horrible, messy illness that killed many and held families at its mercy. *Lord, protect us all, especially Lucille.* He couldn't imagine the consequences if Lucille came down with the disease in her condition.

The next day, a single Pawnee brave rode into camp. He slowly traveled around the inside of the circle of wagons, as if he wanted to be on parade, or maybe he wanted to look for someone.

The striking figure sat on his horse proudly with his back straight and his muscular legs gently guiding the animal. In his left hand, he held a coup stick decorated with mink and weasel skins and feathers of many different birds. He looked cleaner than Jacob had expected, and he looked every inch a regal leader.

He stopped beside Jacob's wagon and stared at Lucille. By now a curious crowd had gathered.

"Don't you worry none," Obadiah said. "He hain't up to no trouble, not iffin he rid in here all by his lonesome."

The brave dismounted in one fluid motion and walked up to Lucille. He reached out and picked up a stand of Lucille's hair with his right hand. She cringed and instinctively drew back. He frowned.

The Pawnee said something in a guttural language. "He likes the looks of her hair," Obadiah translated.

Well, that was obvious. Jacob rather liked her strawberry blonde hair, too.

The brave put out his hand and gently tilted her chin up so he could look into her eyes. He spoke again.

He likes her green eyes too, Jacob translated to himself before Obadiah did. Anyone could see that this man liked the looks of Jacob's wife.

Jacob didn't know of a man who didn't, but he didn't like the way this Indian acted so familiar with Lucille. Surely he wouldn't try anything since he's so outnumbered.

The Pawnee lightly rubbed Lucille's protruding belly. "No," Lucille said and jerked back.

"This has gone far enough," Jacob said. "Tell him to leave."

The Indian and Obadiah had a rather lengthy conversation with Obadiah talking in the strange language and his hands flying all over the place.

"He wants to trade fer your woman," the old man said. "I tried to tell him you wouldn't, 'cause that's not ar ways, but he insists I make you his offer. He offers you fifty horses. Hit's an unheard of price."

Lucille gasped and clutched Jacob's arm so tightly his circulation must have been cut off. Surely she didn't think he'd ever consider such a thing. He would have laughed if the situation didn't seem so serious. Fifty horses indeed! What a ridiculous offer!

"No," he said firmly and shook his head.

The brave said something quickly.

"A hundred horses," the scout translated.

Jacob just shook his head. "Tell him she's not for sale, not for any amount. He can't have her."

"Give him somethang fer comin' in here and makin' the offer," he said. "We don't want him bein' insulted and comin' back with a war party."

"What should I give him?"

"An animal, some food, or something nice of your wife's."

Jacob looked at Lucille. "Go get one of your silk dresses you don't like much—the fancier and brighter the better."

She came back with a red silk ball gown he remembered her wearing to a Christmas dinner. It hadn't suited her as well as most of her dresses did. Jacob took it and gave it to the brave.

While Obadiah explained the gift, the Indian smelled the dress and smiled. He nodded to Jacob, stared at Lucille, and mounted his horse with a single jump. He put the dress in front of him, holding it down with his thigh. He held his coup stick up and rode out. Jacob had never seen anyone who looked more in control than this Indian.

Jacob had just turned to see to Lucille when a guard came running in. "They're gone," he gasped. "The Injuns done stole some of the horses, 'bout a dozen near as I can figure."

"Did you see them?" Marshall asked.

"Not soon enough. We seen the Injun ride in here, and we wuz lookin' this away."

"Those sneakin' no-good scum!" Obadiah exclaimed. "This here wuz jist a die-version soins they could snatch the animals."

"What can we do?" John Brenner asked.

"Not a solitary thang, unlessin some of you're willin' to go after them, and I guarantee hardly a one will be a comin' back."

Lucille gave a deep sigh and leaned against the wagon. She looked unusually pale.

"Are you okay?" Jacob asked as he put out his hand to help steady her.

She nodded. "Just a little weak. I can't imagine what horrors would have befallen me if that savage had taken me."

"I wouldn't let that happen," he told her. "None of the men would."

She breathed in another deep breath and nodded. He helped her into the wagon, but the image of the undaunted Pawnee warrior stayed with him.

The McCraes, Faith's aunt and uncle, were the first the cholera killed. Lena had helped Faith take care of them, because the illness hit both the older couple at the same time. According to Lena, "Only God knows how Faith has managed to avoid the sickness, but thank the Lord she has, so far, anyway."

They buried the older couple on Friday. Lucille felt so bad, and Jacob worried about her, so he didn't go. He did meet with the council at noon, and they decided to lay-by until Monday. Too many were either sick or tired from tending to the sick to move on now.

Time slipped away, and some worried they were behind schedule. Everyone remembered hearing of the Donner Party and what had happened to them when they became trapped in the heavy snows of the western mountains. Some of them had turned to cannibalism to stay alive. Jacob hoped this group of wagons could make up some of the time they'd lost in the days ahead.

A small group of Pawnees came up that afternoon. They had apparently come to trade, but when they learned of the sickness, they quickly left.

Lucille became seriously ill that night. At first, Jacob thought she might have cholera, but when she exhibited few of the symptoms, he realized her labor had begun.

He still worried, because it was much too early, and the baby would be at risk. "Lord, please be with Lucille and our baby. Keep the baby from coming too early, and keep them both safe," Jacob mouthed as he hurried to get Lena.

Lena had come down with cholera, too. "Go get Annie Fischer," the sick woman told him. "She's just had her fifth child, and she knows what to do."

Annie, a robust, middle-aged woman had a no-nonsense way about her. She seemed reluctant, but she left instructions for her oldest daughter to watch her baby and followed Jacob to his wagon. She checked on Lucille and gathered some things she would need later.

"It's going to be a while," she told Jacob. "The first one usually takes longer than the others. You keep some water boiling and come get me again when the pains get closer together and more severe or her water breaks. It's fine if she wants to get up for a spell. In fact, that might speed the process along. If I don't hear from you by morning, I'll come back and check on her right after breakfast."

Jacob didn't like the fact the woman just left. He didn't feel capable of helping Lucille now. Perhaps, if they were closer, it would have been different, but he felt incompetent, alone, and lost.

Lucille refused to get up. "The pain's too bad," she said. "My backbone feels like it's going to break into pieces."

"Should I call Annie back?"

"No, this pain is all the time and not coming in spurts. The contractions seem mild compared with my other pain. Even my legs ache. I'm scared, Jake. I'm afraid I can't do this."

"You'll do fine," he tried to reassure her. "I'm sorry you have to go through this, but just keep your mind on the end, when you'll hold our baby in your arms."

But, he worried, too. Was all this pain normal? Being the youngest child, he didn't know much about all this. How could he reassure her when worry wanted to envelop him too?

Chapter Seven

PROMISES ASKED

JACOB HAD JUST STEPPED OUT of the wagon to go for Annie the next morning when she appeared. Lucille cried out, but the midwife looked unconcerned.

"Has her water come?" she asked.

"No, not yet."

"Did you eat breakfast?"

"No, neither one of us wanted anything."

"It's better your wife not eat until all this is over, but she'll need some water to drink. Why don't you go fix you some coffee? You look like you could use it." She pulled her big frame into the wagon.

She poked her head back out. "Roll up the bottom of the cover on the far side of the wagon to give us more air. We'd probably better keep the one down on the camp side, so Lucille can have her privacy."

Mid-morning, Annie's oldest daughter brought their baby over for her mother to feed and left with the infant afterwards. By noon, Lucille screamed, and Jacob prayed and paced. It had been fifteen hours. Something had to be wrong. He felt it in the pit of his stomach.

"Her water just broke," Annie informed him, "so it shouldn't be too long now."

In four more hours, Lucille's screams had become deafening. After a particularly loud, blood-curdling yell, Jacob heard a different cry. It sounded almost like an angry kitten. The baby!

"You have a fine-looking son," Annie called out. "Wait out there for now." She leaned out a few minutes later and held out a bloody package wrapped in cloths. "Here, go bury the afterbirth, while I finish cleaning your family up."

He grabbed his shovel and took care of the task as quickly as he could, then hurried back to the wagon.

"Come on in," Annie told him.

Lucille looked horrible. Her hair had matted, and she looked whiter than any person he'd ever seen.

"Is she okay?"

Lucille's eyes fluttered open when she heard him. "Name the baby Rudy," she said in a weak voice.

"Well, that's a right fine name," Annie announced. "Maybe he'll have pretty strawberry hair, like his mama."

"Is Lucille going to be all right?" he asked again.

"She lost quite a bit of blood, more'n usual, but she's strong, and she should do fine now."

"Oh-h-h," Lucille groaned. Was she still in pain?

"Here you take your son out, while I check her again."

Jacob took the baby, but as he turned to leave, he noticed the bright red stain already seeping from under his wife. He had a hard time leaving the wagon as his body stiffened with fear.

He looked at his son as he walked back and forth beside the wagon. Rudy would fit from Jacob's elbow to his fingertips—not the tiny baby he expected. How big would he have been if he'd been full-term?

He had light blond hair, the color of corn silk, and it looked particularly pale beside his red complexion. He looked up with deep blue eyes, much darker than Jacob's. The baby stared at Jacob for a few seconds and gave a loud cry of displeasure but quickly drifted off to sleep when Jacob started gently swinging him.

Still, Jacob walked with his baby in his arms. He wanted to know how Lucille fared, but he was afraid to ask. It seemed like ages before Annie came out. She reached for the baby and shook her head.

"I'm afraid we're losing her," she said. "I've tried everything I know, but I can't get the bleeding stopped. She wants to see you. You'd better make it fast. I don't think she'll be conscious much longer."

Jacob leaped into the wagon but slowed when he saw her. She lay in a pool of blood with her eyes closed. She looked ghastly, as if she had already died, but her hand felt warm when he knelt beside her bed and picked it up.

Her eyes opened slowly, as if her eyelids were too heavy to move. She tried to smile, but it came out in a grimace.

"Don't fret," she whispered, as tears gathered in his eyes. "This is for the best. Promise me that you'll take care of Rudy."

"You know I will."

"Promise."

"I promise."

"Promise me you'll throw away all my things without sorting through them."

He hesitated to give her unusual request time to register in his slow, tired brain. He was just getting ready to promise when her body relaxed, and her hand went limp in his. It took a few seconds for him to realize what had happened.

"No-o-o-o! Oh, God, please no."

He felt tears rolling down his face, but his body went cold and numb. He rushed out of the death wagon and ran. He didn't think about where he'd go. He just needed to get away.

He ended up downstream on the river. He stopped, realizing he shouldn't go too far. He'd already run out of sight of the wagons. He sat down on an old cottonwood log and covered his face with his hands.

He wondered why the log hadn't been collected for firewood, but he knew his mind wanted to shotgun from Lucille's death. Dead. He'd had a wife for only seven months, and now she was gone, replaced with a son to take care of. How would he manage? Should he turn back and go home?

Something told him that would be a bad idea. His parents would help him, but he feared Lucille's parents would try to take Rudy. Besides, he couldn't face them after losing Lucille. The seed he'd planted within her had killed her. Did that make him a murderer? He felt like one.

He should have never brought her out here. She hadn't wanted to leave Virginia, and she sure hadn't wanted to leave St. Louis. He should have stayed in St. Louis with her. There'd have been doctors there, good doctors, and she could be just fine now. *Lord, what have I done?* What was he going to do?

Lo, I am with you always, even to the end of the world.

He didn't want to hear that. He didn't want to remember Bible verses, and he didn't want to hear God's promises. Hadn't He said, "Whoso putteth his trust in the Lord shall be safe?" Had Lucille been safe?

Had she put her trust in the Lord? Jacob didn't know. They'd never discussed religion. Why not, since it was of utmost importance? He should know.

"Why, Lord? Why is this happening to me? Haven't I been faithful to follow Thee since childhood? Haven't I done my best and depended on Thee?" The questions wore smooth and slick from the many times he asked them.

Did you turn to God before agreeing to marry Lucille? You knew you shouldn't go to her bedroom, but you were determined to please her, to garner her warmest regard. Did you seek God's guidance before you said "I do," before your marriage started with problems and never got better? Was that God's voice or his own thoughts?

"If I did wrong, punish me," he whispered to the sky above the river. "Don't take her life. You could have made things better between us. All things are within Thy power. You could have spared her life. Rudy needs his mama. I need a wife."

The song of the flowing waters held no answers for him. The silence crushed in on him, as did his situation. He thought of throwing himself into those moving waters and drowning all his cares, but it came in a brief moment of weakness.

He took a deep breath. He didn't want to be a coward, and his son depended on him. He stood and walked slowly back to camp. He didn't want to go back, didn't want to shoulder his responsibility, but it's what he would do. He'd promised Lucille, and, if nothing else, he was a man of his word.

From habit, he started to say a silent prayer and ask God to show him how to take care of Rudy, but he blocked it off. God had deserted him, so he wouldn't pray to Him, but he couldn't silence the Bible verses he'd memorized long ago.

I will never leave thee, nor forsake thee.

Annie took Rudy to her wagon. She said she and her daughter could look after the two babies until after the funeral.

Some women he didn't know came and prepared the body. Lucille hadn't made any friends, unless he counted Iris. The widow had only come to visit when Jacob was also there, and she flirted too much. He got the feeling she was more interested in his wealth Lucille had hinted about. Lena had been a closer friend, and that had been from Lena's efforts and not Lucille's, but Lena still lay in her sickbed.

"Lord, keep Lena safe and make her well."

The whispered prayer slipped out before he thought to stop it. He chided himself. Prayer had become a more integral part of his life than he'd realized. Well, no more.

They held the funeral the next morning. Lena, looking weak and wobbly, came on the arm of her husband. She looked like she needed to be in bed, but Jacob felt better when he saw her.

Annie held Rudy, and her daughter stood beside her with their baby. Jacob hoped Annie would keep tending Rudy for a while. He didn't know of another wet nurse right now.

The graveside service was short and to the point. "The Lord giveth and the Lord taketh away. Blessed be the name of the Lord," the preacher concluded.

The Lord taketh away, all right. Why did He take such a beautiful young woman who had most of her life yet to live?

"She'll make a beautiful addition to heaven," Lena patted his arm.

That was a comforting thought, but he didn't want to examine it too closely. He didn't know if Lucille had been saved. She'd never mentioned it, didn't seem to rely on God, and never wanted to pray, unless he insisted.

He should have witnessed to her more. He should have encouraged her to accept Christ as her Savior. Had he failed her in that way, too?

God seems to have deserted me," Jacob mumbled.

"Nonsense," Lena replied quickly. "God never deserts anyone. It's more like we leave his side. Remember, if you only have faith when everything's going your way, it isn't faith at all. Faith keeps on trusting through the bad times, too – the ones you just can't seem to make heads or tails of."

"I'd better get Lena back to bed," Harlan said. "She insisted on coming, although she is still as weak as a newborn kitten."

"I'm over the worst."

Harland shook his head. "I just hope you don't have a setback."

The preacher announced he would have the regular Sunday service after the funeral. Jacob didn't go.

He'd go get his son every afternoon and keep him until bedtime. He wanted Rudy to know him. He'd tell him about his mother too—how beautiful she was and how much she'd loved him. Jacob had no doubts Lucille loved her baby. Her love for him he questioned.

One afternoon Wayland Marshall and the men from the council came up, along with Annie Fischer's husband. They looked solemn.

"We're so sorry for your loss," Marshall said. "I know it must be hard."

"We've come with a proposition," John Brenner added.

Fischer spoke but didn't look Jacob in the eye. "My wife says she'll feed your baby, but with all our young'uns, she ain't goin' have the time to tend after him. You're goin' to have to make other 'rangements."

"You know Faith Allen's folks died, and she's all alone." Marshall took over. "I don't like the idea of a young, single woman traveling by herself. It doesn't seem quite proper. I think it would solve both your problems if you two hitched up. You could look after her, and she could look after your baby."

"Hitched up?" Did the man mean what Jacob thought?

"Yeah, you know. Married."

"I've already voiced my opinion," Rex said. "I'm against saddling an innocent, young woman with a man like you, Parker."

Lord, Thou can't be asking me to marry this quickly and to another woman I don't know. I lashed out at Thee in anger, but I'm asking for Your guidance here. I want to follow Thy will for me this time.

Whoso findeth a wife findeth a good thing, and obtained favor of the Lord.

His mother had done too good a job at having Jacob memorize Scripture verses. There seemed to be one for every occasion.

"Is she willing?" Jacob stalled for time. He needed to think.

"We haven't asked her yet," Marshall said, "but she's a sensible girl. I believe she'll consider it."

"It seems to me I need someone to care for Rudy worse than she needs a husband. Can't she just care for the baby without us getting married?"

Marshall frowned. "It would be hard enough for her to manage her wagon all on her own. I think it'll take the two of you to manage with a baby. One of you will have to be up all during the night, you know, and something is bound to come up. It wouldn't be proper."

"We've discussed it, and this really is the best solution," John added. "You're also going to need a wife when you get to Oregon. It would be nigh unto impossible for you to start your place and tend to your son by yourself. Once you get there, you'd be in the same fix you're in right now."

That did make sense, and God seemed to be urging him on, at least the Bible verse that came to mind made it seem so. He nodded.

"Why don't you go on over there and ask her," John said. It was a statement, not a question. "A woman likes to be asked all proper like, you know."

"I'd like for the council to go, too. I want y'all to talk to her first and give her your reasoning. In the meanwhile, I'll go visit with Lena Haywood and talk with Faith after you leave."

"Okay, but go by Annie's and carry your son with you. Women always respond to a wee little one," John said.

Jacob didn't feel good about carrying the baby with him, but he'd do it anyway. He didn't like the fact they were trying to manipulate Faith into agreeing. He knew by experience that marriage could be hard enough. If she agreed, he wanted it to be of her own free will and not because some men maneuvered her into it. But at least the baby would remind her of her responsibilities and all that would be expected of her.

"He's just cried himself to sleep," Annie said when he collected Rudy. "The only time he isn't crying is when he's eating or sleeping."

Lena lay in bed, resting but awake, and she appeared some better. She smiled at him and had him come inside the wagon.

"Don't worry," she told him when she noticed Rudy, "I shouldn't be contagious now, but, just in case, I won't hold your baby this time."

"The council has come to me with a strange proposition," he said, "and I wanted your opinion."

"You'd be getting a mighty good woman," Lena said when he explained the situation. "I know it's really too soon for you, but I think it'll work out for the best. She just might be the bridge between the person you are now and where you'd like to be."

"I just buried Lucille. It seems unfitting to me, as if I'm not grieving for Lucille."

"If you're truthful with yourself, your first marriage wasn't what you really wanted. I know you cared about Lucille, but I don't think your love ever developed to the point it should have. If you can let the hurt go, this may be the marriage you dreamed of, and that son of yours does need a mother."

"You think I should do it, then."

"I think Faith would make a farmer an excellent wife. She's used to doing all the work at her family's cabin and small farm in Kentucky so, yes, I think it's a good match. I wish Faith were my daughter. I think that much of her."

"If she were your daughter, would you tell her to marry me?"

"I would. I think a lot of you, too."

"We're through talking with her," Marshall said as he poked his head inside. "She listened to what we had to say and didn't tell us 'no.'"

Faith's worn-looking wagon stood two wagons up from the Haywoods', so he started over to meet her. If he'd ever seen her, he didn't know it, and here he was considering marrying a complete stranger. He looked up to see a young woman who must be Faith heading his way.

She wasn't as pretty as Lucille had been, but not many women were. At least she didn't look homely. He noticed her hair first. She had it braided in two long strands, but with the sun's highlights, it looked like iridescent raven's feathers. Upon closer scrutiny, it appeared dark brown rather than black, but it looked so different from Lucille's reddish curls. As she approached, he saw she looked smaller than Lucille, but Lucille tended to have a more voluptuous figure. Still, Faith curved nicely above and below her tiny waist. He pulled his wayward thoughts back in. She might be attractive enough, but, he knew from experience, beauty could be deceiving.

She stopped when she saw him, and he walked up to her. She looked almost scared. He saw she had warm chocolate eyes under thick black lashes.

"Hello, I'm Jacob Parker. You must be Faith." He smiled at her, and she gave him a tentative smile. Maybe this wouldn't be so bad.

———

Faith looked at the man standing before her. From what he said, she knew this must be Jacob, but he didn't look like what she'd expected. His appearance, his attractiveness, almost frightened her. What would a man like him want with someone like her? She didn't know what to say or how to act. She'd never been around a man she would consider for marriage before.

Jacob looked to be several inches taller than her. He had thick, dark brown hair that almost appeared black, and it curled enough to be noticed. He didn't have either a beard or a moustache, which made him different from the men here, but he hadn't shaved for at least two days and now a heavy stubble shaded the lower part of his face.

She looked into his eyes, and they held her captive. Clear and a bright blue, they seemed to search her very soul. What kind of man stood before her with such an intense gaze? Would he be kind to her? Lena seemed to think a lot of him.

She nodded when he said she must be Faith. Now she needed to say something, but what? She looked at the bundle he held in his arms.

"This is Rudy," he said when he saw where her gaze had turned.

"May I?" she asked and held out her hands for the baby. Anything to give her something to do right now. She felt so awkward.

She loosened Rudy's wrap and looked at his little face. "He's a beautiful baby," she said. Should she have said "handsome?" Was it okay to call a baby boy "beautiful?"

"Well, I guess he takes after his mama, then."

He smiled again, but the smile didn't quite reach his eyes. His eyes never left her, but Faith could get no indication of what he might be thinking.

"Where are my manners? Here I've kept you standing. Won't you come over and sit down by the wagon?"

"No, I need to be getting Rudy over to Annie's. He'll want his feeding before too much longer. I wanted to come over and meet you. I'm going to need some help with Rudy, and Mr. Marshall and the council thought it might help us both out if we married. Are you willing to marry me, Faith, and become a mother to Rudy? I'm planning on starting a farm in Oregon Territory. I'm a hard worker, and I'll take good care of you."

"Are you a Christian man, Mr. Parker?"

"Yes, I guess I am, and please call me 'Jacob.' I surrendered my life to Christ when I was ten years old, and I've tried to walk in His ways ever since." He looked away from her for the first time. After a pause, he continued. "To be honest, I've been questioning God, as to why He took Lucille. My faith isn't at its strongest point right now, but I did pray and ask His guidance in this decision. I'd planned to pull away from God like He'd seemed to pull away from me, but I don't think I can do that. He's been such an integral part of my life for all these years that He's woven into my very being. Praying has been such a daily routine I do it without thinking." He looked for her response.

"I understand. My faith has seen me through everything for a number of years, too. I try to remember when things get their worst and I feel I'm at my wits' end, God resides there. Our tomorrow is always determined by our reaction to God today."

At first, Jacob looked surprised, but then his gaze softened. "I agree that a deep faith is important."

"I wouldn't marry a man who didn't love the Lord, but I understand your struggles and questions. You're going through a hard time now. 'The web of our life is of a mingled yarn, good and ill together.' Are you sure you're ready for another marriage?"

"Is that Shakespeare you quoted?"

"*All's Well That Ends Well.*"

"How is it you know Shakespeare well enough to quote him?"

"When my parents died, and I went to live with my aunt and uncle, I took only Mama's Bible, a dictionary, and Papa's complete works of Shakespeare for books to read. I've read them over and over again."

His eyes showed interest as if Faith intrigued him. "I'd like to have a chance to learn more about you. But to answer your question of whether I'm ready or not, Rudy needs a mother, and I need a wife. It would be hard for me to get a farm up and running without one. I can promise to be good to you, Faith. If things were different, I'd like to court you first, but we'll be pulling out in the morning, and I need help with Rudy soon. Today is the last day Annie will keep him for me all the time."

"I appreciate this talk and your honesty, Jacob. Can you give me an hour to think about this before I give you my answer?"

"Sure, I think that's very reasonable. Mr. Marshall wants the preacher to marry us this evening if you agree. Considering Lucille was just buried, it won't be anything fancy. I'll put on my suit and you don your best dress, and we'll stand up together."

"Okay. You'll come back in an hour, then, so I can give you my answer?"

"I will. I'll take Rudy to Annie, shave, and come back by here."

She nodded, and he walked off. Faith watched him leave. He turned just before he walked out of sight and waved when he saw her looking his way. She waved back.

Faith went directly to Lena's wagon. She'd been headed there when Jacob had approached her. Although she'd heard her friend speak of Jacob with fondness, she needed the woman's advice.

"Come in, my dear girl. I thought you might come."

"You know then?"

"Yes, Jacob came to see me. He told me about the wagon master and council's proposal."

"What do you think?"

"I think Jacob's a good man, a very good man. He put up with a lot from Lucille, but he always treated her with love and respect. Sometimes, when she was in a particularly bad mood, I wondered how he did it. At times, I thought Lucille was so mean-spirited that she could have taught Satan himself some new tricks."

"The marriage wasn't happy then?"

"I'm sure it had its moments, but I don't think it was as happy as it should have been or as happy as Jacob wanted it to be."

"Don't you think it's too early for him to remarry?"

"It is if you're looking for the ideal situation, but out here on the trail nothing's ideal. I think you both need each other in ways you don't even realize yet."

"You think I should marry him then?"

"I think you'd both be getting a partner you can rely on. I have no idea how much love you'll hold for each other a year from now. That's beyond my realm, but I think you could marry a lot worse than Jacob Parker."

"Well, I guess I'll go spend some time in prayer and see if I can get the Lord's guidance."

"Which way are you leaning right now?"

"Toward Jacob."

"Well, if that holds, you come back over here to get ready for the wedding. I want to help you."

Faith went into her wagon and fell to her knees. "Dear Lord, I'm puzzled about what to do, and I'm scared of the future. Everything seems so uncertain right now, and therefore I come to Thee, as I always have. I need Thy guidance on what to do, for only Thou can see the outcomes of the decisions I have before me. Please put Thy loving hand upon me and guide me along the path I should take. I pray. Amen."

A peace flowed through her when she thought of Jacob. Lena declared him to be a good man, and she trusted Lena. It scared her to think of continuing the journey alone. Where would she go, California or Oregon?

Her aunt and uncle had been going to join their son in California, but her cousin hadn't wanted her to come. His parents had refused to go if they couldn't bring her, too, because they needed her to help with the work. He certainly wouldn't want her now that they were dead, and, she'd never met the man, so he remained a stranger to her. It wouldn't even be proper for her to live with him, since he wasn't any closer kin than a cousin.

Where would she go in Oregon? What would she do there on her own? She couldn't go back to Kentucky either. She didn't know anyone else there, and they'd sold the old home place.

━━━━━━━━━━

Jacob took Rudy to Annie. He'd already started crying at the top of his lungs. Good thing he hadn't done that earlier.

"This is what he does best," Annie said as she took him. "You'd better get ready for sleepless nights."

Jacob went back to his wagon. He stood before a small mirror he hung on a wagon hook and shaved, but his mind stayed on Faith. The short conversation they'd just had seemed as meaningful as all of the conversations he and Lucille had put together. She'd complimented him for being honest, but that applied to her, too. She didn't just talk about shallow things, either.

He could tell Christ had become important to her. He wished he and Lucille had talked about their faith before the wedding. It had never occurred to him to ask her how she felt. He'd just assumed she would be a Christian. He knew she'd attended church with her family.

Of course, the situation had been different then, and he hadn't really had much choice.

The worst thing about the situation now was he felt forced into marriage again. Just like the first time, there wasn't much he could do about it. Rudy needed Faith now.

God, I still don't understand what's happened, but Thou knowest all. Forgive me my doubts. Please work this out for good for two people who love Thee and for a little newborn baby.

Jacob didn't change clothes. He'd have time to do that after Faith agreed to marry him, if she agreed. He tried to tell himself not to feel rejected if she refused because she didn't know him, but he knew he would. It didn't make sense since he didn't know if he wanted this either, but he knew the truth of it. He'd just about had all the rejection he could take lately. Well, at least if Faith told him "no," it would be before the wedding and not after.

He had some time to spare before he needed to go back to Faith's wagon, so he strolled through the prairie and picked some wildflowers. He felt ridiculous, but it seemed like a good thing to do. The way he saw it, Faith would be getting the worst of this deal. She would be getting a distraught groom, who had just buried his first wife, and a crying baby, who wasn't even hers. She would be cooking meals, washing dishes, doing laundry, sewing and mending, caring for Rudy, and performing countless other tasks. For all that work, she would be getting his protection and farm work when they got to Oregon—*if* they made it to Oregon.

The more he thought about it, the more unlikely he thought it would be that she'd agree. Why would she want to marry him?

She sat outside her wagon waiting for him. She stood when she saw him, and he handed her the wildflowers.

"To thank you for considering my offer," he told her.

"Thank you." She put the blossoms to her face to smell them. She only glanced at him and didn't look him directly in the eye. This couldn't be a good sign. "After thinking and praying, I've decided to accept your proposal."

"Really?" He couldn't hide his surprise. He'd talked himself into accepting her refusal, and he had to pause to regroup. "Thank you. I'll go check with the preacher, and we'll plan for the wedding to take place about seven o'clock if that suits you."

"Seven o'clock will be fine."

"Would you like for me to come by and walk you there?"

"No, I'll come with Lena and Harlan."

"Okay, I'll see you there."

He paused again before leaning in and kissing her lightly on the cheek. Then, he quickly retreated. Why had he done that? He hadn't thought about it but had just acted on impulse. It had seemed the right thing to do at the time, and he hadn't stopped to think. He smiled despite how awkward he felt. Faith had smelled clean and fresh. How had she managed that out here?

Chapter Eight

WED AGAIN

JACOB HAD HOPED FOR A quiet ceremony, but word had gotten around, and a crowd gathered. The makeshift band played, as he stood waiting for his bride.

She came right at seven, walking between Lena and Harlan and wearing a lovely, pale butter-colored dress trimmed in lace. With her hair tucked up on her crown and a few shorter strands curling around her ears and neck, she truly looked like a bride.

He looked again. Wildflowers accented her hair and she carried a bouquet of them. Were they the ones he'd given her? They had to be. He felt honored.

Jacob didn't remember much of the ceremony. His thoughts were jumbled and he couldn't concentrate. He responded at the proper place and heard Faith do the same.

About the time he said "I do," he noticed the sky had turned a kaleidoscope of color. Pink, rose, fuchsia, purple, gold, and yellow had flung themselves across the sky in royal majesty. It looked as if God had painted them a spectacular wedding present.

He heard the preacher say, "I now pronounce you man and wife. Whom God hath joined together let no man put asunder. You may kiss your bride."

He'd forgotten about this part of the ceremony. How should he kiss her? If he just kissed her cheek would she feel insulted? Would it seem like he considered her as less? He simply touched her lips with his and tried to not make it seem too quick. Still, he noticed how soft her lips were beneath his.

"We would have planned a supper, but there just wasn't enough time," Mrs. Brenner said. "We'll just have to plan something in your honor later on."

"Yes. You'll get to celebrate your wedding twice that way," Marshall patted him on the back.

"Lead your bride in a dance," John told him. Jacob had begun to resent this man he'd thought of as his friend. John sure liked to dictate what to do.

The band immediately began playing a waltz, and he pulled Faith into his arms, but not too close. She seemed to hesitate.

"I've only danced with my father long ago," she whispered so only he heard.

"Just lean into me and go slowly the way I push you."

She did exactly that, and they managed fine. Other couples came to dance after they'd given the newlyweds a minute to lead off.

"Do you want to stay for a while and enjoy the get-together, or would you prefer to go back to your wagon?" he asked when the music stopped.

"I see Harlan leading Lena back, so I'd like to go back, too."

"You look beautiful," he told her, as they walked toward her wagon.

She looked down. "Lena gave this dress to me, and she helped me get ready. The flowers you brought me were a nice addition. Thank you again."

"You're very welcome. I'm glad you appreciate them."

"I have a stew and an apple cobbler already cooked. I fixed enough for Lena and Harlan, but they declined. Would you like to stay for supper?"

"I haven't eaten all day, so I guess I should."

Jacob sat down and Faith dished them up some stew she'd managed to keep warm. It smelled wonderful. She had what she called "shortening bread" to go with it. It seemed like cornbread with pork cracklings in it. He vaguely remembered a cook at the plantation making something like this years ago when he was a small child, but he'd forgotten all about it.

"Would you say our blessing?" she asked, and he did.

She ate in silence, and he felt she waited for him to guide the conversation, just as he had the dance. At first, he allowed himself to simply enjoy the food. How long had it been since he'd eaten? He couldn't remember.

The food tasted wonderful. The restaurants in St. Louis didn't have anything this good. He could at least say he'd married a good cook.

"I think it'll be better if we keep separate sleeping arrangements to start with," he told her. "We have both just buried family, and we don't know each other very well. I think we both need some time to adjust."

She seemed to breathe a sigh of relief. Then, she looked at him and nodded.

"If it's not too much trouble, I'd like for you to start sleeping in my wagon. I'll sleep in the tent."

"All right, but what about this?" She flung her hand out to indicate her wagon and things.

"We'll start sorting through all our things, discarding some, and consolidating others, but that will take time. For now, I'll get someone to drive your wagon. I'll ask Marshall to let you move yours in front of mine in the morning. I'd rather keep them together."

"Oh, I can drive the wagon."

"What about Rudy? You'll have him, too."

"I'll make a sling for him and strap him to me. He'll be fine."

"If you're sure, but I don't want you wearing yourself out. I'll get a driver if it becomes too much. There are plenty of men headed to the gold fields of California, so there should be someone available."

"Did you know we were headed for California, too?"

"No, I didn't."

"Yes, my cousin, Uncle Jed and Aunt Mabel's only living son, went out, got in on the first of the gold rush, and found gold. He wrote and talked them into selling their place in Kentucky and joining him."

"Were you planning to travel to him before you agreed to marry me?"

"No. He didn't want his parents to bring me with them, but they insisted. He doesn't want me."

"So you don't mind going to Oregon Territory?"

"No, I'm looking forward to it."

He sat his empty plate down and looked at the bits of apple cobbler clinging to it. It had tasted so good he wished he had room for more. "This was an excellent meal. Thank you very much."

She looked startled, as if she hadn't expected his praise. "You're welcome."

"If you'll get what you need for tonight and in the morning, I'll go tell Harlan and Lena to keep an eye on your things for tonight. Annie is keeping Rudy."

Lena had already gone to bed, but Harlan and Jacob talked for a while. When he returned to Faith's wagon, she had washed and put away all the dishes, doused the fire, and had her things in a roll.

He walked her to his wagon, kissed her on the cheek, helped her inside, asked if she needed anything, and went to his tent. What an unusual day this had been. He felt as if he'd been pushed off a cliff and still hadn't hit bottom.

Still, since he'd slept so little since Friday, he felt himself dozing off sooner than he expected. The last thing he remembered was the sound of a wolf calling in the night, and another wolf answering the call.

He woke up to the smell of coffee, but it still looked dark in his tent. He got up and peeped out the slit in the tent. The sky had not begun to lighten yet, but Jacob could tell it would soon. Faith had the coffee on, and she sat close to the fire with her Bible in her hand. He hurried to dress and join her.

"Good morning. You're up early. Did you sleep well? Were you bothered by the wolves howling?"

She smiled at him. "It took me a while to fall asleep, but I slept well once I did. The wolves didn't bother me, however. We lived in a cabin in the mountains of Kentucky, and I'm used to night sounds, although some of the ones here are different."

"What are you doing?"

"I like to get up before others and have a time of devotion."

"May I join you, or would you rather be alone."

"Please, join me. I'll pour you some coffee, and I can start breakfast. I'm going to fry pancakes, but I waited until you got up to start."

"Breakfast can wait until daylight. Where are you reading in your Bible?"

"Psalm 118."

"I'd like it if you'd read it aloud."

She nodded and read in a smooth, steady voice, as if she lost herself in the meaning of the words. Psalm 118 thanked and praised God and left Jacob filled with positive thoughts. What a good way to begin the day! Jacob especially liked "This is the day which the Lord hath made; we will rejoice and be glad in it."

"Would you lead us in prayer?" she asked when she'd finished the chapter.

He reached for her hand, and she put hers in his without hesitation. Something felt so right about this, but he didn't stop to analyze it.

"Our Father, who art in Heaven, we do praise Your name. Help us to love and trust Thee more. Please bless our new family. Keep us healthy and safe as we continue on this journey to Oregon. Grant that we may prosper there but be ever mindful of Thy goodness and mercy. Remind us that all good things come from Thee, but the enemy tries to twist our thinking for his evil purposes. Go with us this day and bless it, and may we live it in a manner that's pleasing to Thee and in the center of Thy will. Amen."

"Amen." She gave a slight squeeze of approval to his hand.

Watching her, he could tell she wanted to say something, but she hesitated. He liked the fact she seemed easy to read.

"You can tell me anything, Faith."

A look of surprise flickered across her face. She blinked and gave him a tentative smile.

"I wanted to tell you I appreciate your patience and willingness to get to know each other before we . . . uh . . . "

"Become intimate," he finished for her. She looked down and nodded.

"When we said our vows, Faith, did you mean them? Do you want a real marriage with me, or was this just a marriage of convenience to you?"

"If I answer, I'll expect you to answer the same question."

She seemed to be hedging, hoping to avoid the question altogether. Was he rushing things here?

"That sounds fair. I just think it's best to know where we stand, what our intentions are at the very beginning."

She nodded again but looked down at the Bible in her lap. "I promised to be your wife before God. I take such a promise very seriously. I want to be a good wife to you." She looked into his eyes. "I guess, like most young girls, I used to dream of meeting a special man, falling in love, and living happily ever after. I guess that's not very realistic, but I hope I can have some of that dream. I hope we can make a good life and a good marriage together. What about you?"

Jacob had never once considered Faith's hopes and dreams before. She'd given up her childhood fantasies of Prince Charming, a fairy tale wedding, and happy-ever-after to marry him. He knew those things weren't pragmatic in real life, but he wanted to give her as many of them as he could. They might not have had a courtship before they wed, but there was no reason he couldn't give her one now. Courting her and learning more about her would be a good thing for him, too.

"I totally agree with you. My first marriage didn't turn out as fulfilling as I'd hoped it would be. I'll tell you all about it when I get things sorted out in my mind, but Lucille's death is too fresh and painful right now. I don't plan to keep any secrets between us. I want our marriage to be different, Faith. I want to be the husband you've dreamed of, and I want our love to grow. I take all my promises seriously, especially wedding vows pledged before God."

She smiled at him, a happy, glowing smile that lit up her whole face. At that moment, she looked absolutely gorgeous. She rose to start breakfast, and he needed to get the teams.

"Uncle Jed had six mules to pull our wagon. Any of the men can probably point them out to you."

"Okay. I have an extra team of oxen, but only one extra yoke. If I can come up with more yokes, we can alternate the three teams, so one rests every third day. It shouldn't be too hard to make it so we can hitch either team."

When he came back, she had pancakes, bacon, and a choice of honey, molasses, or black cherry preserves ready. He chose the preserves. It seemed strange not to have to show her how to do anything.

"You're a wonderful cook," he told her. "I don't ever remember eating better food."

"I learned to cook when I was ten years old."

"How old are you now?"

"Nineteen, and you?"

"I'm twenty-four."

He had already hitched up her mules and managed to maneuver her wagon next to his, but he hurried to take care of his oxen, which he'd brought to the wagon. His oxen seemed much more docile and cooperative than her mules.

"The mules seem harder to handle," he told her. "Why don't I drive them and you take the oxen. I think they'd pretty much follow the line without a driver."

"That's okay," she smiled. "The mules are used to me, and we get along fine."

Faith had just finished cleaning up from breakfast when Annie brought Rudy to her. He had fallen asleep.

"He's going to cry a lot," Jacob heard Annie tell Faith. "There seems to be nothing you can do to make him stop. He eats plenty, and I keep his diaper changed, so I'm not sure what's bothering him. I'll send my oldest girl over to get him every three or four hours for his feedings, and she'll bring him back when he's finished."

"Thank you for doing this," he heard Faith say. "If we can do anything to help you, just let us know."

"That's not necessary. Jacob is paying me to wet nurse the little fellow. My Bonnie doesn't take much milk, so I have plenty. Here are six diapers. Consider it my wedding present. I'm sure Lucille has some more in the wagon and some baby clothes, too. Lena helped her make some of them."

Faith turned to Jacob after Annie left. "Is it all right if I go through the items in your wagon to find Rudy's things?"

"Of course it is. Consider anything I have as yours, too. I'd like for you to sort through Lucille's things when you have time. Keep anything you want and we'll trade or throw away the rest."

Faith went into his wagon and gathered up some of Rudy's things. She'd just come out with the baby in a sling wrapped over her neck and shoulder when the signal to line up and start the wagons sounded.

As she went toward her wagon, he noticed for the first time she walked barefooted. He didn't say anything, because he had noticed many of the young women and girls were going barefooted on the prairie.

Faith hurried toward her wagon, and Jacob got up on the wagon seat. He would ride until he got his team in line behind Faith.

About an hour out of camp, he saw Faith stand and start to get off the wagon with it still moving. He held his breath, but she nimbly held Rudy close and got down despite her awkward skirts. Should she be walking beside the front of her wagon? Her mules wouldn't be as docile as his oxen were.

She repositioned Rudy, and Jacob could hear his son crying over the rumble of the wagons. He noticed she wore a hat of some sort instead of a sunbonnet like most of the women. It almost looked like a man's dark hat, but somehow, it suited her. She had also covered Rudy from the sun.

He hopped off his wagon, too. He liked seeing Faith and Rudy in front of him.

He wished she could walk beside him, so they could talk some more. He wanted to learn more about her and how she thought. Maybe they could eventually consolidate their things into one wagon and abandon the other. He doubted Faith's wagon would make the entire trip anyway. It looked old and well-used.

Looking ahead, he noticed Harlan walking by his wagon. Lena must be riding inside. He could tell she hadn't fully recovered and still seemed weak.

Cholera continued to be a problem for some, but there had been no more deaths, so far, and some, like Lena, were improving. Jacob prayed the worst had ended, and his family would be spared.

Carolyn, Annie's daughter, came to get Rudy about ten o'clock. He'd been crying for over two hours. Jacob had seen Faith check his diaper several times, but he must've been dry, for she didn't stop to change it. Jacob wondered how she would manage to change it and still drive her team. Maybe he needed to figure out something else.

They stopped for the nooning, and Faith started warming up leftover stew from last night's supper. For once, Rudy had taken a nap, and she'd laid him in a padded wooden crate under the edge of the wagon, so he'd be in the shade. Jacob hurried to take the two teams to water.

"Let me start milking for us," Faith said as they ate. "I have a cow, also, but she's dry right now and should have a calf before we get to Oregon. I can use the milk and butter in cooking."

"I'm afraid you're trying to do too much. Lester and Morton are milking my cow now and keeping half the milk. With the baby, I think you have your hands full."

"Less and More," she grinned. "That's how I think of them because the names fit. But, I'm used to working hard. If you'll bring the cow up for me morning and night, I'll be glad to milk. I'll cook you some special dishes to make it worth your while." She smiled.

"Trying to bribe me to get your way?" He smiled, too, to let her know he only teased. The fact that they'd come up with the same names for Less and More pleased him.

"Just giving you all the information, so you can make the wisest decision." She gave him a playful look.

"Okay. I don't see how you can cook anything much more special than you have been, but I'd like to taste such a dish."

"Annie sent word for me to take Rudy to her before we pull out," Faith told him after she'd done the dishes. "I'll do that while you see to the teams."

"Do you need more water carried up?"

"We have enough until tonight."

Faith had just returned when two girls, who looked about fifteen or sixteen, came up. They looked only a little younger than she did.

"We're going to take a longer nooning today because there are some new cases of cholera," one said to Faith. "We're off to pick some wild carrots and parsnips for supper. Want to come with us? We won't be gone long. The plants are nearby."

"You go ahead," Jacob said. "When Carolyn brings him back, I'll watch Rudy until you return."

Faith came back with her apron stuffed full of dandelion greens. By this time, Rudy screamed at the top of his lungs, and Jacob walked around with him. She had Jacob untie her apron with one hand, while she held it against her in front. She dumped the plants in the back of her wagon, wiped her hands with the damp dish towel, and took Rudy.

Faith boiled the dandelions greens and then fried them in bacon grease for supper. They and the rest of the meal were delicious.

"I thought you were also going to pick some wild carrots and wild parsnips," he said.

"I intended to, and the others did, but I thought I saw three different plants that looked similar. Since I didn't know what was what, I just picked the dandelions. A woman Aunt Mabel knew once picked mushrooms and got hold of some poisonous ones. They killed her little girl and made her husband and her very sick. Since then, I've been careful to pick only plants I know."

"That makes a lot of sense. There'll be new plants out here, and it's better to be safe than sorry."

"You sound like Lena."

"Is that bad?"

"No, not at all. Lena gives sound advice. She told me she found if she boiled the river water before going to bed and let it stand overnight, the sediment settled out better for drinking. I've been trying it ever since Uncle Jed and Aunt Mabel got sick, and it seems to work."

He saw Faith dig out a hole beside the fire. She raked hot coals into it and set the pot of beans she'd been boiling over it right before they went to bed.

"They'll finish cooking overnight," she told him. "I'll just warm them up and we can eat them at the nooning tomorrow."

Now, why hadn't he thought of that before? It made perfect sense.

"I'm going to sleep under the wagon tonight," he told her. "I don't want you taking Rudy to Annie in the dark, so I'll take him over and rest near their wagon while he feeds."

"I'm sure I'd be safe."

"Maybe, but I don't want to take any chances. I'll take him tonight."

Rudy took short naps but spent most of the night crying. Although Jacob carried the baby to Annie's wagon, he thought he still probably got more sleep than Faith did. She had to stay in the wagon with the screaming boy.

Once he heard her singing to Rudy. She had a sweet, clear voice that reminded him of the ballads people sang in the mountains or the Old Country.

Sometime between eleven and midnight, he was returning from carrying Rudy to Annie, when he heard a shrill scream. Did that come from his wagon? Was it Faith?

Chapter Nine

WILD HEMLOCK

JACOB CAREFULLY PLACED RUDY AND his blanket on the ground beside the wagon and rushed inside. A man bent over Faith, pinning her to the cot, as she fought against him. In the dim light, everything blurred.

"Whatsja doin', Aggie?" the man slurred. "It's jes' me."

Jacob grabbed him by the arm, pulled him off Faith, and shoved him out of the wagon. "What do you think you're doing?" He noticed the man still had his clothes fastened, and he breathed a sigh of relief.

"Jus' getting' in sorta late. Guess Aggie's right mad at her ol' man. Guess I had one ta many tonight, huh?"

"This is not your wagon. Get on now, and don't you dare come back here. I'll kill you if you ever harm my wife."

The man staggered off, Jacob lit a lantern and placed it on the wagon seat, picked up Rudy, and went inside the wagon to see about Faith. She lay on her side, curled into a ball, crying.

Remarkably, Rudy had slept through it all. He put the infant in the crate beside Faith's cot, pulled the lantern inside, and sat down beside her. He gently pulled her into his arms to comfort her, and she yielded willingly.

"Sh-h-h. It's all right, honey. He was just drunk and thought this was his wagon. I don't think he wanted to hurt you. He's gone now."

She trembled in his arms, and he slipped back and pulled her into his lap. He rocked her gently as he stroked her head and back. Her hair fell down her back and felt as fine as silk.

He knew his heart had been warming to Faith, but this had to be too soon. He needed to observe a mourning period for Lucille, and Faith needed comforting—nothing more.

"Would you like me to stay here with you for the rest of the night?"

Faith hesitated, and then finally nodded. "I'd rather not be left alone."

There was barely room for the cot and the baby's crate in the cramped quarters. They needed to get rid of some of Lucille's things to make more room.

He moved Faith to the back of the cot and took off his boots. He'd sleep in his clothes tonight. He noticed she wore a long chemise over her drawers. The soft, thin material did cover her to some extent.

He blew out the lantern and crawled in beside her. She'd slipped as far back on the cot as she could. He turned on his side to face her, and she turned to face away from him, fitting against him like stacked spoons. If he put his arms around her waist, it left plenty of room for both of them on the cot.

As Jacob lay there, with Faith wedged against him, he wished he hadn't told her they would wait until they got to know each other better. He liked her already, and he hadn't slept with Lucille since the night everyone celebrated their first day on the trail. His body responded to Faith in ways he didn't need, not if he planned to refrain from intimacy.

He reminded himself the intruder had scared her, and she didn't need his advances tonight anyway. He heard her breathing change and knew she'd fallen asleep.

He lay awake for what seemed like a long time, but he must have eventually dozed off. He awoke to hear Rudy fretting. Faith shifted and sat up to listen.

"Do I need to take him to Annie?" he whispered.

"Not yet." She lay back down. "He's just making noises in his sleep. When he wakes up hungry, he'll let you know."

"How do you know so much about babies?"

"Aunt Mabel had a baby girl late in life, just after I went to live with them. The little girl died of pneumonia before she turned three, but I took care of her until then."

Faith had been right about Rudy. About three o'clock, Jacob jerked awake to the baby's screams. Faith changed the baby's diaper, while he got up and put on his boots.

"Will you be okay, while I take him to Annie?" he asked her.

"I think so," she replied, "but leave a light burning and hurry back."

He thought Rudy would never get finished, and he rushed back from Annie's. When he got to his wagon, he saw Faith come from the wagon already dressed for the day. She smiled when she saw him.

"I figured there's not much use going back to sleep at this point. It's too near time to get up and start breakfast."

He started the fire, while she lay Rudy down and got the coffee ready to put on. While the coffee made, they sat by the fire and held their devotion.

"I like these special times in the mornings," he told her afterwards. "I'd like to make them a family tradition."

"I'm sorry I got so upset last night," she said, "but I appreciate what you did—pulling him away and staying with me like you did."

"You had every right to be upset, and I'm going to talk with Marshall and the council about what happened. I'm glad I helped. I think you're a very special person, Faith, and I already like you."

"I like you, too."

Jacob smiled as he went to bring up the milk cow. Maybe this marriage would be much better than his first one. Perhaps it could actually turn into a love match. He could always hope. And pray.

He would have never thought he'd be ready for another marriage, especially so soon after he'd buried his first wife. But, perhaps he needed someone to care for him, since Lucille never had. He found himself wanting Faith to fall in love with him. He wanted a real wife and a real marriage. Somehow, it almost seemed like Lucille had just been pretending.

When he related what had happened to the wagon master and the council, they decided to ban drunkenness. Anyone caught drunk would be taken to the council, and if he had indeed been inebriated, he would be kicked off the train.

"I don't think a man should be told he can't have his drink," Jacob heard Rex Caulder complain to Marshall. "The rest of us shouldn't be punished just because Parker can't protect his woman."

"This is no place for drunkenness," Marshall said. "The trip will be hard enough without asking for more problems. No one is banning liquor. We're just saying you can't get drunk, and everyone but you agrees."

Jacob realized Rex had it in for him, and he expected the man would try to make trouble. He shook his head. He agreed with Marshall. This journey west would be hard enough without some making things even harder.

Due to what had happened to Faith when left alone, Annie agreed to keep Rudy with her at night for some extra pay. That would make things easier for Faith and him.

The wagon train held more funerals. Almost the entire families of the two girls who'd picked wild plants with Faith had died. Apparently, the two had picked some poisonous ones, like wild hemlock, along with their wild carrots and parsnips. It caused violent deaths.

The bodies of those who ate it stiffened, and shook so violently they had to be tied down to keep them from hurting themselves. Their jaws clenched tightly, and they breathed with a hissing sound. On the last, blood spurted from their mouths. The father of one family and the son of the dead parents were the only family members spared, and that's only because they hadn't eaten any.

Marshall got everyone together after the funerals and explained to them how to recognize wild hemlock from the others. Everyone noticed how similar the three plants were. Jacob looked at Faith with a new respect. If she hadn't been so cautious and wise, he and she might be in graves now, and Rudy would've been left an orphan.

Things began to fall into a routine. Faith managed to keep up with all the chores, even with caring for Rudy during the days. She had to wash more often than Saturdays with all the diapers and soakers. Sometimes she pinned the diapers to the canvas of the wagons to dry, and the sun helped bleach them white.

Occasionally, after they stopped for the day, she'd start supper cooking and take Rudy with her to the river or else Jacob would carry up water for her to use by the wagon. He recognized how much she did, and he wanted to help her as much as he could.

In any spare moments, she usually sewed more diapers or mended. Jacob started reading the Scriptures in the morning, so she could sew or knit while she listened. He also gave her the material he'd bought in Independence. She cut up the white for more diapers and baby clothes. Rudy would need some larger ones as he grew.

They used as much fresh milk as they could, and Faith churned the rest. She strapped the churning can to the wagon, and by the end of the jostling day, the butter had formed. Jacob thought it was ingenious, although Faith assured him other women were doing the same.

The days had now turned baking hot, but Faith rarely complained. Yet, if another woman drove a wagon every day, he didn't know about it. He hoped they could put their goods together before long, and Faith wouldn't have to work so hard. She had shown herself capable of making the journey on her own, so he wondered again why she'd married him.

The days passed in a monotonous routine. Time didn't seem to mean the same out here.

When they circled the wagons on Saturday nights, Jacob looked forward to the lay-by a Sunday usually provided, but he began to feel an urgency to get Lucille's things out of the wagon. Somehow, if he could redistribute them, even if Faith chose to keep some of them, it would be putting Lucille to rest.

He found himself drawn to his new wife in a way he'd never been to Lucille. Of course, Lucille had kept him at arm's length from the very beginning of their marriage, and Faith didn't. She seemed to genuinely like him. With Lucille, he'd had to watch what he said, or she would constantly be angry. With Faith, he could be himself, and he'd yet to see Faith angry or upset with him. He didn't have to guard his words with her.

He looked forward to making Faith his wife in every sense of the word, and he thought that would likely be soon, maybe in another week. Tonight he planned to kiss her with a thorough kiss. He would be able to tell much about how she felt about him with such a kiss.

She fixed cream of potato soup for supper. It had onions and little pieces of side meat in it. With a mouth-watering cake of cornbread, "tasty" didn't begin to describe it.

"Is this one of those special milk dishes?" he asked.

"If you like it enough, it is," she told him, "but I have others. I also have an egg custard for dessert. With both our sets of chickens, we've accumulated some extra eggs."

"I hope you like fat men, because I may weigh three hundred pounds by the time we get to Oregon Territory."

She laughed. "With the way you walk beside the team and work so hard, I don't think we need to worry about that for years. Not if you plan to establish a good-size farm. I think you can eat anything you want without a concern."

He liked the easy way she laughed. It sounded almost as if she'd held it in for years, and now it tended to bubble over at any given opportunity.

When she started doing the dishes, he rose to help her. She seemed surprised, but he'd already finished his chores for tonight, and he knew Faith had already milked.

"Tell me about your childhood," he said as they worked.

"My early childhood was happy. My parents had married against the wishes of their parents, but they were very much in love and they loved me. My father came from a rich family and was well-educated. His parents disowned him when he married Mama."

"Where was he from?"

"Eastern Virginia, the Williamsburg area. Mama was Uncle Jed's youngest sister, and he became very angry when she ran away to marry Papa. She had been sent to help another sister for a few months because the woman needed help with her coming baby."

Her hands kept busy washing the dishes as she talked. "My parents moved to Salisbury, North Carolina, before I was born, and Papa tutored some students there, while Mama took in sewing. When I came along, Papa declared I would be the best-educated child around. He always said that's one legacy he could give me, that and my faith. I started to read by the time I was three. When they died, I had just turned ten, and I was working on the same level as his best students four and five years older."

"Was that when you went to live with Jed?"

"Yes. The pastor at the church we attended contacted my father's parents first, but they wanted nothing to do with me. My aunt had died, and Jed reluctantly took me in. Mabel probably had a lot to do with persuading him. The pastor personally traveled to Kentucky to take me to them. I never received another day of schooling, but Papa had taught me well enough, and I continued to read my Bible and Shakespeare and study the dictionary."

"Did your aunt and uncle mistreat you?"

"No, but I always knew I had to work hard for my keep. They didn't have much, and we lived very meagerly, pretty much a hand-to-mouth existence. What about you? What was your childhood like?"

"Pretty normal." He looked off remembering. "I was the third child. I have an older brother and sister. By the time I came along, my father had established a well-producing plantation in the Richmond area of Virginia. I grew up secure and loved, especially by my mother. She taught me about Jesus from my earliest memories. When I finished college, I decided to come to the West, because I wanted to farm, and I knew Charles would inherit the plantation, although I'll likely receive some cash. Not long after that, Lucille took an interest in me, we were married that October, and you know the rest."

The look she gave him said "Not really," but she didn't say it. He wanted to establish an intimate relationship with Faith before he told her about his problems with Lucille. He didn't want the past to cast a shadow over their future together.

"Let's take Rudy to Annie and take a short walk before we turn in."

Chapter Ten

NEW BEGINNINGS

AFTER THEY TOOK RUDY TO Annie, Jacob led Faith to the river. He liked the calming sound it made.

"I'm worried about Rudy," she told him. "His cries sound like something is hurting him, and I'm seeing blood in his stools. I asked Lena and Annie about it, but they are at a loss as to what it could be."

"Do you think it's serious?"

"I don't know, but it seems to be getting worse, instead of better. I've tried my best to take good care of him."

"Whatever is wrong, it's not your fault, Faith. You're taking excellent care of him. No one could do better, but I'm glad you told me. We'll pray it's not serious, and he'll get better soon."

She nodded, and he put an arm around her shoulders. They stood side by side looking into the darkening river. Dusk had fallen. He'd brought a lantern, but he hadn't lit it yet.

"I like talking with you and being with you, Faith."

"I enjoy you, too," she said quietly, as if she were unsure she should say it at all.

"You can always tell me how you feel or what's on your mind. I want us to be completely honest with each other."

As he said it, he realized he needed to tell her about his relationship with Lucille, or lack of relationship, as the case might be more appropriately labeled. If things went well, he would ask her to spend the night in his tent next Saturday or Sunday night, and he'd explain everything to her after that.

He pulled her around and wrapped his arms around her. She nestled against him just right. He tilted her chin up and looked into her eyes. It had gotten too dark to tell what she might be thinking.

He lowered his lips to hers and slowly began to kiss her. She tasted sweet, and, when he inserted pressure with his tongue, her mouth opened to his. From that moment on he lost himself in the kiss. He forgot how he'd planned it out; he forgot he'd intended to take it slowly. As she responded to him, his passion rose.

She pulled back first, but he still held her, and she didn't pull out of his arms. Her breathing had grown as heavy as his, and she held on to him as if she needed him for support.

"I hope I didn't hurt you," he said, as he lightly brushed two fingers over her lips. "I'm afraid I got carried away."

"No, you didn't hurt me. I'm just filled with emotions I don't understand. You're the first person to ever kiss me, except for my parents, when I was little."

"I'm glad I could be the first. There's something special growing between us, and it excites me beyond words."

He felt her tense. "What's wrong?" he asked her.

She hesitated, but she eventually answered him. "I don't know anything about the physical side of marriage. I'm afraid I won't know what to do, but I want to please you."

"Oh, Faith, don't be concerned about that. I promise you everything will be just fine. You told me you had never kissed a man before, but you responded to me beautifully. It took my breath away. Just like you automatically knew what to do when I kissed you, you'll naturally know what to do when we come together as man and wife. And I'll guide you. You trust me to do that, don't you?"

He could barely see her head nod in the darkening dusk. She must have wondered if he had, because she said, "Yes, yes I do."

He lit the lantern, wrapped one arm around her waist, and they started back. Now that he had the light, he could see her face. Her eyes were filled with a soft emotion. Could it be love, or had he aroused her that much? He would welcome either one.

He asked her to spend the night in his tent when they neared the camp. He hadn't planned to ask her that tonight, but things had moved faster and farther than he'd planned. The words had come out almost of their own accord, and he couldn't deny his growing feelings for Faith any longer.

"It might be better, so I won't keep worrying about it." She looked embarrassed, but something stirred within him, and he definitely couldn't wait any longer.

He'd planned to have his tent prepared for her with clean linens and maybe some flowers, but that would be impossible now. She was nervous and almost trembling by the time they returned, so he led her directly inside. He knew any waiting would make matters worse for her, and he didn't want a delay at this point either. He'd planned to test her with his kiss and hopefully encourage her feelings for him, but, in truth, that kiss had done something to him. He'd never had a kiss affect him so much, and he'd had his share of kisses.

He turned the lantern down as low as possible, so they barely had light to undress, but he instinctively knew she'd prefer that. They both undressed at the same time. She didn't wear a corset or layers of petticoats like Lucille had. She wore only her chemise, drawers and one light petticoat underneath her dress. With her undergarments still on, she slid underneath the covers and took them off there. He completely undressed and slid in beside her. He helped her pull off her chemise.

She tensed when he pulled her into his arms, but, when he began to kiss her again, he soon felt her relax. In the soft light, he could barely see her dark hair fanning over the pillow like fine strands of licorice. She was so pretty, and he became acutely aware of what a lovely figure she had, not as voluptuous as Lucille's, but still curvaceous in a more slender way. She was perfect.

When Faith moved beside him, he awoke. Morning had begun to lighten the tent. Faith pulled on her undergarments under the covers. He would have liked to tell her to wait, but they needed to get up, so they'd have time to hold their devotion, eat breakfast, and start the day. He knew they needed to get some of the things in their wagons sorted through.

"You were wonderful," he told her and meant it. She'd responded to him in a way he'd only dreamed of.

She lowered her eyes, but not before he saw the joy in them. His heart quickened, and he felt the last hunk of ice melt and fall away.

He kissed her gently and pulled away before his passion grew. It didn't take much for that to happen with her. He rubbed the back of his hand down the side of her face, and she looked into his eyes.

"You make me so happy," he said, hoping she could see the truth of the statement. He knew she needed affirmation that she had pleased him.

"You make me happy, too," she said and smiled shyly.

It took all his willpower not to lay her back down, but it would be too soon, and they had a lot to accomplish this day. They'd better get at it.

He hurried into his clothes and out to start the fire for her. She had shown him how to put some hot coals into a hole covered with a cast iron lid each night, and it made starting the fire so much easier each morning.

Thank Thee, God, for giving me this wonderful woman. I feel Thy blessings poured out and overflowing, and I marvel at them. Never have I imagined anything this amazing, and I thank Thee from the bottom of my heart.

They worked on the wagons after breakfast. Jacob pulled out all their food and utensils. He consolidated some of the supplies to take up less space. He also sorted through and organized all the tools. Anything he didn't think necessary to the trip or his farming, he set aside.

Faith went through Lucille's things. He could tell she had mixed feelings about taking any of his first wife's things, but he assured her he'd never seen most of it, and it wouldn't bother him for her to wear them. She'd probably have to do some minor alterations, but he already knew she could sew well.

She discarded all the silks, except one new dress that had never been worn. She kept the most practical cotton ones. She kept all the new cotton undergarments but threw out all but one of the corsets. When she'd finished, she had condensed three trunks into one, but she also had a pile she planned to rip up for the fabric.

"I'll just rip the skirts off them, fold them flat, and they'll fit in the bottom of the one trunk," she said. "I'll also keep the buttons."

He didn't know how Faith could accomplish as much as she did and still take care of Rudy. He seemed to be crying more and sleeping less. Jacob stopped and said a prayer for his son. He prayed God would heal whatever was wrong and make the little fellow strong and healthy.

"What is this?" Jacob asked when he came to some damp roots wrapped in a small canvas package.

"That's my rose cutting. Mama loved roses and she planted them all around our house. I took one cutting of a pretty red rose to Kentucky. When we left there, I dug up a root to plant in California, but now it will be in Oregon. I've also got some vegetable seeds for a garden."

"That's good. I've got some seeds to plant the fields with, too." Now, if he could just get some work done, instead of daydreaming about his wife.

To Jacob's surprise, Iris Bates came by. He thought she'd been Lucille's friend, not his, and he didn't care for the woman's loose ways.

"I'm very sorry to hear about your wife," she said. "I was sick at the time and didn't learn about her death or your remarriage . . . " She paused and gave Faith a cutting look. " . . . until I recovered enough to get out. I couldn't believe you'd married so quickly."

"I needed someone to take care of my son, and Faith had no one left, so the council thought this would be for the best. As it turned out, they were right." He gave Faith a knowing look.

Iris inched closer to him. Too close. "I would have been glad to have married you if you'd just asked."

Jacob fought a shudder. "That wouldn't have solved Faith's problem of being all alone, and I felt Faith would make an excellent wife and mother." Hopefully, Iris would read between the lines.

She stood for a few minutes, but when Jacob didn't say anything, she huffed and turned to leave. "You should have at least introduced us," she said over her shoulder.

He shrugged. He'd prefer Faith stay away from this woman, and he certainly hoped Iris would stay away from him.

━━━━━━━━━

Faith watched the pretty woman leave in a huff, but she couldn't help but smile. Jacob had not appreciated the woman's flirting, and he'd pretty much told her that he knew Faith would make a better wife.

She leaned back and took a moment just to watch him. She loved to look at the handsome man she'd married, and it pleased her that he treated her so well. She couldn't understand how his first wife could resist him, but, from all she'd learned, the woman must have. Faith's heart swelled just thinking of him and her pulse quickened every time he came near.

He did dozens of things every day to make things easier for her, but she knew he couldn't have named them. He did them naturally as a part of who he was, and she loved him for it. She'd certainly never experienced anything similar in Kentucky.

For so long, she'd methodically hammered out her chores on the nail heads of mornings, noons, and nights. Now, however, joy mixed into it all. Much of this trip had been drudgery, but that didn't hold true with Jacob around.

She didn't have to be quiet or watch what she said around Jacob. She could actually say the things that crossed her mind. Her mother and father used to lovingly tease each other, and she hoped she and Jacob could be like that, too. They were already growing close.

She'd almost told him how much she loved him last night, but he hadn't said the words to her yet, so she held back, too. But, he had shown her he loved her. She smiled at the memory. They had truly become one last night, and she'd liked it, but would Jacob think her a wanton if he knew her thoughts? She didn't know how to begin to tell him how she felt. These feelings were so new, and she hardly knew what she thought herself.

How could she have come to love him so much in just a few weeks? It made no sense, but fairy tales were made of this very thing, and she thanked God for it. After all, Jacob was her husband.

She got up to start supper. "Oh, here are a diary and some letters that came from Lucille's trunk."

Faith handed Jacob the items. He took them and put them to one side, as he continued to work.

She'd already cleaned and cooked the extra rooster, and she would make chicken and dumplings mountain style, one of the special milk dishes she had promised Jacob. She smiled when she imagined what he would say. He was easy to cook for, because he praised everything. She hadn't been used to such praise, or any praise, for that matter, not since she'd lost her parents.

Her uncle and aunt had never mistreated her, but never once had they told her she did something well or thanked her for anything she did. In fact, they'd acted as if she didn't exist most of the time. They'd only spoken to her to tell her to do something or explain how they wanted it done. A blessing had come with that, however. She'd learned the skills it would take to be a helpmate to Jacob, both on the trip to Oregon and in working a farm there.

Her husband made her feel able and competent in so many ways, something she hadn't felt since she was ten. She thanked God for giving her such a husband. He was right for her in so many ways, and, after last night, she thought she might suit him, too. She felt her face grow warm from the memory.

Chapter Eleven

SHOCKING REVELATIONS

"WHY DO YOU WANT TO search Faith's wagon?" Jacob asked.

Marshall and John stood in front of him. They didn't look too happy to be there, but Jacob could easily see their look of determination.

"Mrs. Bates is missing an expensive brooch, and she suspects Faith took it," Marshall explained.

"We don't think Faith took it," John added, "but we thought it best to clear up the matter and put the accusation to rest."

"What makes Iris Bates think Faith would have it?"

"She says Faith had admired it. Faith is from a poor family, and the piece is missing."

Jacob looked at Marshall in disbelief. "Faith is not poor now, and I've never met a more Christian woman than my wife. Besides, I got the impression that Iris had never even met Faith before today. She scolded me for not introducing them."

"I'm sorry, Parker, but will you allow us to search to prove you're right?"

"Go ahead. We have nothing to hide."

Faith walked up from the river where she'd gone to help Lena carry up some water. He told her what had been said.

"I didn't take anything," she said.

"I know that, darling. They should be through soon and see that for themselves."

After twenty minutes of looking in Faith's old wagon, the men came out. Marshall held out a brooch.

"We found this wrapped in the first part of a canvas that held some roots. It fits the description."

"I've never seen that before," Faith said.

Jacob couldn't believe it. Could Faith have stolen the jeweled pin? Would she? No! He knew better.

"We just cleaned out our wagons earlier today, and I unwrapped the canvas with Faith's rose roots and asked about them. Nothing else was in it then."

"I guess she could've moved it since then." Did Marshall think Faith guilty?

"I didn't, and I haven't gone into this wagon since Jacob cleaned it. He put most of the tools in here. We haul the provisions I need for cooking, our clothes, and the bed in the newer wagon. I haven't been in this one for a while until today."

"I'm afraid it's your word against Iris', and we did find the brooch among your possessions," Marshall said.

"But Iris didn't see Faith take it," Jacob said, "and anyone could have placed it in the wagon."

"For what purpose?" John asked.

"Someone who doesn't like Faith or me. Someone who wants to cause trouble." He immediately thought of Rex. Jacob was glad he hadn't come to accuse Faith, too, because he wouldn't have been as nice. Did that mean he might be the guilty party?

"What's the punishment for stealing," Faith asked.

By being on the council, Jacob knew the answer. Ten lashes with a whip. Marshall had said with the open wagons, the punishment needed to be stiff to deter robbery. "Surely you two can't be planning on whipping Faith. If you are, let me take the lashes for her. Mar my back, not hers."

"No, Jacob." Faith sounded frantic. "It's me they're accusing. I couldn't stand to see you flogged."

"As I can't you."

"The case would have to come before the council first," Marshall said.

"Since no one saw the thief," John added, "the evidence is rather flimsy."

"I could agree with that," Marshall said, "but let's see what the council thinks."

The council convened, and they talked with Faith and Jacob about the brooch again. They'd already heard what Iris had to say, and they asked Jacob to abstain from voting.

"We can't make exceptions for anyone," Rex stated. "What would it look like if we let the wife of a councilman get away with stealing?"

Despite Rex's vote to the contrary, in the end, the council decided they didn't have enough evidence to punish Faith. Jacob left wondering who would have put the missing brooch in Faith's wagon. It would've had to have been done after they cleaned the wagons. Who would have had the opportunity and held something against her? Faith couldn't think of anyone. Would Rex have gone to this extent, because he didn't like Jacob? It would seem he'd have tried to frame Jacob and not Faith, and why would he have stolen Iris' brooch to do so, when he could have used anything? Was Iris involved? Questions hovered but no answers.

Two things had kept the day from being idyllic—the accusation against Faith and Rudy's constant crying. Still, when they were together working, Jacob felt at peace. He enjoyed everything he did with Faith, even working to clean out the wagons.

Faith and he tried everything they could think of to quieten Rudy, but still he squalled.

"Just put him in the wagon, so we can eat supper in a semblance of peace," he finally told her. "We don't seem to be helping him any."

They could still hear him but not as clearly. Jacob couldn't wait to take the baby to Annie, so he and Faith could go to bed. He smiled at the thought. He'd had a hard time keeping his mind on the task at hand today. His thoughts kept going back to Faith and last night.

To his amazement, the chicken and dumplings were better than anything Faith had cooked so far. She'd also baked a cherry cobbler out of some dried black cherries she had.

"You're going to spoil me," he told her.

"I hope so," she smiled. "You deserve it."

Did he please her as much as she pleased him? He doubted it, but he wanted to.

After they cleaned up the dishes, Faith held Rudy, and Jacob worked on repairing a harness for one of the mules. Finally, the time to take the baby to Annie arrived. They'd just returned, and Jacob started taking care of the fire while Faith undressed in the tent, when Carolyn came running up.

"Mama says for you to come right away. Something's wrong with your baby."

Faith had heard, and she came out still buttoning the last buttons on her dress. They took off running.

"I was just getting ready to feed him," Annie said. "He suddenly gave out a loud cry and went limp. He died in my arms just that fast. I'm so sorry."

Jacob stood like a stone. He couldn't take in the news. He couldn't take another death. Would everyone he loved be ripped from him? Not Faith! *Oh, please, God, not Faith.*

He felt Faith let go of his arm where she'd been gripping it for strength. Until she let go, he hadn't realized she'd held it. He saw her move toward the baby with tears streaming down her face. He'd never doubted she loved Rudy, but, if he had, that doubt would have been dispelled now.

Still, he couldn't move. His feet seemed rooted to the ground and as heavy as if they'd changed to cast iron.

"You go get the things you want him buried in," he heard Annie tell Faith. "Lena and I will prepare his little body."

Body! His son was really dead. Faith took his arm again and led him away. His feet wouldn't go closer to the body, but they took him away.

She sat him in a chair, but he didn't even have a fire to gaze into. He'd put it out. He knew Faith said some things to him, but he didn't know what they were. He hoped she knew what to do. He didn't. He looked up. The stars were still in the sky. The moon hung half full, or was it half empty?

God, why? Wasn't losing my first wife enough? How much more do You expect from me? I'm not as strong as Job was. I can't take any more.

Faith came out of the wagon with the new baby gown and cap she'd just made. "I'm going to take these to Annie. Do you want to stay here?"

"No, I'll walk you."

He didn't want to be left alone to his depressing thoughts. He didn't want to risk the chance something might happen to Faith. If he had a third loss right now, he thought he'd go mad.

He waited for her as she took the clothes to Annie. Lena had come over, and she walked back with Faith.

"I'm so sorry, Jacob," the older woman said. "He must have been born with something bad wrong on the inside of him. At least he's not hurting anymore."

He nodded. He didn't trust himself to speak. Grief colored everything in tones of black and gray. It gnawed on his insides like a hungry wolf that chewed and shook its angry head as it ripped him apart.

He took Faith's hand as they walked back. He still had her, and she would be a comfort to him.

They went into the tent and got ready for bed. Everything had changed now. He might need physical comfort, but he knew Faith didn't. Tears streamed down her face again. He left his underclothing on and crawled in beside her.

He took her in his arms and held her. She broke into sobs and her body shook with them. He just rubbed her back and drew her close. He couldn't tell her everything would be okay. He didn't know that himself.

She cried herself to sleep in his arms. He lay there with his thoughts ricocheting in all directions.

What if Faith became pregnant after last night? What if having a baby killed her like it had Lucille? Why hadn't he considered these things earlier? Did it take a second death to make him think beyond his own selfish desires?

He'd better not make love to Faith again, at least not until they got to Oregon and off this grinding trail. Would Lucille have lived if they'd not been on such a grueling trip?

God help him, but he didn't wish her back now. He'd never wanted her to die, and he still grieved over her death, but if she and Faith stood before him today, he would choose Faith without hesitation. Was it a sin to feel that way?

Faith turned over in her sleep, and she no longer lay in his arms. He waited a few minutes to make sure she slept soundly, and he eased out of the pallet. He felt as if he'd been wound too tightly to lie still without Faith in his arms. He quietly put on his clothes. As he started out, his foot hit against something. He picked it up. It must be Lucille's diary. He'd thrown it in the tent opening and forgotten about it. He carried it outside and lit the lantern.

There were two letters tucked into the diary. Both of them seemed to be from a man named Rudolph Nester.

He remembered Lucille asking him to promise not to read her things, but he'd never made that promise. He read the letter with the earliest date first. It had been written well before Lucille and his engagement.

My dearest Lucy,

I love how you call me "Rudy," and I shall call you "Lucy." In fact, my darling, I love everything about you.

I can't tell you how much last night meant to me. You are the delight of my life, so beautiful and filled with passion. I can't wait until you can meet me again. Please work that out to be soon. I count the minutes until you are in my arms again.

In your note, you asked if I wanted to marry you. You know that I do. Nothing would give me more pleasure than to call you my wife. Why, I would be the envy of every man who ever saw you. However, with my military obligations, we'll have to wait until I get my commission and assignment. Hopefully, it will be to a post on the East Coast. I would loathe to go out West and fight the savages. That would be no place for someone of your culture and station either.

In the meantime, I look forward to every minute we can be together. Please contact me soon with the welcomed news that you will come to me again.

Yours forever,

Rudolph Nester

Well, Lucille hadn't been a virgin when he married her. But what had happened to her Rudy? Was he the real father of Lucille's baby? Surely she wouldn't have named Jacob's son after her former lover. He read the next letter. The date put it not long before he'd been found with Lucille in her bedroom.

Lucy,

I'm sorry to learn you think you might be in a family way. Regrettably, I won't be able to marry you. It's true I've been assigned to a post in Maryland, but my parents are insisting I marry a Colonel's daughter, and it will be good for my career. If I refuse them, they will cut me off without a penny. I know you'll understand. Marriage to me would be intolerable for both of us if we were without funds, and the money I get from the military now is a mere pittance of what we'd need. The time we spent together was magical, and I'll always re-member them and you with fondness, but, unfortunately, such enchanted times were not meant to last. Therefore, it is with great regret that I must say "goodbye" to you. I am sure you can visit someone in Richmond that can help rid you of the unwanted baby, should you actually be with child.

You know, missing one monthly is not enough to really tell.
I wish you all the best.

Sincerely,

Rudolph Nester

What a sorry excuse for a man! Was marrying Jacob the answer to Lucille's dilemma? Had she entrapped him on purpose? He opened her diary to find out.

The truth cut worse than Jacob had imagined. Despite the ill way Rudolph had used her, she remained deeply in love with the man.

She wrote of how she couldn't stand Jacob's touch, and tears came to Jacob's eyes as he read. Her father had picked Jacob as being naïve but honorable and easy to snare. Lucille had agreed because at least she'd liked his looks, and she played her part in the masquerade to the best of her ability.

She told how she'd had a hard time pretending to be enthralled with Jacob during their engagement. She tried to convince herself, since she couldn't have Rudy, Jacob was as good as anyone. She didn't want to be an old maid, and she did want a good father for her child.

If she told Jacob she was expecting too early, she'd been afraid he'd become suspicious, so she didn't use the baby to get him to stay in St. Louis where doctors might tell him the truth about how far along she was. According to the diary, she'd posted another letter to Rudolph from St. Louis as soon as they'd arrived, but he never answered her.

She had never given Jacob a chance. Their marriage had been doomed from the very beginning. Lucille would have never tried to make the best of things, and Jacob didn't think time would have helped things at all. In all likelihood, things would've only gotten worse.

The betrayal and deception felt worse than the grief ever had. Rudy hadn't even been his son, but, of course, none of this had been the poor baby's fault. He still felt a loss there. He would have treated him as a son regardless. This mess had not been of God, it had been of the devil. But, couldn't God have protected him? Why him? *God, I still don't understand.*

What a fool he'd been! Looking back, the village idiot would have known Lucille's baby wasn't his. Her father must have been right. Jacob had been naïve enough to be fooled. He'd just never considered such an upstanding family like the Statens would be so dishonest.

By the time he'd read the letters and the diary and sorted through some of his own thoughts and feelings, his pocket watch read three o'clock. The call to rise would come at four. It seemed useless to go back to bed. Besides, he did need to stay away from Faith. That would be the only way to be sure he didn't get her with child. He knew he didn't have the strength to be with her at night again and not make love to her. She affected him way too much. He had probably already fallen deeply in love with her, but he didn't want to examine those feelings too closely. Better to save that for a later time.

Thoughts buzzed and stung like angry hornets. Some of them were wild and irrational. Were all women as conniving as Lucille? Could Faith really be trusted? Was she the thief who had stolen Iris' pin? He really didn't know her deepest thoughts and motivations. Why had she agreed to marry him? He really couldn't see a single good reason from her point of view.

Everything that had happened overwhelmed him—first Lucille's coldness, then her death, next Rudy died, and now Lucille's deception and betrayal uncovered. He felt numb inside and hurting all at the same time. How could that be possible?

He stood and built up the fire with the intention of burning the diary and letters, but he decided to hide them in his trunk instead.

He got out pen and paper and wrote a letter to Lucille's parents. He wanted to tell them he knew everything and rant at them for their part in this, but he knew that wouldn't help anything. He wouldn't feel right about doing it either. Losing their daughter and grandchild would hurt enough. In the end, he wrote a short note informing them their daughter had died in childbirth and the baby several weeks later.

He would mail the letter at Fort Laramie. The fort had no regular mail service, but someone headed east would pick up the mail and post it at the first post office, if he left the money to do so. He should write his parents, also.

Faith came out and joined him at four. "What are you doing?"

"I wrote a letter to Lucille's parents and mine to let them know of hers and the baby's deaths. I also told my parents about you."

"I should probably write my cousin about his parents, too."

Faith went about making breakfast, but Jacob could tell she grieved. He wanted to comfort her, but he didn't want to get too close. He needed to pull back for a while. He should have followed his original plan and then their intimacy would have never happened yet.

"Just make some coffee for me. I don't feel like eating," he told her.

"I don't either," she said.

They held Rudy's quick funeral right before the wagons pulled out. Jacob stood beside Faith without touching her. Tears ran silently down her cheeks, but she didn't sob, although she did glance at him with questions in her watery eyes.

They started off, and for once he was glad they had separate wagons. He'd keep it that way for as long as hers would go.

Chapter Twelve

WITHDRAWAL

FAITH LOOKED OVER AT JACOB at the nooning. He had taken a long time watering the teams. When he came back he picked up his plate without a word, ate a few bites, set it down, and said "Thanks." Nothing else.

What was wrong? She knew he grieved over Rudy. She did, too, but wouldn't it be better to comfort each other? She needed him. Why didn't he need her? Did he blame her for Rudy's death? Did he regret taking her as his wife, now that he didn't need her to care for the baby?

"I think I need to be alone for a while," Jacob said when bedtime arrived. "Why don't you sleep in the wagon again. I need some time to sort out my thoughts and work through my grief."

Faith nodded and went to the wagon. What could she say? There had to be more to this than just his grief, or he would welcome her comfort. Something else was going on, but what? Regardless, he had rejected her, and that rejection hurt her to the core. She cried herself to sleep again but not from thoughts of sweet little Rudy. She cried for the loss of Jacob. She realized her hopes and dreams lay in his shadow, so he could easily crush them beneath his feet. She hated the uncertainty she felt.

They'd been seeing signs of buffalo, especially around the riverbanks where they went to water. Faith heard Obadiah going around telling the men he'd found a few stragglers, which were lost from the main herd a mile to the west. He wanted a group of men to saddle up and join him.

"Jacob sent me to drive his wagon until he gets back," Lester said as he climbed up into the wagon. Apparently, the thin man planned to ride instead of walk.

Jacob hadn't told Faith he was going on the hunt. He said little to her and stayed away from the wagon whenever possible. He didn't even come out of his tent in the mornings to have devotion with her now, and, when he said grace, he prayed one or two short sentences. She felt low and heavy, like a sad loaf of bread that wouldn't rise.

Lord, protect Jacob today and ease whatever is wrong with him—with us. Repair our relationship and restore my loving, caring husband, I pray. If I've done anything wrong, if I need to do something differently, please show me. My heart is breaking. Look on me kindly in Thy great love and mercy and help me I pray, in Jesus' name. Amen.

The days were even longer and more monotonous now. The prairie appeared endless in its sameness, as it stretched out before them. Time seemed to either stand still or trickle backwards.

Faith had prayed almost constantly since Rudy had died. If she couldn't read her favorite Psalms over and over again, she said memory verses in her mind, but they weren't soothing her like usual. She had to keep reminding herself God was in control. He would never leave her, and He would see her through no matter what.

Maybe the lesson in all this told her to rely on God and no one else. She'd thought she'd learned that lesson well in the last nine years, but then Jacob had come into her life. She had grown to rely on him for much more than his help and protection on the trail. At last, she had someone to talk with, to appreciate her, to love, and to love her in return—or so she'd thought. Was it all a facade, a lie, a cruel joke?

She knew the Lord was sufficient, but didn't He design man and woman to need each other? Isn't that why He created Eve—to be Adam's companion? She'd had a small taste of how wonderful being Jacob's wife could be. *Please don't take that away now, Lord. It's so much harder to go back to my old life now that I know.* Why did He let her see what could be, only to pull it back again? "I don't understand, Lord. Show me Thy way and will in all this."

"Talking to your mules now?" Lena said with a smile as she walked up. "I saw Jacob leave with the hunt, and I thought you might use some company."

Faith had better not say too much. They had to talk loudly to be heard over the wagon noises.

"Yes, he sent Less to drive his wagon. If I'd known he planned to go, I'd have packed him a nooning."

"He didn't tell you?"

Faith shook her head. She hoped she didn't have to explain.

"Well, I'll be. That doesn't sound like Jacob at all, but I've thought something's been bothering him. I guess it's hard to get over two deaths in such a short time like that."

Faith nodded, but she wanted to say she could help Jacob if he'd let her.

The hunters came back for supper. They'd managed to kill only one buffalo. It had been hard to get close enough to the stragglers, and the beasts were much faster than they looked. Faith learned all this from overhearing Harlan and some of the other men talking. Jacob said nothing about it, but he had brought her a hunk of meat, and they could use the fresh meat.

Faith's fear and worry grew larger with every passing day. She tried to give it to God, but it would keep returning, especially as time passed and Jacob showed no signs of changing.

The wagon train had to keep crossing rivers and their tributaries. The easiest crossings were where they could ford through shallow water or had a ferry, but sometimes there were neither.

They came to a crossing too deep to wade across but with no ferry, so they had to empty out the wagons, patch and tar the cracks, and float

the wagons across. At least Jacob and Faith had already sorted through
their wagons and discarded some of their belongings.

They didn't have the cook stoves or heavy pieces of furniture
some of the others hauled either. Some of those heavy pieces would be
left right here beside the river. Others would probably be left behind
before they got over the high mountains.

Faith watched Jacob for a few minutes and then began to help. She
could work almost as fast as he did, and her hands made the process
much faster. They spent all Thursday preparing the wagons. Friday
they began floating them across.

Faith couldn't swim. There hadn't been a stream deep enough for
her to use near their cabin in Kentucky. They had only shallow creeks
for wading.

The river looked awfully deep here, but Faith felt almost numb
to the danger. She had so much on her mind, she'd let God take care
of this. She wished she could give all her worries to Him, and she
tried, but she kept picking up her troubles with Jacob again. Her mind
couldn't stay away from them or him.

She stared at the raging river. It reminded her of her relationship
with Jacob—uncertain.

Some of the men on horseback took the livestock across first. These
animals had to swim across. They had a hard time getting the animals
started, but once the first one went, the others followed.

Faith watched the first wagons float across. The covers were taken
off to make it easier to guide. Extra men boarded and helped those
with small families. Then, they would use a horse or mule to get back
to the other side. A few of them swam back across, but not many.

They launched the wagon above where they needed to land, because the current would drift them downstream. When their turn
came to go, Jacob seemed nervous, but he said nothing.

"God will see us through," Faith said to him just before the men pushed the wagon in. His face relaxed a little, but he didn't reply.

Once they were launched and into the river, it didn't seem nearly as scary as she'd anticipated. They crossed without difficulty, and Faith thought it would have been fun if she could've shared it with the other Jacob, the one who'd seemed to like her.

Jacob left her there and rode his horse back to get her old wagon. She felt trepidation when she saw him push off. What if the swift current swept him and the horse downstream? What if the rickety wagon fell apart in the raging waters? What would she do then?

What is wrong with you Faith Allen . . . eh . . . Parker? Where is your faith, your trust? You know it's all in God's hands, so why are you fretting? You know better than this!

Jacob got caught in a strong current, and the wagon tilted. Faith held her breath, but it righted again, and Jacob made it across only a little farther downstream. Now if they could just keep their marriage from upturning or drifting off-course.

———————————

Jacob glanced at Faith as he pulled the wagon where it needed to be and got down. She hadn't seemed at all concerned when they were in the middle of the deep river in a vessel designed for land travel. If he didn't know better, he'd almost think she enjoyed this. What an adventurer! He admired her greatly. He turned his head away, stared at the river, and concentrated on stifling his thoughts. Admiring her would take his mind to places he needed to avoid. He wanted to make sure she stayed safe, because he didn't think he could handle it right now if something happened to Faith. God might as well take him, too. He hoped his mother had been right when she said God didn't give us more than we could handle, because he knew he couldn't handle losing Faith right now.

Staying away from Faith had turned into the hardest thing he'd ever tried to do. He thought it would get easier with time, but it didn't. Time gave him more opportunity to think about how great Faith was and how despicable Lucille had treated him.

Sometimes the antithetical sides almost converged, and he felt he could never trust another woman again, not even Faith. He had never been so confused, but the more he thought, the more confused he became. He almost felt numb from the pain and grief of it all.

He barely slept, either, but he usually stayed in the tent. He didn't want to chance having Faith come out in the night and have to deal with that temptation. *Lord, help me to do what's right.*

"You're not eating enough, Jacob," Faith said one morning at breakfast. "Tell me what to fix and I'll do my best to make it something you'll like."

"I like all your cooking just fine. It's not your fault that I don't have an appetite."

He tried to eat a little better, but each bite seemed to grow in his mouth and multiply in his stomach. How long could he go on like this?

He'd found himself too grounded in his faith to turn away from God, but something had pulled him farther away, and he felt more separated from the Lord. He didn't feel as close to anything anymore. Was he doing something wrong? He just wanted to protect Faith, and that had to be the right thing to do.

The trees had long disappeared. The women and children gathered buffalo chips to build their fires. The dry ones had very little odor, and, the best Jacob could tell, the grass particles in the dung caused them to burn well and provide fuel.

Jacob had burned the wood in Lucille's two extra trunks already. His heart still wrenched when he thought of her. How could she have been so dishonest and treated the man she'd married so badly? The hurt stabbed at his heart every time he thought of it. How could it feel in shreds and still grow in love for Faith? Would pulling her close help him to heal? No! He couldn't think of himself first. He wanted to put God first and Faith a close second. He would not put his desires above her wellbeing.

They had a thunderstorm, but no rain came. The sky put on a dark shroud, roared with grief, and lashed out with bolts of lightning, but no tears fell. The stock grew restless, and Marshall sent out more guards. He asked Jacob to go, too.

He saddled his horse and rode the perimeter of the animals. He moved slowly and hummed to try to keep the animals and himself calm, but they were nervous. The light had dimmed, more because of the storm than the setting sun, but he could still see.

He heard the growing rumble before he could see anything. It seemed to sweep across the prairie, but it remained constant and grew louder, certainly not thunder. Everything seemed to stand still to determine what the strange, rhythmic noise could be.

At first, Jacob saw a dark blob moving in the distance, but it covered the entire horizon to the west. Then it became obvious the flowing mass was made up of individual dots. The dots became larger. Buffalo. A buffalo stampede!

They needed to have the livestock in the corral of wagons, but they didn't have time to get them there now. The stampeding herd seemed to be headed straight for the wagons.

"Let's drive these as close to the wagons as we can," Jacob shouted.

He needed to get close to Faith and make sure she remained safe. He sure hoped she hadn't walked away from the wagon. What if she became trapped in the stampede? He prayed a quick prayer as he rode.

The cattle and oxen moved toward the wagons easily, but the horses and the mules had other ideas. Jacob decided the animals weren't nearly as important as the people.

"Some of us need to drive the cattle on up," he shouted, "while others try to round up the horses and mules."

He rode behind the cattle and didn't look to see who followed or stayed. He just looked for Faith.

Because of the way the wagons had circled, they couldn't take the animals toward Jacob's wagons and keep them back, away from the stampede. His wagon sat on the side extending the farthest into the path of the stampeding beasts. He hurried the cattle toward the back side of the circle, which put them between the wagons and the river.

He looked to see three other men following him. "Can you hold them close to the wagons here? Don't give them the opportunity to get scared and run in another direction. I'm going to see to my wife."

"Yeah. Go ahead."

He quickly circumvented half the train. He dismounted at the tongue of his wagon and led his horse over it.

Faith stood behind the tongue of her wagon watching the buffalo come. His heart danced at the sight of her safely standing there. But the great tide of animals seemed to be rushing straight for them. The wagons had started shaking, as if an earthquake had struck, and Jacob could feel the vibration through his boots.

"Come," Jacob said to his wife and put out his hand. She took it, and he pulled her to the center of the wide circle. It was the first time he'd touched her in a good while, and he felt sensations all over his body. Just holding her hand brought back memories of their night together.

"Is it dangerous?" Faith asked.

"I hope not, but I didn't want to take any chances."

The beasts had almost reached the wagons when they turned and avoided contact with the white, canvas-covered tubs. Disaster had been averted.

He dropped her hand immediately. He hadn't meant to keep holding it.

She looked at him as if she wanted to ask a question, but then disappointment took over. "Thank you," she said and walked back to their wagon with her head down.

Jacob mounted his horse and went to see about the livestock. Why did he suddenly feel like he'd let her down? He'd made sure she was safe, hadn't he?

All the cattle were safe, but some of the horses and mules had run off. Faith's mules were among them.

"We need to retrieve the stock quickly before the Indians find them," Marshall said.

A group of about a dozen men saddled up. Jacob volunteered to go, too.

"Let me go tell Lena where I'm going, and I'll join you," Harlan said.

"Tell Faith for me, too, if you don't mind."

"Will do." Harlan threw his hand in the air in further acknowledgment as he walked away with his back toward Jacob.

They found about half the missing stock. Faith's mules weren't among them. It might be just as well. Jacob didn't think they would make it much farther anyway. Even resting every third day, they appeared spent.

He didn't like the thoughts of using all his oxen every day, however. At least he already had the extra yokes.

Maybe he and Faith should consolidate their goods into the one wagon. With them already using up quite a bit of the foodstuff, it would be possible, but that would mean being in closer contact with Faith every day. He'd need to give that some more thought before deciding.

Faith had supper waiting for him when he got back. She had everything laid out and the fire going.

"You should have gone ahead and eaten without me," he told her.

"Neither one of us has been eating much lately, so I decided to cook a simple supper."

She fried corn cakes and served a fried egg on top of them. Jacob had never eaten them quite like this, but they were good. He ate two, more than he'd eaten lately, and Faith looked pleased.

"If I've done something wrong, Jacob, please tell me. I want to be a good wife, but you're making it hard."

"Oh, it's not you, Faith. It's me. There've been too many deaths in such a short span, and I just need some time. Can you be patient with me?"

"It would be easier if you didn't shut me out and try to stay away as much as possible. I'm here for you. I want to help. Let me comfort you."

"I just need some time to sort through things right now."

She looked even more worried. "Are you trying to decide what to do about me?"

What in the world did she mean by that? Maybe, in a way, he was. He wanted to keep her healthy and safe. Was she considering leaving? Surely not.

"Don't push me, Faith. Just be patient and give me some time." He tried to soften his tone, so he didn't sound sharp, but he could tell the words still wounded her.

The next day they passed two dead bodies of men with arrows standing in their chests pinning them to the ground. They'd been dead long enough for their bodies to swell and blacken. It appeared they'd been tortured and possibly mutilated.

"They probably did something stupid to infuriate the Indians," Marshall said. "The natives left the bodies here as a warning. I don't think we have much to worry about. There haven't been many Indian problems recently, not like there were for the first settlers, but we'll be more vigilant anyway."

Faith had to walk right by the site, and Jacob saw her look at the grotesque scene and then quickly look away. He wished he could spare her or at least comfort her. He saw her bow her head slightly, and he knew she was praying.

He used to love to watch her as they walked. Now, it brought agony, because it made him want her even more. He tried to look elsewhere, but, with her right in front of him, that didn't always work. He reminded himself over and over again it needed to be this way. She didn't need to be with child as hard as this journey had become.

"Aren't we going to bury them?" he asked Obadiah as the older man rode by.

The scout shook his head. "They're so fer gone, that no one wants that job, and hit's better to leave well enough alone. We don't want to rile up the Injuns, and hit won't do them men no good now. No, hit's best we keep a movin'."

The plains held plenty of wildlife. Jacob liked the taste of antelope even better than the buffalo. Jackrabbits were also plentiful, and wild turkeys and sage hens gave a welcomed change. Other animals included prairie dogs, owls, rattlesnakes, lizards, and coyotes, but these didn't provide food.

The men had concentrated on hunting buffalo, and there were plenty of them. They could have shot more than they did, but it would be better to take only what they could cook or dry into jerky before it spoiled. They could hunt again when needed.

The bison herds were easy to locate when they were moving fast. They stirred up enormous dirt clouds.

Jacob loved to go on the hunts. Somehow, when he rode fast trying to bring down a mighty beast, he could leave his troubles and focus on the immediate task, and he experienced a brief moment of peace.

Chapter Thirteen

QUICKSAND

THERE WERE STRETCHES OF THE Platte with dangerous quicksand made worse by the fact that it looked harmless. On the Loup Fork of the Platte, Faith watched the men fasten the wagons together with chains and ropes due to the quicksand.

She heard Harlan explain to Lena that this would keep any one wagon from sinking. The wagons in front would help to pull the one behind out of trouble.

Obadiah rode in front, taking care to find a safe route for the lead wagon. She and Jacob were sitting in their wagons to drive them through this. She wished he were in front of her, but she knew he would be following, even if she couldn't see him.

In fact, she wished his wagon always moved in front of hers. Then, she could watch him as he walked along beside the team. She still didn't get to see enough of him. He stayed away from the wagon, as much as he could, and, even when he came near, his mind seemed far away from her. She thought things might be getting a little better between them, but she didn't know for sure. He didn't seem quite as angry, but he hadn't returned to being cordial, either. She worried he didn't want her anymore.

Faith hated all this guesswork. She'd much prefer they told each other what they thought, even if it turned out to be bad. At least that would be honest, but, for some reason, Jacob had no inclination to talk honestly. He had chosen to be sullen and quiet.

Every now and then, he would do something to give her a glimmer of hope. She could almost believe the warm, friendly Jacob still existed somewhere deep inside this new one. She just hoped he would dig himself out soon.

She felt a jolt to her wagon. Had she been daydreaming and got into a quicksand bog?

"Faith, hold your wagon steady and have your team pull hard," she heard Obadiah yell. "Jacob's slid into some quicksand."

Oh, no! Jacob! The cold, stiff fingers of fear clawed at her heart, but she forced herself to concentrate on what she needed to do, instead of letting panic take control. Harlan drove the wagon in front of her, and he had his team pulling hard, too. She wished she could see behind her. Jacob was a good driver, so surely he would get the wagon out.

She finally felt her wagon give a lunge forward, and she knew his wagon had pulled out of the quagmire. She started to slow for a moment, so she could look back.

"Keep 'em movin'," Obadiah shouted. "Don't stop now."

Faith obeyed orders, but she wished she could find out how Jacob fared. Finally, they cleared the marshy area and stopped the teams for the men to unhook the ropes and chains.

Faith jumped down and ran back to Jacob. Without thinking, she rushed into his arms. At first, he gripped her tightly, but then he pulled back and let her go. "That was some good driving you did," he said. "Thank you for pulling me out."

She nodded and walked back to her wagon. At one time he'd have told her he was proud of her. At one time he'd have held her like he never wanted to let her go, instead of pushing her away. Salty tears stung her eyes, but she swallowed hard and pulled them back.

The dust covered everything. Nothing escaped it, and Faith felt as if it even penetrated her heart.

Without Jacob to talk with, the monotony of the landscape grew worse and worse. She needed to talk to someone, so she planned to visit Lena at her first opportunity. That shouldn't be hard. Jacob didn't hang around the wagons any more than he had to, and he got one of the Agner brothers to drive so that he could go on hunts as often as possible.

At least they were having plenty of fresh meat. When she could, she marinated the meat in vinegar water overnight. It made the buffalo steaks tender and took out the strong grassy taste. She also sliced it into thin strips and strung it on the wagon to dry into jerky. It didn't take long in this blazing sun.

Of course, the dried pieces of meat caked in dust, too, but she would rinse and soak what she cooked. She planned to use some of the jerky in stews. She knew they'd occasionally dried meat in Kentucky when they weren't able to cure it. She'd made stews from the dried venison, but she'd had to cook it longer.

How she wished Jacob still enjoyed her meals. He still always thanked her, but he ate a fraction of what he once did, and it showed. He had grown thinner, and she worried about his health.

She wished, even more, he would enjoy being with her again. She'd been granted a few days of warm conversations and one night of Jacob's lovemaking, enough for her to know what she missed now. She'd thought he'd enjoyed that night, too. Had she been wrong? Had she done something wrong? She was too inexperienced to know.

She knew he used to enjoy just being around her. What had happened? What were his thoughts? Why didn't he tell her what had happened? *The Lord giveth, and the Lord taketh away; blessed be the name of the Lord.*

I'll bless Thy name, Lord, regardless, but please don't let Jacob stay estranged. Faith had always turned to the Lord for companionship and comfort. That's what she would do now. He would never turn from her or reject her. He always waited for her with open arms anytime she needed Him. Yes, "blessed be the name of the Lord."

She didn't go to visit Lena. Lena came and got her.

"Harlan has gone off with some of the men, and I thought you might come and keep me company."

Faith picked up her sewing basket and followed Lena. She might as well get some mending done while they sat and talked.

"You and Jacob have been looking right peaked and unhappy lately. What's wrong, dear?" Lena came right to the point.

"I wish I knew. Ever since Rudy died, he's treated me like the enemy. He stays away as much as he can, and when he's about, he doesn't talk any more than he has to."

"Well, he has lost a wife and a son on this trip."

"But, it's more than that. I don't know what it is, but I think it's something that has to do with me. I've even thought maybe he doesn't need me anymore, now that Rudy's gone."

"No, I'm sure that's not the case. I'd say something's eating away at him, though. Have you tried to get him to talk to you about it?"

"You know I have. He just tells me to be patient, give him more time, and not to push him."

Tears started rolling down her cheeks. She tried to hold them back but couldn't. "I'm afraid I've lost him, Lena. Whoever said, 'It's better to have loved and lost than never to have loved at all' was wrong. If I had never known Jacob, I wouldn't know what I'm missing."

"You love him then?"

"I do. God help me, but I do."

"Don't concede defeat yet, child. He's still here on this wagon train, as are you, and you're still married to him. I'm sure he needs someone to talk with and to give him some good advice, and I'm just the person. Harlan says no one has more advice than me."

Faith went to the flap of Jacob's tent that night. She'd seen him go in there, and he'd been avoiding her all day.

"Jacob, could I please talk to you for a minute?"

"I'm tired now, Faith. Can't it wait?"

"No, it can't. If you don't want to come out here, I'll come in there."

He came out immediately. He must have still been fully dressed. She went toward a stool and he followed.

"Jacob, right after we were married you told me you took our wedding vows very seriously, especially since they were pledged before God. You also said you didn't plan to keep any secrets between us, and you wanted to be the husband I'd always dreamed of. You even told me you wanted our love to grow. I don't think you are doing any of those things now. Can't we at least go back to being friends? I miss our conversations and sharing things with you."

She saw him hesitate, and his eyes softened when they looked at her. She hoped she'd finally gotten through to him, but he clenched his jaw and looked away.

"I thought I'd explained. Can't you give me time to get over my losses."

"How much time is it going to take? The rest of our lives? I could give you time if it didn't have to be apart from me. Are you trying to lose me, too? Is that what you want?"

She knew her eyes were watery, but she managed to hold back the tears and keep her voice from cracking. *God, please let him understand, and please let him care.*

"No, I don't want to lose you. That's exactly what I'm doing, trying not to lose you."

He said it quietly, as if he didn't want to say it at all, but his voice had filled with emotion. Yet, he still didn't look at her.

"I don't understand. Please explain what you mean by that."

He shook his head. "Look, just let me sort through some things. We'll talk again soon."

He looked at her then, and he must've seen a look of disbelief on her face. "If you'd like, we'll schedule a time. We'll talk Sunday after the noon meal."

"Okay Sunday, then."

Jacob hadn't slept any that night. Faith knew this, because she'd been awake all night, too, and she'd heard him throughout the night. He had his lantern burning part of the time, and he moved around in his tent part of the time. He looked tired this morning.

After breakfast, he walked toward the Haywoods' wagon. She said a prayer that Lena would have a chance to talk with him.

———————

Jacob had to talk with someone. Faith had been right. He hadn't lived up to his wedding vows or the things he'd promised her, and this bothered him. If a man didn't live up to his word, he wasn't much of a man.

He trusted Lena, but he feared he might not want to hear what she had to say. He hoped she'd have breakfast over with and there'd be time to talk before they had to pull out. He knew she also liked Faith, but he felt she would hold his confidence and not tell Faith what he said. Lena had become a good friend to them both.

She had just thrown out her dishwater when he walked up. She looked happy to see him.

"Where's Harlan?" he asked, and her face fell. "I had hoped to talk to you in private."

Her face lit up again. "Well, come over and have a seat. We should have time. Mr. Marshall said we'll be delayed a bit this morning. We've got more cholera, but we're so behind schedule. He's going to leave the sick wagons behind. When they can travel, they'll try to catch up."

"I'm sorry to hear that. I hope they recover quickly. I forgot all about the council meeting last night, so I didn't know."

"Now, what did you want to talk about?"

Where to start? He told her about Lucille's deceit first.

"Sounds to me you might be feeling a mite sorry for yourself. Remember you're only a victim if you choose to think you're a victim."

Jacob jerked his head up. He'd expected a bit more sympathy here.

"So, Rudy wasn't really your son, and she hoodwinked you into marrying her? I guess you've had a weight on your shoulders. That's for sure."

"No, Rudy had been fathered by another man, but I was a father to him. Still, the situation did hit me hard, and, on top of all that, she still held the cad in high regard. I don't think she would've ever wanted me."

"If you aren't still mourning Lucille, then why have I noticed you being so cold with Faith? When things get so bad you can't see a bright side, you need to polish something to make it shine. Faith would polish up nicely. In fact, if you ask me, she's already a bright spot in your life."

"I didn't know it had become that obvious that I've stepped back from Faith. You know Lucille died in childbirth. Well, I want to make certain the same thing doesn't happen to Faith."

"Are you never going to have children then?"

"I do want to have children eventually, but not until we're settled in Oregon."

"And you've decided all of this without a word to Faith. Of all the idiotic notions! Do you know you're rejecting Faith the very way Lucille rejected you? The reasons are different, but the result's the same."

"I can't stand the thought of losing her. I can't take the chance of putting her at risk."

"What's wrong with you, son? You got your mind so twisted and snarled it's going to be quite a chore to get it untangled. First of all, why are you trying to play God and manage people's lives? If God wanted to take Faith home, do you think anything you might do would change that? You need to seize every moment as the gift it is, because we never know how many we'll have. Life itself is a risk. We're all going to die sometime, and that includes Faith."

She paused and gave him time to absorb what she'd said and then continued. "If you get to Oregon, and something happens to Faith, what have you got? What memories are you making? You need to take your wife and love her, enjoy her, and let her love and enjoy you.

What if something happens to you? What have you given her? How will she remember you?"

"I never thought of it like that."

"You need to wake up and do your best to live every day to the fullest. Don't waste a single one, and that's exactly what you've been doing. None of us are given enough to waste. If you keep holding on to past hurts, you'll miss out on your future. I've always thought you were more mature than you're acting right now. If you're a Christian, where's your faith and trust? The will of God will never take you where the Grace of God won't protect you."

What Lena said did make sense. Listening to her, Jacob wondered what he'd been thinking, too.

"What should I do now?"

"Go to your wife and share everything with her. Tell her about Lucille and what happened there, inform her how your thinking had become skewed, apologize to her, and let her know exactly how you feel about her. You've tried to box up your feelings and store them away from even your wife. It's time you brought them out and shared them. You can't keep a lid on something like that forever. It'll taint everything you do."

"Do you think she'll understand?"

"I think she wants to understand more'n anything. I don't think you realize how hard Faith has had it. Since she was ten years old, she's never had anyone to talk with. Her aunt and uncle just kept her for the work they could get out of her. She was just a little girl, and they never kissed her or hugged her, never tucked her into bed at night, never told her they appreciated her, never showed her any caring or love. They kept her close and guarded her carefully, because they were afraid she might run off like her mama did, and they'd lose their workhorse. That girl desperately needs some love and attention. She needs a husband who'll cherish her and share his innermost being with her. She thought she had that in you, and then you ripped it all from her. We'll never know how deeply you've hurt her."

"I've been treating her as unimportant, just like they did, haven't I? It's not the way I feel about her, but I haven't let her know that."

"Now you're beginning to get your mind straight. You can fix this mess and repair your relationship with Faith. More than anything, right now, she's hoping and praying you'll want to fix it—that you want her."

"I've told her we'd talk Sunday. I'll lay everything out in the open then and tell her how much I care for her. I'll take your advice and make things right."

Lena gave a brisk nod. "Now, that's more like it. I have just one more thought I want to leave with you. I think you've convinced yourself that you've pulled away from Faith to protect her from getting in a family way, but I don't think that's the whole reason. I think you're afraid to get too close to her, because you're afraid of losing her and getting hurt again. I think you're also trying to protect your own heart."

Lena had certainly given Jacob a lot to think about, and she'd been right. He had hurt Faith by loving her once and then abandoning her. He'd stopped doing anything with her or for her. He'd done them both a disservice, because they should be enjoying each other right now.

Chapter Fourteen

STRAIGHTENING

THEY'D STARTED LATER THAN USUAL this morning. Jacob came back from Lena's wagon and said the wagon master had decided to leave six wagons behind. Each family had one or more people too sick to move, and the train had already fallen way behind schedule.

Faith hated the thought of discarding people. She considered staying behind herself and helping to tend the sick, but something had changed in Jacob again. She didn't know in what way, but she hoped things would improve.

He looked directly at her for a change, as if he were searching her inside and out. His countenance and stance didn't look as rigid either. Maybe she just saw what she wanted to see, but maybe, just maybe, he'd talked with Lena, and it had made a difference.

Jacob didn't eat any more than usual at the nooning, but they'd just had cold corn cakes and bacon. It had been too hot to build a fire, and it seemed senseless for no more than they ate. She'd already reduced what she used to cook for them by over half, and they still had leftovers.

"It's been too long since we've had a get-together," she heard John Brenner say to Jacob, "so we've decided to hold that wedding celebration we've been planning to give you. It'll be Saturday night. We should be to Courthouse Rock by then. You just bring yourself and your little wife, and we'll provide the food and music."

Jacob mumbled something under his breath. It almost sounded as if he said he wished he could've had the long talk with Faith before they had their wedding celebration, or it could be just her own wishful thinking again.

Four of the wagons turned east the next morning. They'd had enough of the unrelenting sun, never-seeming-to-end prairie, saturating dust, dirty water, threat of Indians, critical sicknesses, swarms of insects, dangerous river crossings, raging storms, dwindling food supplies, and monotonous walking. It made one tired just thinking of it.

"Do you want us to turn back with them?" Jacob asked Faith.

She looked at him carefully. She wished she knew what he wanted. "I have nothing to go back to," she said. "I have no one."

His eyes fell. Did he want to go back to Virginia?

She wished she knew what he felt. "If you want to return to the East with them, you can. I'll go with you if that's what you want, or I can stay here and drive my wagon on west if you think that would be better."

Jacob looked up with surprise. "No, we'll continue to Oregon Territory if it makes no difference with you. I think that holds better promise for me. There's nothing exciting about going backwards to where you've already been. After all, God did make our toes to point out in front of us and not behind."

He gave Faith a faint smile, but it never reached the rest of his face. The fact he'd said "better promise for "me" and not "us" wasn't lost on Faith.

Jacob had to pull guard duty again that night. Faith always hated it when he had to be gone like that. She still had nightmares of the drunk coming into her wagon that night. She'd hate to think what would have happened if Jacob hadn't been there. No matter how Jacob treated her, he would still protect her. She knew that, and the buffalo stampede had proved it.

She also feared something might happen to Jacob when he pulled guard duty. The Indians always threatened to steal the horses. She couldn't stand the thought of him with arrows nailing him to the earth.

But the other men here could be about as dangerous. Some of them were unskilled with firearms, and guns were always going off accidentally. Why, just this week, a man had been picking up his gun when it went off and shot his own son in the shoulder. A few more inches and it would have hit the boy's heart. What if another guard accidentally shot Jacob? They all carried weapons.

"Stop!" she told herself. Satan caused such negative what-ifs, and she didn't want to listen. There would always be disastrous possibilities, but it would do no good to dwell on them. She would trust God, as she'd always done . . . *whoso putteth his trust in the Lord shall be safe.*

With the exception of the dress Lena had given her for her wedding and the silk she'd saved from Lucille's trunk, Faith put on the prettiest dress she had for the celebration. It looked entirely too fancy for a wagon train celebration, but she wanted to look her best for Jacob and hoped he'd notice. The fawn-colored polished cotton dress with ivory lace matched her coloring and made her hair look brighter.

It had been one of Lucille's more practical dresses. From sorting through her things, Faith could tell Lucille had been the high-society, Southern belle. Faith hesitated to wear any of Jacob's first wife's clothing, but, her own two dresses had become so threadbare, she'd had little choice. Jacob didn't seem to recognize any of Lucille's, however. Of course, he hadn't looked at Faith much lately, either.

"You look lovely," he told her as he helped her from the wagon, and Faith's heart began to pump faster.

"I wish we'd been able to have our talk before this wedding celebration," Jacob told her as they walked to where the others had gathered, "but I have a lot of explaining, and it's going to take some time."

"I wish we could have, too."

"Don't give up on me, Faith. I'm hoping things will get better."

That sounded promising. She prayed things would get better for them.

The food looked good and plentiful. Some of the women had even made cakes and pies for dessert. Everyone seemed hungry and wanted to eat first, so that's what they did.

Mr. Marshall welcomed them all. "Since the Fourth of July came on Thursday this year, the council and I voted to travel on then, because we're so far behind schedule. I'd hoped to make Independence Rock by the Fourth, but we haven't. Today, then, we really have two things to celebrate, our country's independence and Jacob and Faith's marriage. We'd planned to hold their wedding feast earlier, but too much has been happening. We want to rectify that today. Therefore, we extend our belated congratulations and best wishes. Preacher, would you ask the blessing, so we can eat? We'll let the newlyweds go first."

After they ate, Jacob and Faith led off the dancing again. She wished she knew how to dance better because she so liked being in Jacob's arms. He deftly guided her, however, and they slowly moved about, their bodies swaying to the music in unison.

He pulled her close, and she wondered if he could feel her pulse thumping erratically. This felt so good, so right. She lost herself in the dance and forgot all about the people who were watching. She wanted to stay just like this all night, but the dance ended all too soon.

When Jacob led her from the dance area, he put his hand on her back, and she almost cried with joy. He had intentionally touched her.

They'd no sooner sat down than Iris Bates came over and pulled Jacob to the dance floor. It surprised Faith that the woman had come at all since she'd been the one to accuse Faith of stealing her brooch. Why did she want to celebrate Faith's wedding, and, more to the point, why did she want to dance with Faith's husband? Is this the way she planned to cause trouble now? Lena had mentioned that Iris had been as close a friend of Lucille's as anyone on the trip.

The pretty widow had flaming red hair and wore flashy clothes. Her elderly husband had died early in their trip. Rumor had it he'd been a wealthy widower when he'd married the much younger woman. Trying to make more money quickly for his new wife, he'd lost everything with bad investments, and she'd talked him into going to California to strike it rich.

Tonight Iris wore a dress that clung to her voluptuous curves and the neckline cut so low Faith feared she might spill out of it at any minute, especially since the band had started to play a faster reel. Still pulling Jacob along, however, Iris went up to the band, and they changed to a slower song.

Faith gritted her teeth as Iris pressed herself against Jacob. Faith saw Jacob step back and try to keep some distance between them, but Iris would have none of that. She glued herself to him. They did make a handsome couple as they waltzed around with dance steps Faith could never attempt.

When the dance ended, Iris stood on her tiptoes and planted a kiss on Jacob's cheek, which meant her protruding parts rubbed against him. How brazen!

Iris must have asked for another dance, for Jacob shook his head vigorously and came back toward Faith. Faith looked away as he approached.

"I'm sorry about that, Faith," he said. "I should have refused her, but she pulled me up before I had time to think. I didn't want to make a scene, but I almost wish I had come back here, anyway. That won't happen again. Would you like to dance now?"

She shook her head. The musicians were playing another reel now, and she wouldn't know how.

"I'm going to get some cider," he told her. "Can I get you anything?"

She shook her head again. She didn't trust her voice right now, and her silly eyes were beginning to water. She might be making too much of what happened, but she couldn't stop the hurt she felt, although she couldn't say that Jacob had been at fault.

Jacob didn't come right back. She looked over, and he had started to talk with Mr. Marshall.

Lena came up. "I had that straight talk with Jacob. I think he'll be more forthcoming with you now. He's planning to tell you everything, and there's a lot to tell."

Faith wanted to ask her friend some questions, but not here. Did Jacob plan to leave her when they got to Oregon? If he did, what would she do? Would she be able to survive on her own? Maybe some other man would want to marry her, but she didn't want another man. Besides, she knew nothing about divorce, and she wouldn't want to ever remarry even if she did.

"I don't know what to think of Iris Bates," Lena said, shaking her head. "I'm afraid she's looking for trouble, and the person who looks for it will always find it. She needs to understand partaking in forbidden fruits under heated conditions has cooked up many a jam."

Faith recognized the humor in Lena's pun, but she didn't smile. She had a sickening feeling in the pit of her stomach.

When Lena left, Faith couldn't see Jacob anywhere, and the same could be said for Iris. Thinking the worst, Faith went back to the wagon. She would sleep in her old wagon tonight. She moved some things around and made a pallet. She'd just gotten settled when Jacob called. At first, she said nothing, but when he sounded frantic, she answered him. He opened the back flap.

"Why did you leave? Are you sick?"

"I didn't feel well." That was the truth.

"I wanted to dance with you again, and I didn't know where you were."

"I couldn't find you to tell you I was leaving."

"John Brenner wanted to show me some items he'd traded for with the Indians. I didn't stay gone long."

She wanted to ask if Iris had followed him, but she didn't want him to be angry with her for not trusting him. Actually, she trusted Jacob more than she trusted Iris, although he was a still a man.

"Why are you in this wagon instead of the other one?"

"I don't know. I guess it seemed more like mine."

"Oh, Faith. Don't turn from me now. What's mine is yours. In fact, I'd like to put all our things in the one wagon before much longer."

That sounded hopeful. Maybe she'd assumed the worst without reason.

Her hopes fell. He'd decided to use the one wagon out of necessity, not because he wanted to be close to her.

"Please come back over here. I've already pitched my tent, and I want you close in case something happens. Besides, I've got something I want to give you."

She got up and dressed. She wished she had Lucille's wrapper to put on, but it was in the other wagon.

Jacob climbed into the other wagon after her. What was he doing? Was he planning to join her? Her heart felt like it had begun a fast reel of its own.

He went to the trunk that held his things. He reached down the inside and pulled out Lucille's diary and two letters.

"Faith, I didn't have much of a marriage the first time. Lucille could barely stand for me to touch her. I want you to read these. They'll explain it all and let you know some of what I've been going through since I read these. This will make our conversation tomorrow less lengthy."

He handed her the things and hesitated. She took them, and then looked up to see him still standing there. He kissed her cheek.

"Until tomorrow, then, good night."

Faith knew she shouldn't burn the lantern any more than absolutely necessary, so she went out and rekindled the fire. Buffalo chips were still plentiful.

She planned to sit beside the firelight and carefully read what Jacob had given her. She knew she wouldn't be able to sleep until she knew what the diary contained, and this presented the opportunity to understand her husband better. She read the journal first and the revelations there stunned her.

Her heart went out to Jacob. He'd married Lucille to save her reputation, and she'd been carrying another man's baby. She and her family had devised the plan to trap Jacob.

It was all here—the love she'd felt for this Rudolph, his rejection, what she did to ensnare Jacob, how she hated his touch, and how she feared he'd discover she was pregnant too soon for him to think the baby belonged to him. The two letters from Rudolph just confirmed what the diary said.

Faith didn't know a lot about people and relationships since she'd lived such a secluded life, but even she could see Rudolph had never loved Lucille. He had toyed with her and used her for his own base purposes.

She could almost feel sorry for Lucille, but the woman had made poor choices. She'd never recognized the treasure she had in Jacob. He was so much better a man than Rudolph had ever been. Even as Lucille remained cold, Jacob had apparently done his best to make things work. How much had he loved Lucille? Had she completely broken his heart?

Faith wiped the tears from her eyes. This was worse than any Shakespearean tragedy. How hurt and deceived Jacob must feel. Did he think all women were like this? Did he think Faith would play him foul?

This did explain some of the pain he'd been suffering, but it didn't explain how he'd been treating Faith. Surely he hadn't tried to punish her for Lucille's sins.

Well, Jacob might tell her what she wanted to know tomorrow— actually today now.

She went into the wagon to lie down, but she couldn't sleep. Finally, she gave free rein to her tears and cried for Jacob.

Faith must have dozed, because, when she woke up, she could hear Jacob restarting the fire. She got up, quickly dressed, and went out to put on the coffee.

Jacob looked into her eyes, and hers started to tear up again. She looked down.

"Do you hate me?" he asked. "I know you were up reading Lucille's diary last night, because I saw the firelight."

"Why would I hate you?" she managed to get out, but her voice trembled. She held in too much emotion.

"I was pretty stupid to be suckered like that. Perhaps the man who is won by false pretenses deserves what he gets. I was too trusting. I know better now."

Did that mean he didn't trust her either? This had become such a complicated mess, and she just didn't know what to think anymore. "I could never hate you, Jacob."

He relaxed some then. "Oh, what a tangled web we weave, when first we practice to deceive."

"That sounds like Shakespeare, but I know it's not."

"No, it's Sir Walter Scott. Would you like to have our talk after breakfast? I want to get it over with."

What did he plan to say that would be so difficult for him? Did he want to be rid of her and get on with his life? Perhaps, after all that had happened, he wanted to remain single now. It made sense. "I'd like that better," she said. "How hungry are you?"

"Not very. I think I'm too anxious to eat."

"I'm not very hungry either, but I do need some coffee."

"Let's both have some coffee then, and walk away from the camp afterwards. I want to find a private place to talk, one where we're not likely to be interrupted."

"Okay, and, since we're getting an early start, maybe we can still make the services this morning."

"I'd like to begin having our morning devotions together again if that's acceptable to you."

Faith smiled at him. "Yes, I'd like that." Maybe he hadn't planned to rid himself of her after all.

He led her downstream beside the river, and they sat down. Jacob placed his gun to his left side and took her hand in his right.

"Where to begin?" he said. "You read Lucille's things, so you know that sordid story. I knew something was wrong between us from the moment we were married, but I had no idea what. I never suspected Rudy wasn't mine, but I should have guessed."

He squeezed her hand and smiled at her for the first time. "I'm sorry I distanced myself from you. My thoughts got all jumbled up. I thought I wanted to keep you from getting pregnant, so there'd be no chance you might die in childbirth like Lucille did. What a horrible way to go—so much pain and blood." He paused to get a handle on his emotions. "After our wonderful night together, I had nightmares of that happening to you."

"You know, I think a woman would be willing to give up life to have her husband love her, to wake up in his arms every morning for as long as she did live. Maybe without that, it's just existing and not really living at all."

"I think I'm beginning to agree. I've made myself miserable in trying to stay away from you."

"Why didn't you explain how you felt to me?"

"I became so confused and everything seemed overwhelming. There's also the possibility I unknowingly pushed you away because I feared if I got too close, I'd end up losing you and hurting even more this time. I might have been trying to protect my heart from losing a third person. Can you ever forgive me? Whatever my reasons were, what I did was wrong, and I deeply regret how I've treated you."

He must be just feeling sorry for her. He was a good man and wanted to treat everyone right. She couldn't mean anything special to him. "Of course I forgive you, but where do we go from here?"

"To Oregon Territory together," he gave a little laugh.

He'd misunderstood her question. Should she explain or just let it go. He had complained before about her trying to push him for answers.

She decided this might be the only chance she'd have to talk to him like this, so she'd better ask all her questions now. She breathed in deeply, as if the air could give her courage.

"I meant what about us. What do you want me to do, Jacob?"

"I'm hoping you still want me for your husband. I'm praying we can pick up from that one wonderful night we spent together and grow our relationship. I love you, Faith."

Did she hear him right, or did she just imagine it? She looked into his eyes and what she saw took her breath away, but she didn't trust her own perception of things.

"Did you say you loved me?"

"I did. I love you with all my heart." He dropped her hand and looked toward the river. "I know it's too early to expect you to feel the same, but I hope you can come to love me someday." He looked directly into her eyes. "At least you don't seem to have an aversion to me like Lucille had. Do I stand a chance with you? I'll court you, woo you, do anything you want. Just please tell me you might love me one day."

"Oh, Jacob! I love so much right now. I've loved you for a long time. That's what has made the way you've turned from me so hard to bear."

"I had no idea you had such deep feelings for me. I'm so sorry for hurting you like I did. I hurt myself at the same time, you know. It took every bit of willpower I possessed to stay away from you. That's why I stayed gone so much. I could never have left you alone if I'd been near you more. You pull me to you, like a giant magnet."

He took her in his arms and just held her close for a while. She wrapped her arms around him, too. He gave her a gentle kiss, then let her go and stood up.

"If we're going to make it to preaching, I'd better not kiss you as thoroughly as I'd like to right now. We'll save that until later today. Do you have any other questions you'd like to ask me now?" he asked as they walked back hand in hand. "Of course you can ask me anything at any time. I want no more secrets and nothing held back."

"How do you feel about Rudy, now that you know he wasn't your real son?"

"I loved the little fellow. What his mother did wasn't his fault. If he'd have lived, I would've treated him as my son."

She loved and respected this man so much. What a Godly man! She felt blessed to be his wife, and she still had a hard time believing he loved her.

"Did you love Lucille very much?"

"I tried to, but it never grew. I think I cared about her, but I don't think I ever really loved her. Not like a man should love his wife. What I felt for her is nothing compared with what I feel for you. I can't even begin to explain how dear you are to me. Is there anything else?"

She wanted to ask about Iris, but she still felt it would be better not to mention her. She gave a tentative shake of her head instead.

"Come on. I can tell you've thought of something, and we shouldn't keep things from each other."

"What about Iris? She seems to want you."

"Oh, Faith, you have no worries where Iris is concerned. I hated every minute of that dance. Iris is even more forward than Lucille had been when she tried to hook me. Iris is downright embarrassing, and I want nothing to do with her. Even if I wasn't married and in love with my wonderful wife, she would not be my type. Besides being quite a bit older than me, I would never want anything to do with someone who would flaunt herself like she does. I have more respect for God's teachings and myself than that."

I thank Thee, Father, from the bottom of my heart for being true to Thy promises and for giving me my heart's desire in having this amazing man for my husband. Thou art so good to me. Please don't let anything distance Jacob from me again. Let our marriage be as it should be, and let us be a Godly couple, steeped in love for Thee and saturated with love for each other. Amen.

On the way to the preaching service, John Brenner called Jacob away for a quick council meeting. He said it wouldn't last but a minute or two.

"You go ahead and find us a spot," Jacob told her, "and I'll come as soon as I can."

Faith headed that way when Iris approached her. "Oh, good, I've been looking for you. Can we talk?"

"You can walk with me to the service," Faith said.

"Oh, I'm not going to the preaching. Step over here with me. What I have to say needs to be said in private."

Faith reluctantly followed the woman. Jacob might not think too highly of Iris, but Faith instinctively knew the widow wanted him.

"I just wanted to know when Jacob plans to leave you. I mean I know he doesn't need you now that his baby died, and I assume you don't want to stay where you're not wanted. He's the kind of man who needs a real woman and not some slip of a girl that doesn't know the first thing about how to please a man."

Faith was so glad she'd had the talk with Jacob this morning. If they hadn't, she would've probably believed what Iris said.

"Jacob and I are husband and wife. We took our vows in front of God, and we have no intention of breaking them."

"You are naïve, aren't you? We'll just see who knows more about men, but be warned. I've had plenty of experience, and I will get the man I want. I always do." With that, she flounced off.

Faith had a feeling Iris' vast experience with men was exactly what Jacob disliked so much, but the woman had left her uneasy. *Lord, please don't let her make trouble for Jacob and me.*

Jacob joined her not long after she got to the service. He gave her a big smile, as if he were happy to finally be there beside her.

Chapter Fifteen

FLAMING

THEY WERE ON THE WAY back to their wagon when Iris' voice drifted to them. "And, everyone knows Jacob just married her so she'd take care of his baby."

Jacob froze. He looked as if he couldn't decide whether to quickly get Faith back to their wagon or to intervene and stop the gossip.

"It's okay," she whispered. "Let's just go."

"Everyone also knows they don't even sleep together. She stays in the wagon and he pitches his tent. Does Faith actually think that constitutes a marriage? Really."

The girls snickered, causing Jacob to jerk around and head toward the voices. Faith followed behind him, her footsteps slow and heavy.

Iris stood among a small group of women, most of them not yet twenty. They were huddled together and didn't notice Jacob at first. He startled them when he started to speak, and the younger girls ran off at once.

"How dare you insult my wife or my marriage." He didn't raise his voice, but it held indignation. "It is none of your concern what goes on between my wife and me. That's entirely our personal affair, and I'm appalled that you are guessing at such matters and gossiping about them. When I married Faith, I fully intended to make her my wife in every sense of the word, and those intentions have not and will not change. Have I made myself perfectly clear? I hope so, for I do not intend to talk to you about our personal affairs again."

He didn't give Iris time to answer before he turned back to Faith and put his hand on her back. She had never seen Jacob like this. Even his coldness with her couldn't compare to his disdain here.

"But, Jacob, you misunderstood," Iris' voice sounded honeyed and seductive. "Please don't be angry. Please don't turn from me. Remember our dance last night. I hope you enjoyed it as much as I did."

Jacob moved his arm around to encompass Faith and pull her closer as he turned to answer Iris. "Have I not made it perfectly clear that I'm not interested in any woman, other than my wife? And, no, I did not enjoy our dance. The whole time I wished I were holding Faith in my arms. You're not the type of woman who appeals to me. I could use some harsh names if you don't understand what I think of you, but I'd prefer not to use such words."

With that he turned and left, taking Faith with him. "I'm sorry you had to hear that," he told her, his voice now soft and tender. "I know I sounded rather hardhearted, but I got the feeling Iris wouldn't stop trying to make trouble if I didn't make it perfectly clear how I felt. I actually held my temper in check. I can't begin to explain how I felt when I heard her belittling you."

"She actually said some similar things to me on the way to the service."

"Why hadn't you told me?"

"I preferred to do so without so many people around."

"Would you have told me?"

"I think so. I didn't believe the things she said, although I'm glad we had our talk first. Otherwise, with the way things have been, I might have thought you didn't care for me."

"I want you to share everything with me, Faith. Please don't keep anything back, and I won't either. I've learned my lesson about not being completely open and honest with you. I know now that we need to share everything to prevent misunderstandings. I hope you know what I told Iris is absolutely true. You are the only woman I want and the only woman I've ever deeply loved. I tried to love Lucille, but it never grew beyond the initial stages."

They went back, and since they'd missed breakfast, Faith fixed pancakes with molasses for the noon meal. The honey and jams were already gone, and the chickens weren't laying as many eggs.

Their chickens were doing better than most, however. Faith had been tethering them three at a time beside the wagon when they had a lay-by. She tied one end of some twine around a leg and the other end to a stake or wagon wheel. That way the chickens could forage, and they didn't have to feed them as much. They also seemed to lay better and the eggshells tended to be stronger. Jacob seemed amazed that she'd thought of it, but he didn't quite understand how she'd lived in the mountains of Kentucky.

Jacob had known to bury the eggs in the flour to cushion them from breaking, however. Faith just hoped they'd continue to have a few to bury.

She put on a buffalo stew for supper. She still had some potatoes, carrots, onions, and dried green beans her family called "leather britches" to add.

"Come into the tent with me," Jacob said with his eyes twinkling. "I think I'd like a Sunday nap, and I'd like to give my wife a thorough kiss. I've been thinking of it since earlier this morning."

Her heart skipped a beat, as she followed him into the tent, and he tied the flaps together. She understood there would be more than just one kiss, and she smiled.

━━━━━━━

Courthouse Rock, a natural sandstone formation, loomed like a gigantic building on the flat landscape. Chimney Rock could be seen in the distance, but distances were deceptive in such flat land, and one couldn't judge by looking.

The Indian population had changed, too. The Pawnees were no longer the predominant tribe. There were also Lakota Sioux and Arapaho, and the Cheyenne would appear a little more to the west.

Life on the trail stayed too busy to suit Jacob. He would have loved to have a real honeymoon with his wife, but the wagon train moved forward, and with it came the never-ending chores to be done.

By the time the sun went down, they were both often too tired to do more than fall asleep in each other's arms. At least they usually had Sunday as a lay-by day. Jacob had never envisioned the trip to be this demanding or exhausting.

"I know we're living under hard conditions right now," Jacob told Faith. "I wish it were different. I wish I could make things easier for you."

"Shakespeare said 'travelers must be content.' We won't always be on the trail. Things will get better."

At least his and Faith's spirits were not beaten down, as many others were. They had each other and they had God with them all the way. Their love, so newly proclaimed, colored everything brightly with optimism, and they were happy even among dismal conditions.

Many of the emigrants were having trouble with their oxen. The animals' hooves would crack, and their feet would swell. The men operated on them and poured hot tar on the hooves.

So far, Jacob hadn't had this problem, but he'd been able to switch out his animals over the first part of the trip. Now that he used all twelve of his oxen every day, he expected the same malady to hit sometime.

Others were running lower on supplies, too. Some had no more flour and little cornmeal. There were families who had little left but beans.

Jacob and Faith were doing all right, so far. Combining their foodstuffs had helped. Jacob had more store-bought goods, and Faith had more that came from her tiny mountain farm. Her dried fruits and vegetables were particularly good, because they would keep indefinitely and cooked up nicely. She'd had things like honey, nuts, apples, and berry preserves to start with, but they'd eaten all those. They still had enough bacon and side meat, but the fresh meat the men killed along the way offered a welcomed change.

Jacob noticed the grass looked drier and less plentiful, and they began to climb in elevation. He worried about the livestock. He couldn't afford to lose an ox now.

Some people were driving only four oxen on their wagon, but Jacob felt sure those animals would wear out soon. He'd heard of people training a cow to the yoke, but that didn't sound like a good idea to him. A cow didn't seem strong enough or hardy enough to pull a load all day long.

The sun still scorched hot and the flies remained as pesky as ever. Conditions seemed to worsen the farther west they rolled.

"My word, it's hot enough to scald the feathers off a chicken," he heard Lena say.

Chimney Rock now protruded on the horizon like a giant finger pointing to the heavens. The landscape appeared more desolate all the time. The grass didn't grow as high and thick, and it had more gold and brown among the green.

They camped near the rock that night. Some walked to it, which took about an hour. Jacob could think of better things to do than spend over an hour walking to touch a monolith.

He and Faith went downstream and washed in the river. He would've preferred to go in together, but he felt it would be better if he stood guard while she went in. Then, he hurriedly washed off while she sat and toweled her hair.

She had fine, silky hair, and he loved to run his fingers through it. He still marveled at how much she seemed to like his touch and how she responded to him—so different from what he'd known before.

Opportunities to be alone together were rare. When they bathed in the streams, the women usually went in as a group, and the men would do the same at another time. Chimney Rock had drawn enough of the emigrants to its base, however, they'd been blessed to be alone this afternoon.

"Are you hoping we'll have children?" Faith asked him.

He stiffened. How could he answer her honestly?

"I do. Are you trying to tell me something?"

She smiled. "No, since it didn't happen on our first night together, it's not been long enough to tell. I just wondered how you felt about it, after what you said about fearing you might lose me in childbirth."

"I want to have children very much, and I want to have children with you, but, to be honest, I'm going to be very concerned about you, when you're carrying our first child. I hope it's after we get off this grueling journey, but I'm leaving all that in God's hands. It would suit me just fine if Lena and Harlan would settle near us. I'd like for Lena to be there to help with the birthing. That woman has a big heart and a head full of wisdom."

"She's a good friend."

"Did you two know each other in Kentucky?"

"No, I didn't know anyone in Kentucky, except for my aunt and uncle. I met the Haywoods when we started on this trip. Although my uncle didn't like it, he decided it would be better if we linked up with the other families coming from Kentucky with their wagons. We didn't have the money for a train, and we needed to bring supplies from home."

"Were there any your age in the group?"

"Only one young man two years younger than me. All the girls and the rest of the boys were much younger. All the other men were married."

"Did the seventeen-year-old pay you any attention?"

"I think he would have liked to, but Uncle Jed wouldn't let him. I didn't encourage him too much, either. I would have liked to have a friend, but I didn't want Dexter to court me, and I suspected that's what he wanted."

"I'm sure he did."

Faith raised her eyebrows. She had no idea how attractive she was.

"I know how seventeen-year-old boys think, and you're a lovely young lady."

"I think you're biased, husband," she teased.

"I certainly am, but that doesn't make it untrue."

They'd camped for the night in the vicinity of Scott's Bluff. The river here ran nice and clear, and the land provided plenty of grass for the livestock.

This part of the country might be brutal to travel through, but it was beautiful. The sunsets set the sky ablaze with an array of brilliant hues, and they went to sleep talking about the sights.

"Jacob!" he heard Faith call. He jumped up to see her standing at the tent flap.

"I smelled smoke and got up to check and make sure our campfire hadn't sent out some sparks. It looks like the prairie is on fire. Look."

Jacob looked and fear swept over him when he saw how fast the fire consumed the drying grass. It raged in a long line and quickly made for their camp.

"Get dressed, grab two blankets or something we can wet to fight the fire. I'm going to sound the alarm. You take a blanket and lantern and go down to the river. If the fire starts toward you, get into the river and keep a wet blanket over your head."

"All right."

He took his rifle and shot into the air. As he expected, men came running to see what had happened. Most saw the fire immediately and dived into action. Marshall barked orders at those who looked confused.

Faith handed him a blanket, and they hurried toward the river. He wet their blankets, as he ducked himself in the water. He waded to the bank and handed Faith a dripping blanket.

"Now you get in the water if the fire comes anywhere near."

"I will and you be careful. Please be careful, Jacob." She kissed his cheek.

"I will, but say your prayers, anyway." He gave her a quick hug and left.

He joined the throng of men headed toward the fire. The men who'd been guarding the livestock herded the animals toward the river. Why hadn't they raised the alarm?

Some of the men carried torches. That seemed like a good idea, but Jacob hadn't thought of it. He'd assumed the fire would light up things enough. Others brought shovels and digging tools.

The crackling noise surprised Jacob, as the fire consumed the tall, dry grass. The popping almost sounded like gunshots, and there would definitely be a battle fought here. He could also hear a swooshing sound, almost like the wind. The giant, red blob seemed like a living, breathing monster as it snaked its way toward them, devouring whatever lay in its path.

Wildlife ran ahead of the fire, and Jacob wondered how many had already died. He couldn't imagine how much prairie the fire had likely already consumed.

"We need to set a controlled fire between here and the fire to take away the fire's fuel," John shouted. "We'll start it in this low area ahead of the wagons, and hope it will be easier to control. As a precaution, you men with tools, dig a wide ditch, too." He took a torch and showed them what to do. "Go slowly with setting the fire, and keep it beat down, so it doesn't get out on this side, but be quick about it. Remember this grass will burn fast, so don't let it get out of hand or you'll have the wagons burning despite our efforts."

Jacob's thoughts ran with the fire as his hands moved to help. Could they control the fire they were setting, or would it get away from them in the dry grass? If it did work, would it be enough to stop the fire before it got to the wagons?

Jacob's attention turned when he heard someone scream. He looked up to see a woman at the edge of the fire with her dress tail burning.

What was a woman doing out here trying to fight the fire? It wasn't Faith, was it? Other men were wrapping her in blankets and rolling her.

He saw that woman was taller and heavier than Faith. Why did he expect the worst? *Thank Thee, Lord. Keep Faith safe. Keep us all safe and help that poor woman.*

With the long line of men, they had a strip burned before the wildfire got to them. Would it be wide enough, or would the fire jump it?

"Should we get at the edge of the burn and fight any sparks or blaze that jumps the burned area?" Jacob asked John.

"That's a good idea, Parker. Let's do it."

The fire largely stopped when it got to the bare strip. The few fires around the edges weren't hard to control. Fires still raged in the distance, but it had turned to burn away from the wagons, and they'd been spared.

As Jacob walked toward the river and Faith, he realized his hands were burned. He'd thought the burning sensation had come from the heat of fighting the fire. He noticed other men also had singed hair and holes in their clothing. Apparently, they hadn't wet themselves in the river first.

Faith ran to meet him. He put his arms around her, but she noticed him favoring his hands.

"You're hurt," she said, looking at his burned hands.

"They're not bad. You can put some ointment on them when we get back."

John caught up with them and told Jacob that Marshall had called a council meeting to discuss the fire before they started off the next morning. "He's upset. He's discovered all four of the guards had fallen asleep tonight. That's why the guards didn't sound an alarm."

"How do you think the fire started?" Faith asked as she gingerly applied the salve to Jacob's hands.

He tried not to flinch, and he managed pretty well, for the most part. Her gentle touch didn't hurt as much as someone else's would have.

"I'll wrap these in bandages in the morning. I hope you won't have to wear your gloves to drive the team."

"I think I should be all right. They're easy enough to manage. I think I could turn them loose and they'd plod along behind your wagon."

"A bandage will also keep the dust from settling into them."

"I saw a woman out there trying to fight the fire. Her dress caught on fire. I don't know who she was, but I'm sure her legs were badly burned. I'm glad you stayed by the river."

"I never thought of doing anything else but what you told me. How do you think the fire started?" she asked again.

"It's hard to tell. Obadiah believes it's probably from natural causes. He says the Indians usually care too much for the prairie and wildlife to do such harm, although there's been rumors of them starting fires to keep settlers from coming in the past."

"In some wagon trains, guards are shot for going to sleep on duty," Rex said as the council meeting convened the next morning. "We only ask them to stay on guard for four of the eight hours in two shifts, because Obadiah and some of the other men keep a lookout after dinner until the first shift gets there. That's better than on most trains."

"The question is what can we do to prevent this from happening again," Marshall added. "If Jacob hadn't sounded the alarm, we could have all been burnt to a crisp."

"You can thank Faith for that. She smelled smoke and woke me up."

"Well, because of you two, disaster was averted. Did you see the amount of prairie the fire burned? It's scary. We don't have to ask a man to stand guard all that often, so there's no excuse for going to sleep on the job."

"The problem is the trail tires everyone out," John said. "The day's so exhausting, it's easy to fall asleep."

"Maybe it would help to shorten the shifts," Jacob said. "We could have four two-hour shifts instead of two four-hour shifts, but a man's turn would roll around quicker."

"It's worth a try, I guess," Marshall said. "I haven't heard a better idea. We'll give it a try starting tonight. Maybe they can stay awake for two hours better than four."

"It won't help," Rex grumbled. "You'll see. Now we'll have to be on guard more often. You should flog those men and make an example of them."

When Jacob got back to the wagon, he realized Faith stood on the other side talking to someone. He started to go over and join them when he heard a male voice.

"If you needed to marry, why didn't you come to me? You know I liked you. I would've taken good care of you, Faith. I couldn't believe it when Mama told me you were married. Since we're in the other division of wagons, I haven't been able to see you like I'd planned. Pa and I were sickly when your wedding took place, and I didn't even know about it until yesterday. Your uncle wouldn't let me near you when he was alive."

"Jacob needed my help with his baby, Dexter, and Mr. Marshall didn't want me traveling alone. Our marriage solved both our problems."

"But it ain't right, marrying all of a sudden like that. You deserve to be courted, Faith."

"Because I married quickly, doesn't mean Jacob hasn't courted me. He's brought me flowers and done dozens of things each day to treat me special."

"He's good to you then?"

"He's very good to me."

"But do you love him?"

"Yes, I do. Jacob and I are happy. You're such a special man, Dexter, I know God has someone special picked out for you, too. Just be patient, and you'll meet her."

When Jacob went around the wagon, Faith had her hand on Dexter's arm. She quickly pulled it back.

"Here's my husband now," she said. "Jacob, you remember me telling you about Dexter coming from Kentucky with my family. Dexter this is Jacob."

Jacob put his left arm around Faith and reached out to shake Dexter's hand with his right. "Pleased to meet you, Dexter. I hope things are going well for you."

"They could be better," he said and looked at Faith. "I guess I'd best be going. You take care, Faith."

"You, too Dexter, and tell your family I send my regards."

"I'll make sure Faith's well taken care of, young man."

"You must have heard most of the conversation," Faith said after Dexter had left.

"I guess so. It startled me, so when I heard him say he wanted to marry you, I stopped in my tracks."

"I'm sorry, Jacob. I certainly didn't expect this."

"I'm not all that surprised, but I thought you handled it well."

"I wanted to be kind but let him know I'm taken. You didn't mind?"

"I don't like it that he wanted to steal my wife, but you told him I treated you special, and you loved me, so I can't mind too much."

He looked down at her and smiled. When she looked up at him with her dark brown eyes glowing, he bent down and covered her lips with his.

Saturday afternoon Faith gathered up the laundry and turned to him. "What's this all over your shirt?" she asked him. "It looks like long, red hair. Jacob?"

He looked up from cleaning his gun. "I don't know. Let me see it."

He'd pulled the shirt off yesterday, knowing Faith would want it to wash today. Even he could see the strands of long, red hairs, and only one woman he knew had hair like that.

"I know it looks like Iris' hair, but I promise you I have no idea how it got there. I haven't seen her, since I gave her a piece of my mind, and you were there then."

He met Faith's gaze and let her search his eyes. He looked into hers too, trying to determine if she believed him.

"If she sneaked into the wagon and planted some of her hair on your dirty shirt, Jacob, that's scary."

"Yes, it is, but I think she might be capable of that."

"You know, I do, too."

He breathed a sigh of relief. She believed him. He stood and took her in his arms.

"It's you I love." He smoothed her hair back away from her eyes. "I don't need or want anyone but you."

"I believe you, Jacob, and I love you, too." She smiled as she picked up the basket of clothes to take to the river. "I'll be sure to wash your shirt with extra care. I want to make sure I get it clean."

He laughed. He liked her saucy spirit. He'd never noticed this side of her before.

Chapter Sixteen

FORT LARAMIE

THE LAND NOW ROSE IN rolling plains and hills. To the south, dark, mysterious-looking mountains wiggled in the heat on the far horizon, looking like mystical mirages.

As they got closer to Fort Laramie, the Indians they encountered were Arapaho, Ute, Cheyenne, and Sioux. Most of these would probably be represented at the fort.

The Sioux, a large nation, wandered over most of the plains, and they would be at the fort, also. These Indians saw many of the other tribes as their enemies, but, in the past, some of them had occasionally joined forces to fight the white settlers. The Blackfeet had always considered the Sioux their arch enemy, and the Sioux once announced they planned to wipe out all the Pawnee to the east.

Jacob thought the Indians would have had a better chance of standing against the settlers' invasion if the different tribes would band together. However, if that had happened, he probably wouldn't be traveling west now. Although the Indians were always a threat to the emigrants, things were not as volatile as they'd been over the previous decade. More Indians were trading with the white man rather than fighting them now.

Most of the travelers wanted to get to a place where they could buy some provisions. Jacob knew he and Faith could use a few things too, but they could make it a while longer without restocking if they had to.

Fort Laramie sat amid rolling hills and the slow-flowing Laramie River, which the wagons would need to cross to get to the fort. A tributary of the North Platte, its crystal green waters reflected the sun's rays like flashing jewels.

Indians camped outside the gates of the fort. They were everywhere. Obadiah said so many of them set up their teepees there because the fort limited their presence inside. Over five hundred lodges of Sioux were also camped out on the river, more than a mile away.

Fort Laramie had not been established as a military post, but it had been the first of the fur trading centers on the trail to be converted to one. This had happened just last year, as the California gold rush swelled. Marshall said the fort had started as a log cabin in 1841.

It now appeared as a squat, white fortress built around a square. The trading rooms were on one side and the living quarters on another. Debris seemed to be scattered about most of the area—some of it apparently discarded from passing wagons. With the mountains waiting ahead, Jacob could understand why.

The wagons set up camp back from the fort, and the people walked in. The place teemed with activity, and this group would just add to it.

"It's more crowded than I expected," Faith said. "These are the most Indians I've ever seen."

They found a mass of people inside the fort, too. A few old mountain men sat back and watched the others or tried to bargain in trade. Pretty Cheyenne and Sioux girls with sleek black hair, calico dresses, moccasins on their feet, and plenty of jewelry, walked close to their white men patrons and silently stared at everything. A few men in suits stood in stark contrast to the rugged mountain men, staggering drunks, or blue-clad soldiers. Clerks stood behind the counters helping customers, and even some of them had Indian wives.

Jacob and Faith stared at it all. It seemed a lot to take in and "a sight to behold," as he heard Lena say.

Besides the trading center, the fort also housed a dry goods store, blacksmith, and cobbler. Jacob noticed the stains on the walls and floors near spittoons, where men's aims had been off the mark.

Prices were exorbitant. Jacob decided he would limit his spending, but he might get a few things. The prices would probably be even worse at the forts farther west.

"We have to transport everything we sell," one shopkeeper told them. "It takes a lot to get them here. That's why the prices are high."

Jacob and Faith decided to just look around today. They were planning to stay one more day in the hopes the wagons they'd left behind with the sick families might catch up. They could come back tomorrow to buy a few things.

As they started back to their wagon, Jacob noticed Iris on the arm of a lieutenant. Good. Maybe she'd leave him alone for a while or, even better, stay here. When he noticed how the officer treated her, however, he decided the man probably didn't plan to marry her.

Jacob decided to throw out some more of their things as others had done and consolidate everything into one wagon. Faith's wagon wouldn't make it much farther. It had grown more rickety with each mile, and he didn't want it to break down on the trail, especially in the mountains. It might even create a dangerous situation for Faith. Besides, when they did this, Faith could walk along beside him, and they could talk.

The more he got to know his wife, the more she intrigued him. Considering what Lena had told them, it was a wonder she had as many social skills as she did. Perhaps her early days with her parents had started the foundation and gave her some self-confidence. She seemed naturally out-going, but she tended to be shy at times, which probably stemmed from her environment in Kentucky.

Faith had a better education than most women, although she hadn't received a day of schooling after she'd moved in with her aunt and uncle. She especially knew the Bible and Shakespeare. He had a couple of the classics stored in the bottom of his trunk he hoped to share with her over the winter. There wouldn't be time to read during this trip. Perhaps he could give them to her for Christmas. He knew she'd be delighted.

She was smart, too. When she picked up new information, she remembered it—another reason to have her with him more. Being together would break the monotony, and the days would be less boring for them both.

Since the fort had begun to run low on some items, especially those needed in California, Jacob decided to trade some of their things, either inside the fort or with some of the men around the place. They had duplicates of many of the tools, and more than two of some of them. Since weight would be a problem as they climbed the mountain trails, Jacob thought it might be wise to dispose of any unnecessary items while he could get something for them. It would be better than leaving them beside the trail.

They walked to the fort, carrying armloads of tools when a grubby looking man approached them. "Ya don't happen to have a tent, do ya?"

"We do," Jacob said, "but we've been using it."

"Wouldja be willin' to let it go? I got me a hankerin' to go to Californy, and the fort's all outa tents, though I got the other thangs I needed."

"I might. What are you offering?"

"I ain't got no money or nothin'. I git paid more fer my furs iffin I take it in trade at the fort, but my squaw's got some real nice buckskin jackets, moccasins, baby boards, and sech."

"I've used my tent most of the way here."

"Makes no never mind to me, as long as it don't leak none."

"Let us take these tools to the fort, and we'll meet you back here, say in about thirty minutes. You can take a look at the tent. If you want to bring a leather jacket and some moccasins that would fit Faith and some leather gloves for both of us that would make things go faster."

"I'll do that very thang." He nodded his head.

They did manage to trade their tools for a bag of flour, sugar, and some potatoes. Considering how much the supplies cost, Jacob was pleased.

"Anything else you need?" he asked Faith.

"No, I have everything I need," she smiled in a way that made him think the statement had a double meaning, and he smiled, too.

"I brung a boy's size jacket fer the little lady," their new friend said as they walked back to camp together. "Hits goin' to be cold in them mountains, so I thank ya have a good idee here. I brung two pairs of leather gloves fer y'all. Figgered ya could make good use of them, too."

They made the trade quickly, and Jacob helped him take down and fold the tent. The jacket looked similar to the one he'd gotten in Missouri, except for the size. They both were made with leather and had fringe across the front and back.

"I used to wear a jacket styled like a man's when I went out hunting," Faith said. "I made it, but it wore out, and I didn't have it to bring. I do have Lucille's wool cloak, though."

"I'm thinking you may need to wear them both."

"In July?"

"We'll be seeing snow on the mountains soon enough. You hunted in Kentucky?"

"I did. Uncle Jed went with me most of the time, but I could shoot better than he could. On the last, he let me go alone and said he felt too poorly to get out in the cold."

The moccasins for Faith were soft and well-made. She'd already thrown away the shoes she'd brought. The uppers were even too far gone to resole them. She'd been wearing Lucille's, but the soles of them were falling apart. Jacob had left them at the cobbler's, but they didn't fit Faith well, and he thought the moccasins were a good idea.

He and Faith took boards from the old wagon and attached them near the top of Jacob's wagon bed. In that way, they made a platform, where they could make a sleeping pallet. They were lucky enough to find a recently discarded feather mattress still in good shape, and they lay it beside their wagon to let the side that had been down sun and air out. Now, they could store things throughout the wagon bed, under the platform, and still have a bed for the two of them.

He also took the cover from the old wagon. Although it had been well patched, Jacob thought it might come in handy for something.

Like most of the wagons, they used every bit of wagon space. Things were suspended all over the wagon, inside and out, but they were traveling light next to most of the emigrants.

They decided to walk around the fort one more time before they left. Even with the crowds milling about making it hard to walk at times, it gave them something different to do.

Some of the men were getting together a shooting contest and had gathered some items to use as targets. A small group stood practicing before the match started, but Jacob decided they were probably novices. The veteran marksmen seemed to be standing around waiting for the action to begin. They watched the practice for a while.

"I can outshoot any of them," Faith whispered.

Jacob thought he probably could, too. "Why don't we enter," he said. "Even if we don't win, it should be fun."

"But it costs a whole dollar for each entry."

"We've got the money. Since we traded for what we got here, we can afford two dollars for an hour or so of fun."

"You don't mind me entering? I'll be the only woman."

"Not as long as I'm with you."

They asked at registration if they had time to walk back and get their rifles. They did, so they paid their fee.

"With this wagon train being in," the man said, "it's going to be a big pot. We already got more than fifty entries. Organizers will get ten dollars, and the rest will go to the winner."

Jacob collected his rifle, and Faith got her Uncle Jed's. The gun she pulled out was ancient, but, if she could shoot with it, that's all that counted.

"My old one's not firing right," she told him. "This one's better."

In the first round, each shooter had to shoot a tin can as near to the center as possible. The fort saved all cans for just such a purpose. There must have been about sixty-five men and one woman starting off.

Each man picked up his can and held it to determine the best shots at the end of the round. They chose the twenty top shots.

The men looked stunned when Faith stepped up to shoot. Some of them began to heckle her.

"Don't you never mind, little lady," one of the old mountain men told her. "You just show them what you can do and hush them up."

Jacob didn't think most men thought Faith would even hit the can, but she did. When she brought her can up, the hole sat dead center. She really could shoot.

Knowing how well Faith had done, Jacob took special pains with his aim. He would be okay with Faith outshooting him, but he surely didn't want to go out in the first round. Both of them made the top twenty. As near as he could tell, no one had done better than Faith, although some might have tied her.

For the next round, they were to shoot the top off a glass bottle, as near to the lip as possible and still not have any lip left on it. After this round, there would be only ten left in the match.

No one teased Faith when she stepped up to shoot this time. At the end of the round, Faith still remained in the contest, but Jacob didn't. He'd shot the top off his bottle, but it had been too far down the bottle to make the cut.

"Win it all for us," he told Faith. "I'm proud of you."

"The mountain men here can sure shoot," she replied.

"So can you, sweetheart. Do you want to use my rifle now? It seems to be a better gun."

"No, but thanks for offering. I'm used to firing this one, so I'll stick with what I know."

For the next set, ten rocks were laid out on a board. The small rocks were nearly the same size, but to have no arguments about it, the contestants drew numbers out of a hat to determine their shooting order. Each one could determine which rock they wanted to shoot.

Jacob didn't understand this one since they wouldn't be able to tell who hit their rock nearest the center. When he saw men pick up the crates and board that held the stones and move them into the distance, however, he knew. It didn't matter, because the feat would be to hit a rock at all. Jacob could barely see one.

Faith drew number three. She stood steady as she pointed her barrel, although the old rifle had to be heavy for someone her size. She had no trouble shooting her rock. By now, some of the men, including the old mountaineer who had championed her, were cheering after her shots. Jacob clapped the loudest. He looked at her in awe. At the end of the round, only four shooters had hit a rock.

"This will be the last round," a man announced. "We have a piece of wood attached to a rope. The rope will be swung from the same position and the person who shoots the piece of wood closest to the center will win. In case of a tie, we will continue until we have a winner."

The rope with the wood attached suspended from an inverted L-shaped pole that looked like something used for a hangman's noose. The wood would be brought back against the pole and released. A shooter could only shoot on the swing back. This gave the man who started the pendulum time to get out of the way and prevented a shooter from waiting until the swing slowed.

"I'm used to shooting a moving target, like squirrels," Faith whispered to Jacob. He smiled. It looked to him as if she could hit anything.

"Ladies first," the old mountaineer hollered, and the crowd of watchers agreed. Jacob didn't know if it would be better or worse to go first. It turned out to be better.

Faith stood ready. The man released the wood and rushed out of the way. Jacob held his breath. Faith shot as soon as it started its second swing, and the wood fell from the swing. Most of the people looked puzzled.

The man who started the pendulum walked over to the wood and looked up. He smiled and pointed to the rope. "She's shot the thing right in the center, where I tied the rope around the wood. I don't guess you can get much more in the middle than that."

Cheers broke out everywhere, and Jacob picked Faith up and swung her around. She had set a very high standard for the others. They couldn't beat her, only tie her.

It took about ten minutes to hang another piece in the exact same position. They had several pieces of wood the same size ready if needed.

They didn't need a new piece after the second shooter. He seemed nervous and missed the entire piece of wood.

The third marksman hit very near the center, but he didn't hit the rope at dead center. The fourth man barely hit the end of the wood.

The official declared Faith the winner. Many of the people stood around shaking their heads. It was hard for Jacob to believe, too. His wife continued to surprise him.

"Honey, I'm so proud of you I could bust," Lena said and hugged her.

"I didn't know you were here," Faith said.

"I hadn't planned to be, but news spread through the wagons fast that you were going to be shooting, so most of us came out. You did us folks from Kentucky proud."

"I sort of figured you to be a mountain gal," the old mountain man said. He'd been standing to one side waiting to congratulate Faith. "People who hunt in the mountains learn to shoot in any conditions. Why, I've seen a mountaineer hit their prey with so much fog you couldn't see a tree at ten feet."

"We didn't have powder or balls to spare, either," Faith said. "I was taught not to waste them."

"Well, that's the best shootin' I've seen in a long time. I'm right glad I didn't enter this time, although I'd have counted it worth a dollar to see this. I don't expect too many of the other riflemen will be over to congratulate you, 'cause you really showed them up. Did you notice we didn't have a single soldier in the last round? Are you folks headed to Oregon?"

"We are," Jacob said. "I'm planning to farm there."

"Well, I'd say you've got yourself a right handy helpmate here."

"Indeed I do, and she can cook just as well as she can shoot."

"You don't say. I don't know why all the best ones are already taken when I meet 'em. I sure wish you folks the best."

"You too, mister." Jacob shook the man's hand.

"Well, we made money on this stop," Jacob said while smiling at Faith as they started for their wagon. "We traded for all our purchases, and you made fifty-seven dollars."

"You're crazy to let your wife take part in a shooting contest, Parker," Rex said as he passed them. "What were you thinking?"

"That she's talented."

"There you are, Jakey." Iris seemed to be headed for the fort. "Wasn't it nice of you to let Faith win the match. I hope she's going to share her winnings with you."

"I shot my best today. Faith won all on her own."

"And the winnings will go for things we need on the trail or in Oregon," Faith added. "Jacob and I keep our funds together."

"Well, at least you have some funds to keep," she muttered as she continued on her way.

"I think she may have just given us a hint of what's she about," Jacob said. "I think she's looking for a man with money."

He'd told Faith about the extra cash, and he'd showed her where he had hidden it. They'd better also find a good hiding place for this fifty-seven dollars. Most of the people now knew they had it.

All but one of the wagons left behind due to sickness pulled in at dusk. They had lost three people, the parents in one wagon, and a son in another. The surviving parents had taken in the three children of the dead parents. They'd buried the dead in unmarked graves due to the Indians, taken three more days for some of the sick to start recovering, and started out. They'd made better time than the larger train, and even traveled on Sunday, but here they were. They said they'd be ready to pull out in the morning.

Chapter Seventeen

FORT BRIDGER

"INDEPENDENCE ROCK IS NINE OR ten days west of Fort Laramie," Marshall told them. "Most wagon trains have been able to reach it by the Fourth of July, but instead it'll be more toward the last of July for us. I'd like to believe we can make up some of the lost time, but the roughest part of the journey is still ahead. Right now, we're about three hundred miles from South Pass. The South Pass is at the Continental Divide that marks the half-way point of our trip."

A rumble of disbelief and discouragement followed. How disheartening to realize they hadn't completed half the journey yet. By the looks on their faces, many questioned if they could even make it.

"If we lose any more time, we should probably start traveling on Sundays. The only problem with that is we'll need a lay-by day even more as the trip gets harder. We have the mountains coming up."

"I wish we hadn't come."

"This is harder than I ever imagined."

"Are we even going to make it?"

"I'm so tired now I don't know where I'll find the energy to keep going."

The pessimistic comments flew. Jacob looked at Faith, and she smiled at him.

"We'll be fine," she said. "This will be an adventure we can tell to our children."

He raised his eyebrows to ask her the silent question. She laughed.

"No, you don't need to worry. Not yet."

The rest at Fort Laramie had refreshed Faith and Jacob. As they started off, Jacob enjoyed the fact his wife now walked beside him. He should have abandoned the second wagon sooner. Now the oxen could be rested every other day, and that would help. The mountains and the remainder of the journey would be hard on the livestock, too, and Jacob feared finding them places to graze would become an increasingly difficult task.

"You surprised me by how well you can shoot. What else can you do that I don't know about?" Jacob asked Faith as they walked along beside the wagon and team.

"I don't think there's anything else. I lived on the little mountain farm, and we mostly lived off what we had."

"Can you skin rabbits, dress out a deer, tan leather, or clean fish?"

"Yes on all of those."

"What would you like to do that you can't?"

She thought a moment. "Well, Aunt Mabel liked to spin and weave, so she took care of those, and I never learned. I did all the dyeing of the yarn, though. I also remember Mama embroidering and doing fancy needlework, but Aunt Mabel didn't see the worth of fancy needlework. She had me sewing and mending instead, but I'd like to know how to do the pretty stitching, too."

"If you could have any small item that you don't have, what would it be?"

"Some writing implements and a diary or paper." She answered right away this time. "I used to love to write when I was younger, but I didn't write well then. I read my books and studied my dictionary when I moved to Kentucky, but I never had a way to write, except in the dirt with a stick. I think I'd like to keep a journal or do something to improve my writing. Why all these questions?"

"I want to get to know you better. I think your shooting talent made me realize there's still a lot I don't know about you, and we've been so tired at the end of most days we haven't been able to carry on lengthy conversations."

"That may be even truer for me. I don't know much about your childhood, your college days, or what you were thinking when you met Lucille. Is it okay to ask about Lucille?"

"It is, but I have to admit that wasn't the best period in my life, and I'm not proud of what happened or why it happened, but you can ask me anything. Let's see now." He paused to decide how to condense his story down.

"My childhood was pretty normal for a Virginia planter. Mama taught me until I turned twelve. She also taught me about God and the Bible. At twelve, Charles' tutor started teaching me in preparation for college. I attended William and Mary because that's what my parents expected. I liked to learn, so I didn't mind. I never really fit in, because many of the other students liked to frequent the taverns and participate in other activities in which I wanted no part. Others liked me well enough, but I didn't belong to any groups nor did I have any very close friends. I spent most of my time studying, and I did quite well academically."

"I'd known of Lucille for most of my life, since she lived in the Richmond area, like me, but I'd never been around her often. Even on the occasions when she and I did attend the same affairs, she never noticed me. She always had plenty of other admirers hovering around her. When she wanted to walk in the garden with me at the harvest ball held at her house, I felt flattered. You already know how she tricked me into marrying her. Her father took me into his office and told me, since I'd been alone with her in her bedroom, marrying to save her reputation was the only honorable thing to do. I'd been in the bedroom with her for less than five minutes, but I knew people would still gossip about it. Since she'd always been so sought-after and had turned down innumerable other offers, I felt proud to marry her. I should have remembered pride goeth before a fall. She remained demurely flirtatious and seemed to dote on me until we were married. From the moment we said our vows, everything changed. You read her diary, so you know what I mean."

"But you didn't love her?" Faith asked softly, apparently unsure if she should ask again. He understood her need for reassurance.

"I thought I did at first, but the longer we were married, the harder it became. I knew I didn't feel the deep love I wanted to have for my wife, but I hoped it would grow over time. It didn't grow at all, but I tried to be a good husband anyway. I was happy and proud when she told me she expected our baby. I hoped the newborn would pull us closer together. I never suspected Rudy wasn't my son. I should have, because there'd been clues. Her father had been right about me being naïve. They picked the right man to hoodwink."

"I think your problems with Lucille and my problems with my aunt and uncle were preparing us to be the right people for each other. I think because of our pasts, we're better able to appreciate what we have now. I love you, Jacob, and I have no doubt that you're exactly the right man for me."

"That's a good way to look at things, and I think you're right. You're what I need in every way, and I love you more deeply than I thought possible, but still, my love continues to grow."

They talked about everything: their pasts, likes and dislikes, hopes and dreams, academic topics, current affairs, expectations, and their faith. They didn't consider anything taboo and they listened, as well as talked.

Jacob had always thought his parents had a good marriage, but he and Faith were so much closer, so much more in love. This exceeded anything he'd ever dreamed of.

In the nine days of traveling it took them to get to Independence Rock, Faith left his side only once to walk with Lena for about an hour.

Independence Rock looked like a giant sleeping animal from a distance. When they approached it, it looked like an enormous mound, perhaps a turtle in its shell. If they'd made it here toward the first of July, they'd have had a lay-by day and a huge party, but, since they were running behind schedule, they would move on in the morning. Still, many in the train wanted to carve their names on the rock before dusk.

"Would you like to leave our names there, too?" Jacob asked Faith.

"It's close, so I wouldn't mind walking there and doing that."

Faith put some meat on to be simmering, and they went to the rock. Some of the younger ones tried climbing the rock, but Faith and Jacob just walked around it, carved their names in a place they could reach, and walked back to their wagon.

"Did it get its name because wagon trains could make it here by Independence Day?" Faith asked.

"Yes. I understand the first wagon train to carve names here arrived and had a big celebration on July the Fourth. They named it Independence Rock."

They left the Platte and entered the Sweetwater Valley. The aptly named river ran clear and tasted much better than the muddy Platte. However, the river had supposedly been named for the time trappers were crossing the river with pack mules, and their sugar spilled into the river.

"Are you still going to boil your drinking water?" Jacob heard Faith asked Lena. "This water doesn't seem as muddy."

"It doesn't," Lena agreed, "but it's still river water, and I can still see particles floating, so I think I will. The boiling does seem to help settle the dirt out better and maybe that's why none of us have been sick recently. It can't hurt any; that's for sure."

The next landmark would be Devil's Gate. There the Sweetwater River had carved an almost four-hundred-feet deep canyon from granite through the spur of a mountain. It did look like a gate, arch, or entranceway, but it stood about half a mile from the trail. Since they hadn't laid-by at Independence Rock, Marshall gave them a longer nooning, so there'd be time to walk there.

"I don't like its name," Faith said. "I certainly wouldn't want a gate for the devil. Who'd want to let him in?"

"Some people do seem to choose to do evil," Jacob said.

"True, but they pay for it, don't they?"

"The pity is sometimes others do, too."

They began to see rattlesnakes regularly, and they were unnerving. Jacob heard someone say they were prairie rattlers. One of the children on the train had been bitten by one and died. Faith said venomous snakebites were more dangerous for children, because they were smaller, and that did make sense.

Jacob liked their new sleeping arrangement inside the wagon. He found their makeshift bed more comfortable than the pallet in the tent.

"I've got second shift guard duty tonight, so I'm going to need to get in bed as soon as possible," Jacob told Faith.

"I thought you had the first shift."

"I did, but one of the men wanted to switch with me."

"Go on in and I'll be right behind you," she said.

When Jacob sat down on the edge of the bed to pull his boots off, he saw the cover at the foot of the bed move. He stood up and looked under the covers. A snake! He threw the covers back down. It almost looked like a rattlesnake, but he hadn't heard a noise. He didn't want to look again for fear he'd disturb it. It needed to stay right there until he could figure out what to do. How could he get rid of it without getting bit or shooting up his wagon? *Lord, I could really use Your guidance here.* Maybe he'd better get some help. He started out of the wagon when he met Faith coming in.

"Stay out here until I get back. There's a snake in the wagon and I'm going for help."

Jacob saw Obadiah ride into camp and called out to him. The scout dismounted, and Jacob explained the situation.

"Well now, iffin that don't beat all. Let me take a gander at this here snake."

Jacob led the scout into the wagon and watched as he pulled down the cover. The snake raised its head.

"Well now, hit sure does look like a rattlesnake," Obadiah said as he stared at the snake, "but you're okay. This here's jist a bull snake. He's not dangerous atall."

Obadiah picked up the snake by its tail and flung it from the wagon. "That one ain't all that big, fer a bull snake. They can git some size on 'em."

"How would it have gotten into my wagon and into my bed?"

"I'd say moren likely somebidy's tryin' to play a trick on ya. Yes siree, that snake got here with some two-legged critter's help. I'll let Marshall know 'bout this."

Jacob thanked Obadiah and went out to get Faith. He was still dumbfounded. What reason would someone have for putting a snake in their bed, and who would do such a thing?

"Do you think there are any more snakes?" Faith asked.

"No, but at least it wasn't venomous."

"I'd have been scared to death if I'd found it here when you'd gone to pull guard duty. I'm not that afraid of the non-venomous snakes, but I don't want them in my bed, and, like you, I wouldn't have known for sure this one was non-venomous."

They got into bed. Jacob hoped he could get to sleep now. The man he would be relieving would come wake him in two hours. The guards took turns doing that until all of them had been replaced.

He wanted to talk with Faith about who might have put the snake in here, but that would have to wait until tomorrow. He needed to get as much sleep as he could. The day after guard duty always seemed long and tiring.

"Obadiah thinks someone put that snake in our bed," Jacob told Faith as they walked beside their team the next day. "I can think of only three people who might possibly do such a thing."

"Iris and who else?"

"Dexter or Rex Caulder."

"I know Rex doesn't like you, but surely Dexter wouldn't do such a thing."

"Well, it does seem like a boy's prank to me, and he probably doesn't like me that well, since I have you."

"Whoever did it might have been trying to scare me, not you. After all, you were supposed to have the first guard duty."

"That's a good point. I hadn't considered that. I guess it will be hard to ever know for sure. I hope this isn't just the beginning, but I want you to be extra cautious, just in case. I'd like for us to stick together, as much as possible."

"All right. I like sticking close to you anyway." She gave him a playful look, and he couldn't help but laugh.

They crossed back and forth through the Sweetwater several times, but most of the trail moved away from the water. The terrain had become dry and dusty, and the snow covering the mountains in the distance teased them by its very presence.

They had to walk through dry sage and sandy plains. Their shoes and boots filled with so much sand, they'd have to stop and shake them out. The sage made travel too rough to go barefooted through, and the sand could become hot enough to scorch feet bottoms.

There'd been no more buffalo chips to burn in this area. Since trees were still scarce, the campers burned sage. It burned up more quickly, but it made a hot blaze and the embers would stay hot for a long time.

"I feel blessed to have you cooking for me." Jacob wanted to let Faith know he appreciated her. The things Lena told him about how poorly Faith's aunt and uncle had treated her still bothered him.

"I've had plenty of practice," she told him. "I know some people today are using a cast iron kitchen stove. A few are even trying to haul something like that to Oregon. We always cooked in the fireplace, however, and there's not much difference in cooking in a campfire. In fact, we used an outside fire for such things as making soap or rendering lard anyway."

Walking along in the exhausting climate became drudgery, and tempers tended to flare at the smallest disagreement and sometimes without any provocation. Seemingly happy people weren't immune.

"Why can't you have us something warm to eat at mid-day once in a while, Lena?" Jacob and Faith heard Harlan yell one day.

"You mean to tell me you want something hot to eat in this desert? Are you daft, man?" Lena replied.

"I said 'warm' woman, not hot. Faith manages to have Jacob something warm to eat most days. She'd not dare serve her husband hardtack and cold bacon."

"Well, maybe you'd better start looking elsewhere for your meals if I can't suit you. If you can show her you have money or the prospect of some, I'm sure Iris Bates would be eager to cook for you, and she won't even care that you're a dried-up, old fool."

"Woman, you've got a tongue sharp enough to fillet trout, and if you keep giving everyone a piece of your mind, you're not going to have any left. It seems to me that day is just about here."

"It's too bad your mouth's the best-exercised muscle you have. You sure do keep it flapping, but it's all just nonsense."

Jacob knew the Haywoods would likely make up before the day ended, but some people's rage grew worse. Two brothers got into an argument over whether or not to leave a desk behind. One pulled his gun, and the other shot him. The council deemed it self-defense, but how sad.

Jacob almost bit his own tongue a couple of times to keep from saying something too sharply. If Faith ever had the same problem, she didn't show it. She seemed to manage to stay optimistic no matter the circumstance. Jacob wondered how she could always be in a good mood. When he asked her she quoted him what Paul had said in the Bible.

"I have learned, in whatsoever state I am, therewith to be content. I know both how to be abased, and I know how to abound: everywhere and in all things I am instructed both to be full and to be hungry, both to abound and to suffer need. I can do all things through Christ which strengtheneth me."

"You certainly know your Bible," Jacob told her.

"It's the book I've read and studied the most through the years. Knowing it is much easier than applying it, however."

"Your parents aptly named you. You have a strong faith."

"I hope so, but I think my parents gave me my name because they intended to instill a strong belief and trust in God. I thank them for giving me such a strong foundation, and I want to do the same for our children." She looked at him and laughed.

"No, not yet," she answered before he could ask the question. She knew he wondered every time she mentioned children. She didn't know he also tried to keep track of the possibility himself. Unlike with Lucille, their relationship now stayed close enough he could have some idea.

The trail got rougher as they crept up the rocky slope in the Wind Mountains. The climb was more gradual than Jacob had expected. He guessed the steep mountains would come later, but he knew they would come. Once they crossed the South Pass, all the rivers would start flowing west to the Pacific, instead of east to the Mississippi and the Gulf.

Trekking over the rocks became so hard, most of the drovers, including Jacob, tied skins over their oxen's hooves and foot areas to try to protect them more. They were shod, but the rocks would still fray them until they were raw and bleeding.

The people had difficulty, too, and no one went barefooted now. Faith put on Lucille's old shoes because the soles were thicker than hers, but Jacob knew they wouldn't last on the rocky trail.

Everyone focused on getting through South Pass, because, then they would be descending into Oregon Country, although they'd be only half-way to their destination near the coast. Oregon Territory covered a huge area of largely unsettled land.

Once they came to a marshy bottom where ice lay beneath a layer of grass revealing an ice spring. They dug out the ice and enjoyed wonderful ice water.

Finally, they made it to the South Pass, but they were too exhausted for a celebration. Now they'd be descending into Oregon Territory, and the end seemed in sight. No one would be turning back now. After this, the distance would be shorter to the Oregon coast than going back to Missouri.

The pass didn't look as Jacob had imagined it. The barren pass sat at the high point of a sagebrush plain. Antelope were plentiful and hawks abounded, as they looked for prey in the wide, open space. No steep grades led to South Pass, but the land gradually ascended, until, at the pass, the view became incredible, except for its sameness.

They headed down into the Green River Valley. The pines and evergreens attested to the high elevation, but it lifted their spirits to see the greenery.

"We had woods all around our cabin in Kentucky," Faith told Jacob, "and I think that's what I've missed most as we crossed the plains. I loved to walk the old Cherokee trails in the forest. I went hunting or gathering nuts or roots as an excuse to go there."

"We had a lot more trees in Virginia than the plains have, too. There were plenty of trees on the plantation. We had forests where Charles and I went hunting every fall. In fact, Charles taught me to hunt."

"Did you have slaves?" Faith asked.

"We did, and the house and stable slaves seemed like family to me. I never had much contact with the field hands, but I felt sorry for them. The idea of slavery has always made me uncomfortable. I understand Oregon Territory is supposed to be a free area where there'll be no slaves, and I'm glad."

The nights were especially cold now, and Jacob and Faith were using their buckskin jackets. They piled their bed with all their coverings. Jacob had brought blankets, and Faith had quilts.

When they got up in the mornings, ice would be covering the water in the barrels. Now Jacob understood why Faith had been working so hard to knit them more socks. Of course, with all the walking, they wore them out quickly, too. She knitted fast like she did most tasks, and she'd managed to have them scarves made, too. They would need them again in the mountains yet to come.

They'd been following Little Sandy Creek, which would lead toward the Big Sandy and on to Green River. Sometimes Green River became so deep they'd have to raise the wagon beds with green willow saplings growing by the water to cross. This usually kept their goods from getting too wet.

At least they were able to catch some fish now. Bacon had become their main meat, and they welcomed the taste of the fresh fish. The ones Faith fried made Jacob's mouth water.

Jacob had done well in geometry, and he helped the men determine how much rope would be needed for a fording. He would draw his triangles in the dust to do his calculations.

Marshall said a shortcut would save them three days, and the councilmen held a long discussion on whether or not to take it. On the shortcut, they'd have to go fifty miles without water or grass for the livestock, and the toll on the animals and people could be high. In the end, they opted for the safer route, and Jacob was glad.

Of course, Rex had disagreed. "I see no reason to prolong this trip," he said. "I say take the short-cut and get to our destination sooner."

"The important thing is to get there," Marshall had commented, and everyone else had voted for the safer route.

They left Green River Valley and headed south toward Fort Bridger, following the longer route. They began to see more Indians—Crow, Shoshone, Bannock, and a few Paiute. Obadiah said the Shoshone were the more peaceful Indians. Many of the fur trappers from here westward chose Shoshone brides.

Fort Bridger looked as busy as Fort Laramie had been, but Laramie had more Indians around it. This rustic stockade sat at the dividing waters of Black's Fork, which provided icy cold water, fresh from the snowy mountains. Fort Bridger also had broadleaf trees again.

The fort itself seemed more rundown than Fort Laramie had been. Bridger had been the first fort built on the western side of the Mississippi especially for emigrants heading west. It had been built of dried clay applied over poles and had some twenty cabins for traders and their Indian wives.

Prices here at the fort were atrocious. Flour sold for fifty dollars a sack, and sugar went for a dollar a cup. Jacob and Faith were almost out of coffee, and they had to pay an outlandish price for it at the fort.

Jacob just thanked God they had the money for what they needed. So many of the families didn't. Of course, he wanted to save as much as he could to put into starting the farm. They would have to build a cabin and have some furnishings. Then he'd need a barn, outbuildings, and a few things for the farm.

Some of the men at Fort Bridger were having another shooting match, but they refused to let Faith join them.

"It jist ain't no place fer a woman," one of the trappers grumbled. "Leave the shootin' to the menfolk."

Jacob wondered if they'd already heard about Faith's shooting skills at the Fort Laramie competition. Whatever their reason, they were adamant. Since Faith couldn't participate, they went back to their wagon. Jacob hadn't intended to shoot anyway.

When they got back to the wagons, someone had stolen things from many of the families. "I should have posted guards," Marshall said, "but I thought enough of us would be here at any given time we wouldn't need that."

"Maybe we should check the Parkers' wagon," Rex said. "I heard Mrs. Parker tends to take things that don't belong to her." Iris agreed with him, but no one else said anything.

The only thing Faith could find missing was some of the clothing she'd hung out to dry. Others had much more taken, especially foodstuff. Obadiah said the Indians here might be less dangerous, but some of them had become adept at thievery.

Jacob had started back from checking on his livestock when a shot rang out. It sounded much closer than the shooting match. Besides, the contest should be over by now. Faith came running as soon as she saw him.

"I think someone just took a shot at me," she told him, as she tried to catch her breath. Her eyes were wide with fear. "The ball whizzed awfully close to my head."

"It could have been a stray shot," he told her but realized he didn't know if he believed it himself or not. "There are a lot of people around."

"I guess so."

He put his arms around her and pulled her close. He hoped the shot had been unintentional. He didn't want to think of the danger and what might happen otherwise.

They stayed at Fort Bridger for two days. The animals and people needed the rest, and they hadn't had any delays in the mountains. The lay-over helped, and they started out again with a little more vigor.

Marshall warned them about what was to come. They'd gone through a stretch of desert-like land already, but Jacob feared the great basin would be a real test for them. He wasn't looking forward to it, but he did want to get it over with.

Chapter Eighteen

FORT HALL

AFTER A LONG PULL UP Muddy Creek, they came to Bear River, which provided a lovely campsite. They should be about ten days out of Fort Hall. Thankfully, they made camp on Saturday, so they could stay there through tomorrow.

Jacob led Faith down to the river's edge. Here the river had a wide span with banks so low it resembled the Atlantic coast. The sky used the river for a mirror, turning the water a vivid blue. The reflections of tall evergreens sent fingers into the water. The beauty of the place could almost steal one's breath.

Faith sighed. "I like it here."

"It does look like a landscape painting."

Jacob stood behind her and put his arms around her. She leaned back against him.

"Let's come down here and have our devotion tomorrow morning," she suggested. "Wouldn't this be a good setting to worship our Lord?"

"It would indeed. Maybe we could also do some fishing tomorrow afternoon. I'm sure we could catch enough for supper."

"I'd like that. You and I have never found the time to fish together."

Three of the families decided to stay instead of continuing on. Dexter's was one of them. He approached Faith when he thought he had Faith alone. He didn't know Jacob was in the wagon looking for another shirt.

"You can stay here with us, Faith," he said. "You don't have to continue."

"I want to continue. I would never leave Jacob. It would break my heart."

"I just thought I would ask and make sure."

"I'm sure, but thank you, Dexter. I wish you the very best."

For a fleeting moment, Jacob wondered if Faith would have told the young man exactly the same thing if he hadn't been near. Of course, she would. He had no reason to doubt her.

"He doesn't give up easily, does he?" Jacob said, as he stepped from the wagon. "Doesn't he know how immoral he's acting? You are my wife."

"Yes, I am, but I feel sorry for him. I hope I didn't hurt him in my refusal, but he must understand I love my husband. I've told him more than once."

"I can understand his fascination with you. I'm pretty fascinated myself." He put his arm around her shoulders and pulled her out of sight for a kiss.

Jacob and Faith did carry their coffee and Bibles down to the river Sunday morning. Their time of devotion in the quiet morning and peaceful setting soothed Jacob. He almost hated to leave.

They also made it back before supper to fish. Faith caught as many as he did, and they enjoyed the time together away from the others.

"I hope the remainder of the trip isn't too difficult," Jacob said.

"Are you expecting it to be?"

"Marshall and Obadiah say the worst is yet to come."

"Do you think we should stay here instead of continuing?"

"Is that what you want to do?" *Stay here near Dexter.*

"It is beautiful here, but we know we can obtain land near Portland. That's been your goal, Jacob, so I think that's what we should do, unless you've changed your mind."

"No, I haven't changed my mind, but I want to consider your wishes, too."

"I'll be happy anywhere you are."

"I must admit, I'm a little jealous of Dexter. It bothers me he still asks for you when he knows you're already married. Aren't these people Christians? Between Iris and Dexter, I'm beginning to wonder what this world's coming to."

"You're right. I'm also a little jealous of Iris. I trust you, but I don't trust her."

"I don't trust her either. She seems to want to cause trouble, and she's headstrong enough to not take my 'no' for an answer."

The conversation left Jacob feeling more at peace. Faith's comments let him know he had nothing to fear from her.

They caught enough fish for supper, and still, they lingered. When they went back, it would be to start the routine tasks of another week on the trail. Jacob pulled Faith down into his arms as they reclined beside the river. He rolled over and kissed her long and completely. He would have liked to continue their lovemaking, but, although they were secluded, anyone could walk up, so that would have to wait until tonight.

They got to their feet and had began gathering their things when something hit Faith in the temple. She fell to her knees and clutched her head. Blood trickled between her fingers and down the side of her face.

Jacob panicked and grabbed her for a better look. A short, deep gash ran along her hairline. He gently tucked a stray strand of hair behind her ear and pressed his handkerchief to the side of her head to staunch the blood.

"What was it, darling?" he asked, trying to appear calm. "Did you see anything?"

"I think it may have been a rock, but I can't be sure because it happened so quickly. I didn't see anything else."

"Come on let's get you back and get you bandaged."

Jacob looked around as he led Faith back. He didn't see anything either.

Lena stood outside her wagon starting supper and noticed the blood on Faith's face as they walked by. She came over to take care of Faith's cut. It took more pressure to finally get the bleeding to slow enough to bandage it. The spot had already started to swell and discolor.

"I'll cook supper tonight," he told her.

"No, you won't," Faith told him. "I'm fine. It's just a little nick." *Stubborn woman.*

She baked small potatoes in the edge of the fire, as she fried the fish and made cornbread. She got out the last of their pickles, and they ate supper. Jacob couldn't believe how good it tasted.

Jacob thought Faith felt worse than she was letting on, because she went to bed after they finished the dishes. She even let him do the milking, which told him a lot.

He took care of the fire and got ready for bed himself. He crawled in beside her and pulled her close. The more he thought about what had happened, the more his fear grew. *Oh, God, please don't let anything happen to Faith. Please keep her safe. I need her, and she's Thy greatest blessing to me. I feel so helpless in this situation, but I know Thou can do all things, so please protect us both and grant us many years together to serve Thee. I pray. Amen.*

Jacob went to talk with Marshall before they pulled out the next morning. There'd been too many incidents lately—the snake, the gunshot, and the rock. Jacob might be getting overly suspicious, but he had even begun to wonder if someone had started that prairie fire.

Marshall didn't have any answers. "All I know is to keep a close watch," he said. "If I were you, I'd talk to Lena and Harlan and have them watching, too. If it is someone and they continue their mischief, they're bound to get caught sooner or later."

Jacob just hoped it would be sooner. He couldn't stand the thought of Faith being in danger and threatened like this.

Dear Lord, keep her safe.

Someone had started rumors about Jacob, and he remembered what he once heard his mother say. "Rumor runs faster and hangs around longer than the truth ever does." It did a lot of damage, too.

The grapevine said Jacob had lost his first wife and his son, and now unexplained things were happening to Faith. It insinuated Jacob was trying to get rid of his wife, as he had Lucille. Some people seemed to believe the ludicrous tale.

Faith dismissed them. "Surely they don't think you would put a snake in your own bed, and you couldn't have hit me with the rock. You were right beside me."

"You need to be concerned about the incidents, Faith. I'm afraid someone is trying to hurt you. We need to be vigilant."

"I am concerned, but it will do no good to worry. I plan to be careful, but there's only so much we can do. I refuse to live in fear and feel I have to look over my shoulder all the time. I'll trust in God to protect me. He always has. 'The Lord is on my side; I will not fear; what can man do unto me,' as Psalm 118:6 says."

"I wish I had your faith. I think I do until times like this, and I find myself worried that something will happen to you."

The next morning, Faith read Deuteronomy 31 for their devotion. Verse six read, "Be strong and of a good courage, fear not, nor be afraid of them; for the Lord thy God, He it is that doth go with thee; He will not fail thee, nor forsake thee." She must have picked that verse just for him.

Jacob tried to leave everything in God's capable hands. He spent time in prayer each day as he walked beside the oxen team, but, especially at night, he tended to pick the worry back up. Hadn't the reason given for Faith marrying him been that he would protect her? Rex might be right. He didn't seem to be doing a very good job.

Not far from Bear River the wagons came to the Soda Springs. These were a group of mineral springs with Steamboat Springs being the most impressive. The geyser shot squirts of water up two to three feet with a whistling sound, like a steamboat. Jacob and Faith stood hand in hand and watched the strange sight. She gave a little bounce and laughed when the water whistled.

Jacob rather liked these soda springs. Faith took the last of her dried black cherries, poured some of the fizzing water over them, and let them soak for a delicious cherry soda drink. Water from the springs also turned out to be good for making bread.

The women washed clothes in the warm springs. Some of the springs were hot, some were warm, and others had cold water.

When they spent a night near one of the springs, some of the boys went swimming. Jacob would have liked to go in privately with Faith, but he saw no opportunity.

They moved on to Fort Hall. They'd made up a little of their lost time by not spending as much time at the landmarks or forts as some trains did, but summer slipped by.

Fort Hall had been constructed of wood encased in whitewashed, sun-dried adobe bricks. A pair of towers, looking a little like squat sentinels, stood at the front. The United States flag flew over it and looked a little out-of-place in the dismal setting.

Like Fort Laramie, Fort Hall had been a fur trading post, but the Hudson Bay Company had pulled out when it became part of the United States last year. It was now a military post kept especially for travelers on the trails.

They pulled in around noon. They would spend the rest of the day here and leave early in the morning.

Like the other forts, this one had its share of Indians and mountain men. A few of the women had piles of clothing made from deer and antelope skins for sale.

The prices at Fort Hall were high, but not as expensive as they'd been at some of the other forts. Jacob and Faith bought some more flour and cornmeal.

Iris caught up with Jacob as he went to the stream to get water. "Jakey, I need to talk with you."

He wanted to tell her to stop calling him "Jakey." It reminded him of Lucille every time she did, and he didn't want to talk with her at all. Instead, he asked, "What do you want?" The words seemed to take an accusing tone he didn't mean to show.

"You know I'm planning to leave the Oregon Trail where the California Trail splits off unless someone makes me a better offer. I had hoped you might make that offer. I could make you happy. I know I could."

"I'm happy with my wife. You need to find you a single man."

"I'd rather have you. I'd go on to Portland with you, or better yet, you could come to California with me. We would have a good life either way."

"I'm not interested. Find yourself someone else. By trying to take another woman's husband, you let me know what kind of person you are, and it's not a good one. You're proposing adultery." Several other words came to mind, but none of them were Christian.

"You'll change your mind, Jake Parker." She stomped her foot. "You just see if you don't."

Jacob trudged back to his wagon deep in thought. He considered not saying anything to Faith about what had just happened, because he knew she didn't trust Iris with him, but he decided he'd better tell her. He didn't want to keep secrets, and, if he did, and they were discovered, it would make him look guilty of something he hadn't done.

"Talk about not giving up. Dexter at least stayed by Bear River," Faith said.

"Well, ideally, Iris will head for California, and we'll continue on to Portland. The trail will split not far from here, so I'm hoping we'll be rid of her."

"Is the same person still driving her wagon?"

"As far as I know. It's some boy. I don't know who he is, but I've seen him a few times. He looks young, but I guess he's about fifteen or sixteen. I think his father might have died around the same time as Mr. Bates. I'm sure I heard Marshall say the boy and his father had planned to farm in Oregon. We've lost quite a few people on this trip, and it isn't over yet." He paused realizing Faith's aunt and uncle, as well as Lucille and Rudy, were among that number.

Faith looked at him with sympathy flooding her eyes. "It's been a long, hard journey, hasn't it? I'd never even been off our Kentucky farm since I went there at ten, so this is very different for me."

"Are you exhausted, honey?"

"No more than anyone else. I intend to see this through. I'll be walking right there beside you, Jacob Parker, all the way to Portland." She smiled.

Chapter Nineteen

MISSING

JACOB HAD TO STAY WITH the livestock the last two hours of the night. He asked Harlan and Lena to keep an eye on Faith and their wagon.

When he returned to the wagon at four, the fire hadn't been started. Faith usually tried to have the coffee going by the time he got back when he had watch duty during the last shift.

"Faith," he called at the wagon flap. No answer. He crawled inside. The bed stood empty. His heart sank to his toes.

He rushed to the Haywoods' wagon.

"I didn't hear a thing," Harlan said. "Maybe she walked out for some reason. If there'd been a struggle, I'm sure we'd have heard it. Lena's a real light sleeper."

Jacob started going from wagon to wagon. Marshall, Obadiah, and John helped him search. No one had seen Faith.

"I'll go get some of the soldiers from the fort to help us search there and the outside area," Marshall said. "I'm sure she'll turn up."

At six o'clock they still hadn't found her. Jacob saddled his horse and began searching with the soldiers.

"We're running way behind where I'd like to be," Marshall said. "Normally, I'd hold the wagon train up for you, but I'm still afraid of the possibility the train might be caught in the mountains in a snowstorm. I'll give you to eight o'clock, but then we'll be pulling out."

"You do what you need to, but I'm not leaving without my wife. We'll catch up with you if we can."

Jacob felt as if he were riding in circles, as he gripped the reins so hard his knuckles turned white. He tried to keep a soldier in sight but spread out enough to be useful.

His mind rode in circles, too. Rattlesnakes had become common. What if she'd been bitten? Had someone taken her off? He couldn't imagine she'd gone anywhere on her own. Perhaps an Indian had kidnapped her, but then surely Harlan would have heard a struggle or something.

The worry gnawed at him like a plague of infested rats. He tried not to think he'd lost Faith like he had Lucille and Rudy, but the thought nagged at him anyway. If that happened, he didn't know what would become of him.

Dense darkness fell underneath a cloudy sky with still no sign of Faith. After asking at the fort one more time, he reluctantly walked back to his wagon. When he got there, the Haywoods' wagon stood beside his.

"We didn't want to leave you and Faith," Lena said. "We thought we'd wait and see if we could help. Then, the four of us can travel together to catch up with the others."

Jacob had to fight back the tears, and his throat became sore from swallowing them. *Oh, God, please may the **four** of us be going to catch up with the others. Protect Faith wherever she is and help me to find her, I pray. Amen.*

Lena offered him some supper, but he couldn't eat. His stomach had tangled into knots the moment he'd found Faith missing.

"I know you haven't eaten anything all day," Lena said. "You need to eat to keep up your strength. You can't find Faith if you keel over."

He forced down a bite, but he had a hard time swallowing it. He kept wondering what he would do if they couldn't find Faith or if they found her dead. The grief of just thinking about it pulled at him like a raging river or that quicksand they'd struggled through, and he felt as if he were being towed under. He put the plate down in despair.

He didn't try to go to bed. He couldn't lie in that bed without Faith. Lena and Harlan had wanted to keep him company, but he needed to be alone. He didn't feel like talking.

He toyed with the idea of lighting a torch and continuing his search, but the soldiers had said finding Faith in the dark would be near impossible, and they needed some rest to continue in the morning. He knew it would be futile for him to try alone. He worried that they hadn't already found her, because he knew the longer it took, the less likely it would be to find her unharmed.

He sat beside the fire for a long time, but he knew his body had moved beyond tired. Eventually, he grabbed a quilt and lay under the wagon, but he didn't sleep.

He got up before daylight and rekindled the fire. He sat staring at the blaze for a long time before he made some coffee and tried to read his Bible. He couldn't keep his mind on the words, so he gave up and prayed. He poured his heart out to God, but it still felt raw and bruised when he finished.

At daylight, he walked to the fort. The officers had asked around but hadn't found a single clue or lead. How could someone just disappear without a trace, especially his Faith? He knew she would have wanted to stay with him, so something must have happened to her. He tried to push down the panic that thought caused, but it proved too strong.

He went back to the wagon and saw Harlan with the oxen. Jacob hadn't even thought of them. Thankfully, Harlan had.

The three of them were discussing what they should do when Marshall came riding up. He had to know something. Jacob held his breath.

"We've found her," he said before he'd completely dismounted. "She's been tied, gagged, and hidden in Iris' wagon, but she's okay."

"Glory be!" Lena shouted.

"What happened?" Jacob asked.

"Kenny, that's Iris' driver, went to your wagon and told Faith you'd been hurt and needed her. She ran off with him, and he led her to their wagon. They hit her over the head, dragged her into their wagon, and bound and gagged her. Iris covered her with a quilt. I don't know how long it took for the poor girl to wake up, but Kenny got concerned. He finally came to me and told me what had happened."

"Why in the world would Iris do that?" Harlan asked.

Marshall shook his head in disgust. "If Faith never showed up, Iris thought Jacob would go with her. I think she planned to send Kenny on whichever trail Jacob didn't choose to take. Faith would have gone with Kenny, but Iris hadn't told Kenny that part yet. I really think Iris has gone mad with her obsession to get her way. None of this makes a lick of sense. I don't think they even thought about what they'd do with Faith in the long run."

"She must have been responsible for the other mishaps, too," Jacob said.

"That's true, although she had Kenny do part of the mischief. He put the bull snake in your bed, but she thought you'd be on guard duty, and Faith would receive the scare. Iris shot the gun close to Faith herself. Kenny shot the rock with a slingshot. He says he meant to scare her, not hit her in the head. Iris also admitted to planting the brooch in Faith's wagon."

"Did she start the prairie fire, too?" Jacob asked.

"No, that must have started on its own."

"Why did Kenny agree to all this?" Harlan asked.

"He thought they were funny or harmless pranks to begin with. He knew the snake was harmless, and he didn't mean to actually hit Faith in the head with the rock. She either moved or his aim was off. After the kidnapping, though, he realized things had gotten out of hand, and that's when he came to me."

"Where are the wagon train and the others?" Harlan asked.

"They're going to wait for us. Obadiah is with them, and I put John Brenner in charge until I get back."

"Let's get going," Jacob said. "I want to see Faith."

"You saddle up your horse and ride on, son," Marshall said. "Just follow the wagon trail ruts. Faith's with my missus for now. I'll hitch up your team and bring them on with the Haywoods."

"Thank you, sir."

As Jacob rode the southwest stretch, he realized he hadn't asked Marshall what would happen to Iris and Kenny. Well, that wasn't important when compared to Faith. His wife had been found alive, and he now rode toward her. *Thank You, Lord!*

Faith sat in a chair beside the Marshalls' wagon peeling potatoes. He saw her before she saw him, and he rejoiced at the sight. As soon as he dismounted, he looked up and saw her come running to him.

He caught her in his arms and held her tightly. He didn't ever want to let her out of his grasp again. He felt her tears and pulled back enough to see her face.

"Did they hurt you, darling?"

"Not seriously. I have a sore knot on my head and rope burns from where they tied me up, and I tried to wiggle out, but I'll be fine. I'm sorry, Jacob. You told me to be careful, and I didn't think this through before I ran off with Kenny. Of course, I didn't realize who he was at the time, but I guess I should have. When he said you'd been hurt, I panicked and rushed so I didn't even notice where he took me."

"Sh-h-h. It's all right as long as you are. Don't worry. We're back together now, and that's what matters. I've worried enough over the last twenty-four hours for both of us. I made it, barely, by prayer and supplication. God granted my requests this time, or maybe He granted yours, but I have you back, and that's what's important."

She looked as tired and worn-out as he must. He wanted to take a nap with her in his arms, but their wagon hadn't returned yet. Instead, he borrowed a quilt from Mrs. Marshall and they spread it under a small tree beside the nearby stream. There he lay beside her and held her close. She seemed to need this as much as he did.

"Go to sleep if you can," he told her. "We both had a rough night."

"Yes, I remained too cramped to sleep. They tied my feet and my hands behind me and then tied a short lead to Iris' cot. I lay on the floor of the wagon bed all night."

He picked up her hand, saw her red, raw wrists, and kissed the inside of her lower arm just above the rope burn. He felt a slight tremble run through her. The way she responded to him never ceased to thrill him.

He kissed her tenderly. She'd been through a lot, and she needed his gentleness now.

She lay on his shoulder and he saw the goose-egg-sized knot even through her hair, but he didn't touch it. It looked ugly, bruised, and sore.

"Does your head hurt?"

"A little. I hardly notice it now that you're here."

Jacob lay still hoping Faith would fall asleep. Much later he heard the two wagons come in, and he sat up. Faith looked up at him, and he hoped she'd been able to take a nap.

He helped her up, grabbed the quilt, and they walked back to camp. Lena ran and hugged her gently.

"All of you eat with Wayland and me," Mrs. Marshall said. "I fixed enough."

They ate fried potatoes, beans, and cornbread. The potatoes weren't bad, but the beans and cornbread were not nearly as good as what Faith cooked. He realized anew how much God had blessed him.

"Your second cow had her calf last night," Harlan said. "She seems to be doing fine, but you might need to see to the calf. I also milked the other one for you, but she's not giving much milk now."

"Thank you. The cows slipped my mind. This trip's been hard on them, too, but they've made it so far. I'll keep the new mama tied behind my wagon where we can see to her calf until it's stronger."

"We might as well stay here and move out first thing in the morning," Marshall told them.

"What's going to happen to Iris and the boy?" Lena asked.

"The council will meet and decide," Marshall said, "but I don't think the men will want to hang or severely whip a female. At least, they didn't seem to when Faith came before them accused of taking Iris' brooch. I don't rightly know what else to do with Iris, though. What do you and Faith think, Jacob?"

"I think Iris needs some punishment," Jacob said. "The shot could have killed Faith or someone else. Kenny's should be lighter, because he did eventually let you know what was going on. But kidnapping is serious, and I think Iris meant Faith harm."

"I'm willing to forgive and forget," Faith said, "as long as the trouble is really over, and Iris isn't our neighbor, where I have to contend with her."

"That's very reasonable of you, Mrs. Parker, but are you sure? Jacob is right. What Iris did is serious."

"I'm just happy that she didn't cause any permanent damage, and my Bible tells me that God expects us to forgive. As long as Iris won't try anything like this again, I'll be happy."

"Well, we'll see what the council thinks. In any case, I'll have the pastor speak with her."

The council met that evening, but Jacob didn't go. He stayed with Faith, as it would be better to let the others handle this matter. They knew how he felt.

Marshall stopped by after the council meeting. "Iris has promised to leave with the group going to California. Lester and Morton Agner have agreed to look after her until they get to California, but they told her they wouldn't put up with any of her shenanigans. They told her, if she didn't mind herself, she'd be left on her own. The council took how you felt into consideration, Faith. If you and Jacob had pushed for punishment, I think the council would have gone along." The wagon master shook his head. "I've got a feeling she'll end up marrying some poor soul who's struck it rich and spend his gold for him."

"I assigned Kenny to help the preacher's family. He's not a bad kid. He just needs some guidance. I think he became infatuated with Iris and wanted to please her. That's probably how he got so involved in all this, but I really do think he's learned his lesson."

Jacob held his tongue, but he didn't feel the justice in this. Iris needed some kind of punishment. Otherwise, it looked as if what she did didn't matter, but perhaps it would be better to leave it all in God's hands. That's what Faith would say, anyway.

Jacob lay beside his wife in the wagon and thanked God for the privilege. Being around Faith was helping him see what strong faith really entailed. If he understood why God did things, then he wouldn't need trust and faith. When he didn't understand but chose to trust anyway, his faith grew the most.

Faith snuggled against him, and he scooped her closer. He felt a tug on his heart and realized he loved her so much it almost hurt.

They reached the California cut-off without incident. The wagons camped by the nearby Cassia Creek. In the morning the two groups would go their separate ways, so the women decided to have a good-bye party for supper.

Faith cooked biscuits, the last of her dried green beans she called 'leather britches,' and apple cobbler from dried apples. Jacob hadn't tried to tell her not to overdo. She'd already resumed her normal tasks, and he knew she wouldn't agree to taking it easy.

As usual, everyone ate first. If Jacob and Faith hadn't been near the front of the line, they wouldn't have gotten any of Faith's dishes. Hers were cleaned out early.

"Every waltz is mine," he whispered when they heard the music start.

Iris came, but she sat demurely off to the side and only danced if someone asked her. She danced three reels, one with each of the Agner brothers and one with Obadiah.

Most of the people were ignoring the fiery redhead. Jacob noticed she didn't look nearly as provocative as usual, a definite improvement.

After they finished eating, Faith wanted to speak with her, so Jacob followed. Iris stood when she saw them approaching. She looked skittish, almost scared.

"I wanted to say goodbye and wish you well on the rest of your trip," Faith said. "I hope California is good to you, and I hope you find out what an awesome friend Jesus is the way I have. Do you know how much He loves you?"

Iris only gasped a little more than Jacob. She seemed at a loss as to what to say, so she extended her hand tentatively. "Thank you, but don't worry about me. I can assure you I'm absolutely devoted to self-preservation."

Faith hugged her former enemy. "Learn from all this, Iris," she whispered. "Learn, change, and make the right choices."

After that, it seemed the atmosphere became more relaxed and others spoke to Iris, too. Jacob realized he'd just witnessed many of Jesus' teachings put into action, and he swelled in pride for his wife.

"I believe everyone has a heart for God," Faith said when he told her how he felt. "I think we're all born to yearn for Him, but some folks just prefer not to recognize it."

When Jacob pulled her into his arms for a waltz, he felt as if they were dancing on air. It surprised him to realize being with Faith thrilled him even more now than it had in the beginning. He had begun to understand that a love like theirs only grew stronger over time. *Thank you again, Lord, for all Thy many blessings.*

Chapter Twenty

SNAKE RIVER

NINETEEN WAGONS TOOK THE CALIFORNIA Trail the next morning. A few more headed for Portland. The California group had elected a new wagon master and scout. Marshall and Obadiah would continue northwest.

They would be following Snake River for a big portion of the rest of their journey. This area lay in the northern part of the Great Basin, a high desert. Even with the river near, water would be scarce. Obadiah explained the Snake often lay at the bottom of deep gorges and canyons, too far down to collect any water.

To make matters worse, waterfalls on the Snake abounded. Therefore, they could be parched and the livestock dying of thirst, and they'd hear the water roaring in the distance, but there'd be no way to get to it. Those falls could be heard as far away as forty miles.

Now they faced an arid stretch, where there would be little but sand, desert scrub, jackrabbits, and rattlesnakes. Rotting bodies of dead cattle lay along the side of the trail as a stark reminder of hardships to come. Persistent buzzards circled overhead, as if forecasting imminent doom, and they blackened the decaying bodies of animals along the trail.

After the horrible sights, Faith became more determined than ever to get their animals through, especially the calf and its mother. Jacob prayed for them all.

In addition, dark gray lava and basaltic fields stretched out in murky beds to bring on feelings of doubt and fear. However, Obadiah said the wagon train would be skirting most of those.

The sun blazed above them with a vengeance. As they wound farther along, lips cracked open because of it, and hands and arms became raw. Even with hats or sunbonnets, their faces burned, and skin turned dark and rough, reminding Jacob of walnut hulls.

They rubbed grease on their lips, but then, the dust caked to them so thickly, that became uncomfortable, too. Even without wind, the wagons kicked up clouds of dust. Jacob and Faith had stopped talking as they walked along. Even without conversation, however, Faith's very presence comforted Jacob. Her eyes smiled at him, even if her lips were too sore to move.

The mountains, which sometimes were barely visible in the distance, looked more like mirages. Their wavy outlines wiggled in the baking heat.

A family in the back of them lost an ox from the conditions. They butchered it and shared some of the meat.

Marshall announced everyone needed to lighten their loads or more animals would die. Jacob and Faith emptied their two trunks and tied the contents in sheets. They burned the wood from the trunks.

Jacob hoped he would be able to keep his plow. As the heaviest thing he hauled, he would need it when they got their land. No one hauled a cast-iron stove or heavy pieces of furniture anymore. They'd all been abandoned.

The high desert demanded suffering. It might not be a textbook desert, because much of what Jacob had read called it semi-arid, but it came as close to being one as he ever wanted to see. The water barrels were running low, and the livestock showed it. Almost all those with mules lost at least half of them. Jacob could have sold an ox for any amount of money people had, but out here money wasn't needed, and his oxen were. Although he felt selfish, he knew he needed his extra team. He had Faith's well-being to consider.

The hunting had also dried up. The animals seemed to know better than to come to such a place. They were lucky if they saw a few sage hens or rabbits. The coyotes they heard at night probably got most of them. Obadiah said they could eat the rattlesnakes, but most of the emigrants weren't that desperate yet.

The cattle had become hard to control. They could often smell the water from the river, and they'd grown dehydrated and thirsty, but the river wasn't accessible. The number of drovers had to be increased, and those driving the teams had to work harder to keep the oxen on the trail.

"You know why we decided to go west, woman?" Jacob heard Harlan answer a question Lena asked him. "We wanted some good, fertile land, and this is available." He raised his voice in frustration.

"Yeah, well you know we'll pay for it dearly in the long run," she answered. "We might not have to give a lot of money, but mark my words. We'll pay for every inch of that land in toil, sweat, and tears."

"Well, quit your fussing. We've come too far now to turn back."

"Harlan, I think you've got just enough Irish in you to make a mule look cooperative."

Faith walked up beside Jacob. "She's just venting some of her frustrations. Lena doesn't really mean to be so negative. I'm sure she'll snap out of it. She's not usually so pessimistic."

Jacob put his arm loosely around Faith. She had a rare ability to take things as they came and make the best of them. Nothing seemed to get her down.

"Sit down," she told him, "supper's almost ready."

Faith sat quieter than usual during supper, but he guessed the day had been tiring on them all. He looked forward to getting in bed himself.

"I'm beginning to be a little nauseated in the mornings." Faith looked at him carefully.

"Are you getting sick, honey? What do you think's wrong?" She had been so strong on this trip. Was that about to change? Worry gripped him. What could he do to help her? Maybe he should go get Lena.

"This time I think the answer is 'yes' to your unspoken question."

It took a moment before he could make sense out of what she was saying. "You're expecting a child?"

"I think so," she nodded. "I've missed my last monthly, and now I seem to have morning sickness. I threw up this morning after you went to collect the team."

So she knew she couldn't keep the fact from him much longer. He should have known. The desert hardships had caused him to be less observant. His heart fell into his stomach, but he took a deep breath and tried to collect himself.

Hadn't he learned to trust in the Lord for all things? Just because Lucille died in childbirth, it didn't mean Faith would. But, with the worst part of the trip coming up, it'll be hard on any woman, much less one who's expecting a child, a nagging little voice whispered inside him. He tried stuffing that insistent little voice into an inner crock and holding down the lid.

"This journey is rough, and you'll need to take it easy," he told her.

"No, I won't. I'm strong, and, from what I understand, it will be better on me to continue walking and doing my regular chores. Lena says staying active is better than lying around like some women try to do."

"You already told Lena about the baby?" He felt hurt she hadn't told him first.

"No. I wanted you to be the first to know, but Lena and I have talked about birthing in general. No one had ever explained female things to me before. Aunt Mabel only told me about private things as they happened."

Despite what Faith said, he hoped he'd be able to take some of her load and help her more. At least they should be in Portland before she started getting big.

"When do you think the baby will be born?"

"I'm guessing sometime in May or June. It'll be a spring baby, and that should be a good time because the weather will be warming up."

"I'm very happy," he told her, because he knew she needed to hear him say it. "I'm looking forward to being a father." That was true.

"Really? You feel good about this?"

"Yes. I want our baby very much, but I admit I'm still worried about you. Since both of us want children, however, I'm going to do my best to leave this in God's hands and trust in Him. He's kept you safe for me so far, and I believe He will now."

The smile she gave him rivaled the noonday desert sun. When she rose, he did also and gathered her into his arms. The day might still be warm, but a man needed to kiss his wife at a time like this.

Morning sickness hit Faith hard. She couldn't eat or drink anything when they first got up. Frying bacon also made her sick, so Jacob told her he would make himself some coffee, and it would be enough breakfast for him. She disagreed.

She fixed biscuits, pancakes, or corn fritters. She'd serve Jacob but saved hers to eat cold much later in the morning. Dry bread seemed to stay down better than anything else. By noon, she usually felt much better, and she stayed fine for the rest of the day.

Jacob always made sure she went to bed as soon as they finished supper. He knew the nausea left her weaker, the heat exhausted her, and the work of the day drained her strength. At times, he couldn't understand how she managed to stay on her feet. He wanted her to ride more, but she knew the animals were struggling in the heat, and she rarely did.

He took care of the dishes. They no longer needed to milk. The milk cow had gone dry, and the other one barely gave enough for her calf. Jacob felt as if he moved on sheer determination, or maybe it was God's strength. It couldn't be his own.

American Falls announced its presence long before they came to it. The wide waterfalls foamed, sprayed, and slammed loudly down onto a rocky part of the Snake.

Several miles later the Twin Falls made a less noisy splash, but they were unique. Here the Snake River divided into two streams, which curved as it poured over huge rocks into a churning pool below. The twins were not as tall as the American Falls, but they were wider and Jacob thought prettier.

Twins? Could Faith be having twins? Two babies at one birthing might not be so bad, as long as two didn't tax her more. On the second thought, maybe one at a time would be better.

The next falls were even closer, and at Salmon Falls, a small encampment of Indians had salmon to trade. Jacob traded Faith's oldest rifle for enough fresh salmon for three meals and some smoked salmon for later. Some of the others complained about the taste of the salmon, but he and Faith liked it. He smiled to himself. Maybe they just needed Faith to give them some cooking lessons.

They were losing livestock. Some fell due to the heat, minimal grass, lack of water, and exhaustion. Others rushed to drink from a poisonous alkaline pool. One of Jacob's oxen got into the bad water. Jacob and some of the men tried to save him. They forced charred remains from the campfires down his throat and gave him some fresh water, but he became bloated and had so much trouble breathing he finally drew his last breath.

Their milk cow died next from the harsh conditions. Grazing had become sketchy, and the cow had lost so much weight her ribs showed. She just wobbled, shuttered, and fell over one day. Jacob gave her to Obadiah to butcher, and the scout butchered it and gave them back a shoulder and a shank.

They still had Faith's cow and calf. Jacob had babied the calf and taken it in the front of the wagon part of the trip. He thought it had a good chance of making it if its mother kept giving enough milk.

In a region this dry, the wood on the wagon wheels shrank, and the iron rims would roll off like children's old-fashioned hoop toys. After Jacob saw this happen the first time, he tried to pour water over his every chance he got. Of course, he had to wait until they had easy access to water. It was too precious otherwise. He did use any dirty water from washing something, however.

They'd all get to soak their wooden wheels at Three Island Crossing. Others were saying it would be the most dangerous and difficult water crossing in the entire journey. They'd have to cross it, however, if they stopped at Fort Boise, and the northern side of the river would be much more favorable for travel than the dry, dusty, baking southern route. The river might be so deep they'd be forced to remain to the south, but they'd soon know.

Jacob slept little the night before the crossing. Try as he might to leave all his anxieties with God, he found it almost impossible to do. Now he not only had Faith to worry about, but also their baby, and he acutely felt the responsibility to keep his family safe.

He told himself he should be concerned, and it didn't mean he wasn't putting enough trust in God. As he lay beside Faith, who slept soundly, however, he wondered.

The rushing, green waters of Snake River were divided into four channels by three islands. The river spanned wider here, but, due to the islands, each single vein looked narrower than any other place in the river. Obadiah reported that it also ran shallower here. Three times the wagons could rest upon dry land before they continued the crossing.

Eight wagons crossed at a time. Jacob's wagon waited in the second group, which suited him. He watched the first group carefully. A man rode on each side of the lead oxen with ropes to help guide and steady them if necessary. The loose livestock would be driven across last this time.

Jacob's wagon made it across the first part with no difficulty, and his anxiety ebbed a bit. Faith looked over at him and smiled, as they pulled onto the first island. Had she been worried, too? He couldn't tell. He was especially glad they just had the one wagon now.

When Jacob drove his wagon into the second stream of water, he could feel the stronger pull. The first channel bent more as it moved around the widest of the islands, and the bank curved also. This must have slowed the water to some degree. The second crossing appeared to be shorter than the first, however, so with a deep breath, a quick prayer, and intense focus, they made it to the middle island.

This island seemed much longer than the other two, but it wasn't as wide as the first one. Obadiah said it was shaped like a crescent moon, but Jacob didn't know how the scout knew this. Jacob sure couldn't tell. Perhaps there were hills ahead, which would afford such a view.

They didn't always take the most direct route across. Riders went into the river first to determine the best path, according to the depths and currents. The bottom had uneven places with deep holes. Sometimes the team would get off the path, and the riders would have to pull them back.

All the wagons made it to the islands, but the last crossing to the land looked the farthest. It also seemed to have the strongest current.

Jacob saw wagons in the first group wobble and tilt as they limped across the hazardous water. If something were going to happen at the crossing, this would be the time and place.

He felt cold inside as he urged his team forward. His concern grew as the water lapped his wagon ten inches above the bottom of the bed, as if the river wanted to swallow them up. He had to keep the oxen moving. If they tried to stop, they'd be more likely to be swept away.

At one point the wagon swayed so much, Faith had to clutch the seat to keep from falling out. Jacob braced with his feet and legs. He held his breath more than once, but with the help of the two riders, they finally made it. *Thank Thee, Lord, for Thy constant presence. Thank Thee for seeing us safely across this raging river. Continue to protect us as we resume our journey. I pray, in Jesus' name. Amen.*

The first wagon in the last group got into the middle of the channel, tipped onto its side, and hurled down the river. Jacob didn't know them, but he, along with everyone else, watched in stunned silence as the disaster unfolded before their eyes. The only sounds were from the river and those in the wagon, as the oxen bellowed and the people screamed. Rescuers, hoping someone might have been able to make it to shore, tried to find survivors. There were none to be found.

When the last emigrants attempted to cross, one of the wagons looked as if it would wash downriver too, but the driver yelled at his team, the riders pulled, and the wagon made it. All but one had made it across. That night they camped on the north side of the Snake.

Fort Boise lay ahead, and everyone needed some rest, including the animals. Jacob and Faith had only a rooster and three hens left from their chickens, and none of the hens were laying. He hoped the four would make it all the way with them, and they'd be able to rebuild a flock.

Lena said she'd be glad to see Fort Boise. "If we don't soon stop long enough for me to wash and dry clothes, we're going to drown from all the dirt we're carrying on the next crossing."

The clothes weren't the only thing that seemed dirty and stiff. Jacob felt that way himself, and he knew Faith did, too. They weren't as bad off as many of the travelers, however. At least they didn't have oozing boils breaking out all over their skin.

They started traveling well into the night, both to find grazing and to make up some time. Marshall sent boys carrying lanterns out in front of the lead wagon to light the road.

Then, each wagon used a light, and the train could inch its way forward in the darkness. Sometimes a full moon would help light the way like a giant lantern.

According to Obadiah, the fort and Boise River were named from a French word meaning "trees." He said the first trappers were overjoyed to finally see trees again. Jacob could understand that. The terrain looked dismal and bare without them.

The green valley welcomed them after the almost three hundred miles of black rocks and barren desert. And, as an added bonus, rabbits were plentiful and easy to hunt here.

Jacob was glad he and Faith had bought some flour at Fort Hall, because it cost much more at Fort Boise. The Indians around the fort were friendly, however, and had more salmon to trade.

Like Lena, Faith went to wash clothes. Maybe the dust wouldn't be as bad for the rest of the trip, and they could actually feel clean again.

Faith still felt nauseous in the mornings, but it seemed to be wearing off earlier, so maybe her morning sickness would soon subside. Jacob tried to help her as much as possible without being too obvious. She didn't like to be coddled.

Jacob threw caution to the wind, and they went to bathe in the river together. Since there were trees and bushes in spots along the river, he led Faith to a place out of sight from the fort and the wagons. They left on their under clothing, just in case, but it felt wonderful to get in the water, and it refreshed them.

At first, the cold water almost took their breath, but it gave Jacob a reason to hold Faith close. In the end, they laughed and played like children. He could tell Faith's waist had thickened, but she still wasn't showing otherwise.

When they got out and sat in the sun to dry before they put on clean clothes, Jacob felt the most relaxed he had in a good while. Laughter proved to be good medicine.

They only stayed at the fort for one full day. They were about a month from the Dalles, but Marshall felt pushed. He said if they were delayed any, and winter came early in the mountains, it could spell danger. Jacob would like to have remained longer, but he also wanted to get this trip over.

Not far out of Fort Boise, the road started climbing. Once the grade became so steep, one wagon went at a time to prevent skidding accidents affecting more wagons. One wagon lost a box from the cargo shifting, but nothing else happened.

The temperatures also dropped as they climbed. They'd definitely left the red, hot desert behind them, and, by the looks of the mountain-tops, snow lay ahead. At least they now had plenty of trees and firewood.

Jacob looked at the mountainside before him. He stood waiting for the wagon in front of him to climb the steep grade. They were yoking up two teams to each wagon in order to be able to make it up.

Faith sat in their wagon watching. When it became their turn, he'd help her down and she would walk beside him. She knew never to be behind the wagon in case it got away. It hadn't happened to anyone yet going up, but it could. Their progress had slowed, but they inched forward bit by bit. Going down would be almost worse.

It took time to double team the wagons. They had to keep hitching and unhitching the second team. Going down a steep grade, they removed all the oxen and put a pole through the spokes in the wheels to act as brakes and keep the wheels from turning. They tied ropes to the wagon and wrapped them around trees. Then the men would gradually let out the ropes to ease the wagon down the mountain. If they lost their grip or the ropes broke, the wagon would tumble down and crash into a thousand pieces. Jacob saw this happen more than once. In an instant, the family lost every possession they owned. They'd end up walking the rest of the way and eat and sleep at the mercy of their fellow travelers.

After the steep up and down, a band of Indians met them wanting to trade their smoked fish. The Indians they met were usually in small groups and seemed peaceful. Obadiah said they were Cayuse, but the Nez Perce might also be around.

Occasionally the Indians also had venison, pumpkin, corn, potatoes, and peas or beans. The vegetables were even more welcome than the fish, because most of the emigrants had run out of fruits and vegetables long ago. Most liked venison better than the smoked fish, too. The Indians would trade for any type of tool, fabric, or clothing.

Some of the Nez Perce had camas roots. Camas, a type of lily, resembled a small onion but tasted sweeter. The Indians ate theirs raw or ground and made into patties, but most of those in the wagon train just roasted them.

Faith had cooked all their carrots to keep them from becoming too rubbery through the desert, but they still had a few shriveling potatoes, some dried apples, and a little dried pumpkin. Like everyone else, however, dried beans bought by the pound had become their staple.

She made some fried pies from the dried apples that were delicious and Jacob's favorite. He especially enjoyed them at breakfast with his morning coffee. His wagon had been stocked with some spices in Saint Louis, and Faith used them to add extra flavor.

Some of the emigrants were almost completely out of food of any kind. The Parkers had more because they had used the two wagons for half the trip, and they had provisions from both families.

"If I stay well-fed," one man laughed, "I'm going to be naked by the time I get to Oregon City from so much trading with the Indians."

Chapter Twenty-One

MOUNT HOOD

ONE NIGHT JACOB AND FAITH were just finishing supper when a loud commotion sounded from the other side of the camp. Jacob cautioned Faith to stay near their wagon and get inside if need be, picked up his gun, and went to investigate.

The scene astounded him. A huge grizzly lumbered around camp and didn't want to leave.

"Don't shoot it now," Obadiah yelled. "You wound that critter and he's jist gonna git mad and hurt somebody. Hit'll take moren one shot to brang him down. Shoot into the air."

The men did, and the bear stopped, trying to figure out the noise.

"Beat some metal together," Obadiah continued to bark orders. "Yell and make as much noise as you can."

With the noisemakers behind him, Obadiah began to swing his rifle back and forth at the grizzly. The bear gave a mighty growl of annoyance, but he turned and plodded off.

"Guess he decided he wanted his supper cooked and served up tonight instead of doin' his own huntin and fishin'." Obadiah shook his head. "And I guess we jist changed his mind. He probbly come where he smelled the salmon fryin'. Y'all need to be on the lookout for sech unwanted visters."

"Hey, Obadiah," one of the men called. "Where're you from? You almost sound like a Southerner."

"Well now, I've been a mountain man so long I don't know as I can rightly ree-collect, but near as I recall I wuz born in Carolina."

"North or South?"

"Back then it was probably just one," one man joked, and they all laughed.

Jacob hurried back to make sure the grizzly didn't decide to circle around to the quieter side of camp. Grizzlies! One more danger to watch out for.

The wagons had to cross other streams in their westward crawl, but most of them were small and easy, although two of the rivers still presented a challenge. They were headed toward the Columbia where Jacob and Faith would have a decision to make.

"You seem happier, Faith," Jacob commented one morning, "not that you ever seemed unhappy."

"I'm over being sick in the mornings, so I do feel better. It's different, of course, but this land reminds me more of the Kentucky hills I know. I think I'm going to like it in here."

"We haven't had a dance or get-together in a long time," Jacob heard Lena say to Harlan.

"Everyone's too tired," he replied.

How true. Most of the people were using their last stamina to climb the hills and mountains. The animals were still dropping from exhaustion. The temperatures were much cooler, almost too cool, but the steep climbs were still hard.

The Blue Mountains had loomed before them for days. They were dark with evergreen forests and white with snow in places. The Grande Ronde Valley, which nestled between mountains, looked inviting.

"Wonder why some people haven't just stopped here to make their home?" Faith asked.

"I'm not sure. Perhaps they're afraid to settle out here since it's so isolated and there's always danger from Indians."

"I've heard some people talk of going to Oregon City and others to Portland. Which one are you planning to go to?"

"I think they're so close together, it won't matter. I believe settlers came to Oregon City first, but Portland grew up beside it. We can make that decision when the time comes. I just want to get there."

"We're getting close, aren't we?"

"Closer every day."

It rained while they were in the valley, a cold, drenching rain. The muddy mess made everything slick, and the going became miserable and slow. The group lost several more oxen as they strained to pull in the quagmire.

Some of the emigrants cut their wagons in half and made two-wheeled carts, so fewer oxen were needed. The contraptions could even be made so the family could pull it if required.

They hit snow several times, but they were flurries with only light accumulation. As they crested another mountain, the snow thickened and the wind picked up.

"Hit might look bad," Obadiah said, "but I've seed hit much worse. We should git through this without havin' to hold up. That's the important thang."

The cold stung and Jacob worried about Faith. He didn't want her to suffer frostbite. She wore two dresses and a petticoat, besides her other under things and two pairs of stockings. He had her wear a pair of his socks over her stockings, because the only footwear she had were the moccasins. Her other shoes had fallen apart in the rocky, rough walking on the high desert plain. On top of all this, Faith wore her buckskin jacket, a knitted scarf tied around her head, and Lucille's wool cloak with a hood.

He worried about her walking in the slick snow and possibly falling, so when the ground leveled out, he sat her in the wagon with a quilt around her. She alternated between riding and walking, because she said the walking helped warm her. At night, they huddled together under all their covers.

Jacob always got up first and had the fire roaring and the coffee on before Faith got up. She seemed to have mixed feelings about it.

"I really like getting up with you," she said. "You don't need to be waiting on me."

"Yes, I do. I want to take good care of you and our little one. I think it's part of my responsibility as a husband. Besides, I love you and like treating you special. You deserve it."

"I don't know what I've ever done to deserve you as my husband."

"Oh, you deserve much better than me, but I'm glad you're stuck with me anyhow."

"I hope I'm stuck with you for a long, long time."

"We're going to be at the Dalles soon, and we have a big decision to make. I've prayed about it, and it's been on my mind a lot, but I can't decide what's best. We can float down the Columbia River from Dalles to Ft. Vancouver, which isn't too far from Portland. The waters are perilous, but we'd have professionals taking us down. It is rather costly, but we have the money. We couldn't take all our livestock, and we'd have to disassemble our wagon if we took it."

"The other option is to go the Barlow Road. It's a harrowing hundred miles, which crosses the Cascade Range by the south shoulder of Mount Hood at Barlow Pass, follows Camp Creek and Sandy River, and goes on to Oregon City. This trail is going to be rough, mountainous, snowy, and cold."

"If you're asking me my opinion, my first inclination is to take the Barlow Road. We'd just continue with our wagon and teams and not have to rearrange for the river ride. I have no strong feelings, however, so anything you decide will be fine with me."

"If I could see into the future, the decision would be easier. Either choice has dangers. It's hard to know what would be best for us."

"Remember I come from the Appalachian mountains." Faith smiled at Jacob. "Ten to fifteen more days around a mountain doesn't sound all that bad. We could talk with the Haywoods and see what they plan to do."

"That's a good idea. I'd feel better if I knew they were with us. We could help each other."

Lena and Harlan joined the discussion. No one felt strongly about either choice, but in the end, they decided on the land route.

After crossing the John Days and then the Deschutes Rivers, Jacob decided he was glad they weren't planning to go down the Columbia. He wanted to be through with raging rivers.

The Deschutes certainly fit that description. It spread out wide between its banks and had a violent current, but after that crossing, they'd be close to the Dalles.

When the wagons pulled close to the Dalles, the wagons separated. Most of the people were tired and preferred the shorter, eighty-three mile trip down the Columbia where they didn't have to do all the work. However, several didn't have the hundred dollars for the river trip, so they'd go overland. A few planned to build their own ferry from logs and float themselves down. Since they wouldn't be familiar with the river and reports told how dangerous it could be, Jacob thought they were crazy to attempt it.

Seven wagons would be going over Mount Hood. Besides the Parkers and the Haywoods, the preacher and his family, including Kenny, would be among them.

Jacob wanted to get an early start in the morning. Delay now could mean the difference in making it through the pass or not. With Harlan's insistence that they needed a leader, the group elected Jacob as its wagon master. He didn't really want the responsibility, but it'd be only for a few days. He hired Obadiah to guide them the rest of the way. Wayland Marshall planned to travel down the river, and those taking that route wouldn't need a guide.

After breakfast the next morning, Jacob brought everyone together. "This is new to all of us, except Obadiah," he said. "I'm so thankful he agreed to lead us the rest of the way. Let's bow our heads for a word of prayer. Preacher, would you lead us in asking the Lord to guide and bless us?"

Jacob thought he would divide up the extra livestock and tie them to the backs of the wagons, but Kenny volunteered to drive them behind the small train if he could ride Jacob's horse. Jacob agreed since the horse looked to have recovered from the toll the desert had taken on it. For a time, Jacob had feared it wouldn't make it, but it had. He never tried to ride it during those days, and that helped. Kenny looked to be pretty light, so he hoped the horse wouldn't be too burdened.

Most of the others didn't have much stock left. Jacob had the most, but he knew starting with a complete extra team had saved his oxen. Having six, instead of four to pull the wagon also helped. Still, he had lost four and had only eight left of his original twelve.

They'd also managed to keep the one cow and calf alive so far, perhaps a miracle in itself. They still had the rooster and two hens, too. Faith had kept their coop shaded most of the day through the desert, and she wrapped a quilt around their crate at night in the cold of the mountains.

"The first day has gone well," Faith said as they cleaned up the supper dishes. "I heard Obadiah say we've covered almost fifteen miles."

"The first day will usually seem easier, but I'm glad today went well. I'm just praying we don't get stuck on Mount Hood. Obadiah said many had when their wagon broke down or a snowstorm hit."

"I'm glad Obadiah agreed to join us for supper tonight. I like to hear him talk. His speech reminds me some of the mountain dialects in Kentucky."

"I'm glad you thought to invite him, because I don't think I would have. He sure did seem to enjoy your cooking." Jacob paused to consider what Faith had said. "Why don't you talk more like him if the people around you did?"

"Papa always insisted that I know and use proper grammar. He'd helped Mama to correct her speech, and I grew up learning to talk correctly. When I went to live with my aunt and uncle, I made an effort not to pick up their speech patterns. I felt I could honor my parents this way, and I tried to continue my education on my own for the same reason. Of course, I had very limited resources, but I did the best I could with what I had. My aunt and uncle expected me to do so many chores that I rarely found the time to study, but they allowed me to read on Sundays, and I had more time for studying during the winter months."

"You have a better education than most women. Your parents would have been proud of you. I know I am."

"I'd know much more if Papa had lived. He was determined to make a scholar of me, despite the fact that I was female, or maybe because of it. Papa liked to challenge others' prejudices. Both my parents would have loved you. Mama would've especially liked how caring and gentle you are with me, and Papa would appreciate your sharp mind and strength of character."

"Thank you. I wish I could have known them." Did Faith really see all those things in him? Jacob hoped she never became disillusioned. He knew how often he fell short of what God wanted him to be.

The Barlow Road did become harder. Jacob began to realize, not only did they have to go up and down the slopes of Mount Hood, but they also had to cross the rocky, volcanic cliffs where a wagon could easily roll from the ledges.

"Don't you worry none," Obadiah encouraged. "Many a man's made hit o'er this here mountain. Why, before that Barlow fellow did hit, thar wuz Injuns. That's what he done, followed ol' Injun trails to git across."

Devil's Backbone turned out to be the worst place Jacob had ever seen. He could see where it got its name, because the narrow road looked like a giant backbone on a skeleton. He didn't even see how a wagon would fit on it. To make matters worse, a high drop-off loomed on both sides. At least this natural bridge looked relatively level.

Taking a deep breath after a heartfelt prayer, Jacob led his team across first. He walked at their front, leading them slowly across. Faith followed at the rear. Neither of them had room to walk beside the wagon here.

As they crept along, the wheels would throw loose rocks, which would go tumbling down the almost vertical sides, a warning to anyone brave enough to try to cross. It did take courage. Jacob's left him when the rear wheel on one side of their wagon started to slip over the edge, and he could do nothing to stop it. To try to hold or push the wagon from the edge would be foolish. A fall would mean he'd tumble off the ledge and down the deep ravine with the wagon.

He kept the team moving forward at a steady pace and hoped the momentum would pull the wagon where it needed to go. It must have been the right thing to do, because the slipping wheel found the road again, and they continued forward.

"I prayed hard when our wagon started to slide down the cliff," Faith told him after they'd crossed the Devil's Backbone and got to a portion wide enough to walk together again. Jacob smiled at her. He could put a lot of trust in his wife's prayers.

As they neared Barlow Pass, another problem presented itself. The temperature dropped even more, the wind picked up, and heavy, dark clouds began to move in.

Jacob remembered what Obadiah had said about snowstorms in this area and the earlier Donner Party. Although this road hadn't been opened at that time, the wagons in the Donner Party had become stranded in the Cascades from heavy snows which made travel impossible. Most of them died and the survivors had resorted to cannibalism to stay alive. It was an even more frightening story, considering this group's present circumstance. Jacob watched the skies.

"Hit's agonna snow," Obadiah forecasted. "Hain't no doubt about hit."

The questions were "when" and "how much." A whiteout hit right before they got to the pass. The wind swirled the falling snow so that no one could see where to go. They camped on the road leaving enough room between the wagons to build fires. At least this part wasn't so narrow, and that made the situation less threatening. If such a storm had hit on Devil's Backbone, Jacob didn't know how they would have survived. He felt sure they wouldn't have.

The fierce winds made for a rough, cold night. They tied their wagon flaps together and tightened the canvases, but the snow still seeped in. The gusting wind shook the wagon, and Jacob feared some of the canvases would rip apart. Counting the ones in use, he still had three, so he could replace one if he needed to.

He got up and double checked to make sure the tops were securely tied down. He certainly didn't want to completely lose their wagon's covering in this storm. Even if he did have another, it would be a losing battle to replace it in this weather.

The storm raged so fiercely they slept little. Jacob and Faith stayed in bed under heavy covers and shared their bodies' warmth. They held each other close and managed to nap a little, but they lay awake more than they slept.

Jacob worried about what tomorrow would bring. Would they be able to get through the pass, or would it be closed off? What if it remained closed until spring? It could happen, especially if they kept getting more snow at this high elevation.

"We'll get through," Faith told him. Could he now add mind reader to all her other talents?

The morning light revealed a thin layer of snow on the top quilt covering them. It surprised him he wasn't any colder. His body seemed fairly warm, but his feet were cold and his nose felt frozen. The cold air stung as he breathed it into his lungs.

The snow seemed to insulate the mountain in muffled silence. Nothing appeared to be moving about as Jacob climbed from the wagon.

Obadiah had gone out exploring as soon as the light began to push back the darkness. Things didn't look quite as bleak this morning. The snow must have been fine flakes because only about six inches lay on the ground, but drifts were much higher in places. Still, it could've been much worse.

One of Jacob's oxen had run off in the storm, but he decided not to take the time to look for it. He wanted to get off this mountain as soon as possible.

He worried about how the other livestock would fare, too. They couldn't graze here, and no one had any grain for them left.

"The snow's drifted through the pass," Obadiah reported, "but I thank, iffin we've got enough tools, we ken shovel through hit. The back side of the mountain is gonna be slick iffin thar's much snow on hit, but maybe the wind blowed hit offin most the road."

"Should we wrap the animals' legs in strips of wool to help them in the snow?" Jacob asked.

"Iffen hit wuz much worse, I'd say do that, but I'm ahopin' we're gonna be outa this here mess soon. I'd ruther git movin' instead of takin' the time."

The drifts in the pass weren't over waist high in any place, and most of that lay closer to the sides of the cliffs. They only needed to shovel what stood about knee-high. They took turns shoveling the snow, and inched forward as they dug, in case the wind came up again. Jacob found shoveling snow could be a good way to stay warm.

Faith drove their team when Jacob took his turn at shoveling. As it turned out, they got through the pass without too much trouble, but it took time.

"Should we make an early camp or continue on?" Jacob asked Obadiah.

"I'd say the sooner we git down some, the better. When we get offin this here mountain the goin'll be much easier."

They had to shovel only now and then as they descended. The snow seemed more powdery than icy, and that made travel easier, too. When they camped for the night, less than three inches of snow stood around the wagons.

They ran out of the snow the next day, and their speed picked up some. They didn't have to use ropes anchored around trees anywhere, but they did put poles through the wheels to brake the wagons at the steepest places. Once or twice Jacob also had ropes attached to the back of the wagons, and two men would help hold the wagon back. He told them to let go if the situation became dangerous, but he needn't have worried. There were no runaway wagons.

Camping also grew easier as they descended. More open areas for camping and the gradually warming temperatures helped.

With the mountain to their rear, Jacob felt encouraged. The animals could now find some grazing, and the worst of the journey had been left behind. They were getting close to Oregon City now.

He realized it would be hard to leave friends like Obadiah. At least Harlan and Lena planned to stay near Faith and Jacob.

Chapter Twenty-Two

THE WILLAMETTE VALLEY

DESPITE THE FALL SEASON, THE Willamette Valley still looked lush and green. The freezing weather hadn't reached here. What a beautiful sight for the travel-weary settlers to behold! It was the end of October, but they'd made it, and God had blessed them to get over Mount Hood without too many problems. They could have been trapped there.

Oregon City bustled with the new emigrants coming in during the fall. Jacob wished they could have gotten here in early spring, so he could begin planting soon, but that would've been impossible. They wouldn't have been able to travel in the winter without grass for the animals.

Now it would be six months before he could start planting. In the meantime, he'd need to secure their land and build a cabin and barn. He looked over at Faith. They probably both needed to rest up before they jumped into such heavy work as preparing fields and planting, anyway.

Good news awaited them in the city. Congress had just passed the Donation Land Claim of 1850. It enabled every white male citizen eighteen years or older to settle on three hundred and twenty acres in Oregon Territory for free. If the man had married, he and his wife could both claim the acreage. The wife could even own her half in her name, and this would be one of the first laws in the country to allow a woman to own property. This meant Jacob and Faith could claim six hundred and forty acres between them.

Six hundred and forty acres! Why, his father didn't own many more acres than that with the plantation.

Jacob was glad they'd come out this year. The Donation Act would only apply to those filing a claim by December the first. They had made it with only a few weeks to spare. He assumed Congress had meant the act for those already here or almost here and not for those who might leave after they passed it.

Harlan and Jacob rode out and found a pretty piece of property with a good-sized creek running through it. They filed adjacent claims. Other homesteaders in the area, who already had their cabins built, came out and helped them fell the trees and put up the cabins. They'd decided to put their cabins within sight of each other.

"You won't have to rush to get your barns up," they were told. "We have fairly mild winters here."

The house raisings turned out to be a party. The women cooked while the men felled and trimmed trees. Neighboring women brought baked goods, and they helped cook on campfires. The two families were living in their wagons until the cabins were completed.

Faith acted surprised she fit in so well with the women, but Jacob wasn't. Faith had a caring, humble, lovable nature. If anyone ever disliked her, it would be from jealousy.

Although her stomach had begun to round, it still didn't protrude, and she said she felt wonderful. Jacob knew she looked it.

The cabin they built had just one big room, but it had a nice, stone fireplace. Harlan and Jacob built their furniture from stripping cedars. Each cabin had a table, two chairs, and a bed. They were also working on two more chairs and a bench with a back to place in front of the fireplace.

"I know it's not much of a house," he told Faith, "but we can add to it after the spring planting."

"It may not seem like much to you," she said, "but it is nicer than what we had in Kentucky, and I'm happy with it."

If Faith felt happy, then he did, too. God had blessed.

Faith stood in the middle of the cabin and looked around. Her home. Unbelievable. After the wagon, it seemed so spacious and new. She loved the smells of the cedar and pine. She smiled widely as memories of yesterday flooded her.

When they'd seen the Haywoods off to their own nearby cabin, and she'd started back into the cabin, Jacob had scooped her up into his arms and carried her inside. She'd wrapped her arms around his neck and laughed.

"What are you doing?"

"Carrying my wife over the threshold of her new home."

She couldn't protest he might hurt himself. Jacob was strong, and he carried her as if she were no more than a baby.

"I've been in and out of it a hundred times already."

"I know, but this will be our first night in here, and I wanted to welcome you properly."

She snuggled close to his chest and enjoyed the moment. Instead of setting her on the floor, he'd put her on the bed.

"I wish it were better," he said as he sat down beside her and rubbed her hair back from her forehead. "It will be someday soon. You deserve nothing but the best."

He still never understood this was plenty fine to her. Coming from a prosperous plantation background, it was Jacob who saw it as lacking.

"I have the best," she told him. "I have you."

"You definitely have me. I'm glad you see it for the best."

She could read the hurt that flickered across his eyes and knew he thought of Lucille and the fact that his first wife didn't want to be married to him. She reached up and stroked his cheek to erase the bad memories. When his lips covered hers, neither one of them thought of anything else.

Faith wanted Christmas to be special this year. With plenty of evergreens all around them, Jacob cut down a pretty tree. Faith made some fabric ornaments, and she planned on baking some cookie ones, too. Lena had given her suggestions, because Faith's aunt and uncle had never had a Christmas tree. They'd considered it a waste of time. However, Jacob's family had always had one, and he wanted one in their new home. Faith liked that about him, and she enjoyed the tree's scent so much that she had Jacob gather some small boughs for the mantel and window sills. He insisted he didn't want her to do too much, especially outside.

Packages wrapped in feed or flour sacks and cloth sat under the tree waiting to be opened. The Haywoods were coming for the midday meal, and they would open presents then.

Faith had been roasting a large goose on a spit all morning. She'd turned it regularly, and had it far enough above the flames to allow it to cook slowly. They'd been able to buy some potatoes, and Jacob had rigged her up a drip pan to collect some of the juice dripping from the goose, so she could make gravy. With biscuits and a spice cake, they'd have a nice meal.

Faith wished they had more vegetables, but they wouldn't have those until a new garden started to produce. She could hardly wait.

"That tasted too good," Harlan said after the meal, as he pushed back from the table. "I feel stuffed."

"Now it's time to open presents," Lena smiled.

The Haywoods gave Jacob some fruit and nut seedlings. "We brought a few fruit seeds and nuts across and planted them in containers to have to set out in the spring. They're just coming up," Harlan said. This present hadn't been under the tree.

They gave Faith a beautiful quilt top Lena had made prior to starting out from Kentucky. "We'll get together and quilt it when we get some batting, and these men have enough time to make us a quilting frame," Lena told her.

The Parkers gave Lena some cloth to make her a dress, and Jacob had carved an ax handle for Harlan, because he'd broken his. They also promised them several chicks when the hens hatched some eggs, likely in the spring.

Harlan gave Lena some beautiful baskets nestled together, one inside the other. He'd traded for them from the Indians in the area. Lena had made him a shirt.

Faith also gave Jacob a shirt she'd made, plus a new pair of pants. He seemed very pleased.

When she opened her present from Jacob, she clutched it to her chest. He hadn't let her handle it, so she had no idea what the package contained. Inside were not one, but three books: *Oliver Twist* by Charles Dickens, *Twice Told Tales* by Nathaniel Hawthorne, and a diary for her to practice her writing in. She almost cried she was so moved that he'd remembered what she'd said months earlier.

"I have some pen and ink for you, too," he told her.

"Oh, Jacob, I'm speechless. This is too much. I can't believe it. How did you manage?"

"Well, I brought the books with me from Virginia. I hope you don't mind that I've already read them. The journal I managed to find in Oregon City. It's the only one they had."

"You having read the books makes them all the more special. We can discuss them that way. Thank you so much. I can't wait to get started."

"Now let's read about the greatest gift of all," Jacob said, as he reached for his Bible.

The winter passed quickly. Faith had mixed feelings when spring came. She loved the pretty scenery, as everything turned green and blooms burst forth, but she knew she would miss Jacob being in the house as much. She also felt trepidation as well as anticipation at the coming birth of their baby. She thanked God for Lena being nearby.

Faith had planned with Lena to get Jacob out of the house when her labor started. If he wasn't already out in the fields, Lena would have Harlan take him somewhere.

If he hadn't been so apprehensive, she'd have loved to have him there with her, although Lena said that just wasn't done. As her time neared, however, she realized he would likely be experiencing as much pain as she did, just a different kind.

He tried not to show his growing apprehension, but she knew him well now. He feared he would lose her and perhaps their baby, as well. Although she had some nervousness, too, because she didn't know exactly what to expect, she wasn't petrified like Jacob.

She'd tried telling her husband God would be with them no matter what. He agreed, and he tried to trust everything would be fine, but his past always came back to haunt him. She prayed Lucille wouldn't always cast her dark shadow over Jacob. She felt if she could just get him through this one birthing, things would be better.

Dear Lord, please show Jacob Thy faithfulness to Thy children. Help Jacob to not despair through my birthing. Help him to rely on Thee and be his strength, I pray. May everything be normal and may our baby be strong and healthy. Pour out Thy loving mercies, and bless us. I ask these things in Jesus' name. Amen.

Jacob remained so gentle, kind, and helpful. As she got large and awkward, he did more things to unburden her. He made sure she put her feet up, like Lena told her, as her feet and legs began to swell. He tried to do many of her chores, as well as get his fields ready and take care of the animals.

The calf had been weaned, and they were milking the cow now. The hens were setting, so they should have plenty of chickens soon.

This land turned even more beautiful in the springtime. The grass greened, flowers popped out in the fields, and native plants promised a bountiful harvest of berries, fruits, and nuts. This was the nearest thing to the Garden of Eden Jacob or she had ever seen.

Her first labor pains began just as they went to bed. Lena had told her the birthing process would be slow and it would take hours, so she didn't say anything. She hoped she could wait until morning and she could get Jacob out the door first. She knew Lena would be over to check on her after she cleaned up from breakfast.

It became difficult to lie still, however. Knowing Jacob still slept from the sound of his breathing, she eased out of bed.

"What's wrong, darling? Are you all right?" He must have been listening for her, even in his sleep.

"Everything's fine. Go back to sleep."

"What do you need? Let me get it for you. Would you like some water?"

"No. It's just hard to stay in bed, and I need to get up and stretch a bit."

He shot up immediately. He lit the lamp and came to her side. A sharper pain hit and she grimaced.

"Are you in pain? Is it time?"

So much for hiding anything from him. "It might be starting."

"I'll get Lena." His voice shook.

"Not yet. It's not that close, and I don't want her to come over and have to wait so long."

"Shouldn't you lie back down?" He took her elbow to help support her.

"I need to walk some first."

Jacob walked beside her. She could tell he grew more nervous with every step.

"Jacob, please calm down. It makes me tense when you're so nervous."

"I'll try." He sounded apologetic.

"Darling, everything's going to be fine. I'm going to be fine. I'm sure of it."

He stopped and pulled her to him as best he could with her girth. He stood a little to the side of her and held her gently in his arms.

"I love you so much, Faith. Maybe too much."

"I know, but I have a feeling that our love is going to grow even bigger when we hold our child in our arms. Can you imagine it, Jacob? A part of you and me made from our love. I need you to focus on that. You're not going to help me if you fall apart. Let me focus on the birthing and not have to worry about you. Can you do that for me?"

He took a deep breath. "I'd do anything to help you in this, Faith."

About one o'clock the pains became much worse. She told Jacob to go for Lena.

"Let me help you to bed first. I don't want to worry about you falling while I'm gone."

Lena came and pronounced things looked normal. Harlan had come to take Jacob out to the barn.

"Can't I stay here?" he asked.

"You'd just be in the way," Lena told him. "You go on out in the barn and leave this to us women."

"Please, Lena. I need to know what's happening. I promise I won't be a hindrance, but I need to know she's all right minute by minute."

He gazed pleadingly at Lena, and she glanced over at Faith. Faith looked at Jacob and saw the truth in what he'd said. He needed to be beside her or the worry would drive him mad. She nodded.

"You'd better not get in the way," Lena huffed. "This is no place for a man, even if he is the husband."

"I'm going back to the house, then," Harlan said. "Jacob you're welcome to come join me any time if you change your mind."

Jacob just nodded. He went to the kitchen area, picked up a chair, and set it beside Faith's head.

Lena put the second pillow under her head and a folded, extra sheet under her. Then, she busied herself getting things ready.

Jacob picked up her hand and held it in his. When a pain hit, Faith clenched his hand and pulled. He hung onto her.

"That's it, sweetheart, pull on me," he whispered near her ear. "Let me be your strength."

An amazing thing happened, because he did become her strength. He had Lena hand him a damp cloth, and he bathed her face with his right hand, as he held her hand in his left. Between pains, he whispered encouragement. When the pain intensified and she began to groan, he told her to yell, if it would help.

"Do whatever you need, whatever helps," he told her. "Don't worry about upsetting me. Just take care of your needs."

"I'm beginning to see the top of a head," Lena said, "and that's a good sign. It shouldn't be long now."

Jacob smoothed back her hair. "You're doing great, Faith."

About four o'clock in the morning, Faith gave her first mighty scream and baby Parker made his way into the world. He was none too happy with his new environment and let his displeasure be known.

"You have a beautiful, little son," Lena announced.

Lena cleaned the baby, while Jacob moved to sit on the side of the bed and wash Faith's face and neck. She saw him look at the sheet under her, and she knew he checked to see how much blood had come. Then, he looked at her so tenderly, she felt like crying like the baby. He gently kissed her brow.

"See, I was right," she told him in a voice much weaker than she wanted. "Your son and I are both fine."

"Thank you for my son, and for his mother. I am so thankful you were right."

"Here you hold your son," Lena held out the wrapped bundle, "while I see to your wife."

Jacob sat back down in the chair and moved the baby with a gentle swaying motion.

"What are you naming him?" the older woman asked.

"Jonathan," Jacob told her. "It was Faith's father's name."

"You surprised me, Jacob," Lena told him. "You were calm and helpful in here."

"I just wanted to help Faith, and I am learning to trust the Lord more."

"Hallelujah!"

Everything finally grew quiet. Faith had fed Jonathan. Harlan had come to see the baby, and he'd helped Jacob with the necessary chores, while Faith dozed. Lena had cooked a stew and biscuits to have later, when they wanted to eat, and the older couple then left.

Faith lay with Jonathan tucked close to one side. She looked up to see Jacob standing at the foot of the bed watching them. His bright blue eyes were soft and filled with emotion, but he looked exhausted.

"Put Jonathan in his cradle," she told her husband, "and come here." She patted his usual place on the bed.

He shook his head. "You need your rest."

"So do you. Let's take a nap. I'm sure Jonathan won't let us sleep too long."

"You were incredible, Faith," he said as he moved close beside her. "I am so proud of you."

"I could say the same thing about you. You were pretty incredible yourself. I'm glad you were beside me."

"Does that mean I passed the test? Can I stay when another such time comes?"

"You'd better promise me you will. I wouldn't want to go through it without you now that I know how much help you can be. I love you so much, Jacob."

He told her he loved her, whispered just before he gave her a gentle, loving kiss, which reiterated the words.

EPILOGUE

FAITH AND JACOB STOOD ON a rise where they could see the house and fields in the distance. Jacob put his arm around his wife and pulled her close.

"It's changed some in almost nine years, hasn't it?"

"It has. You've worked hard and accomplished a lot."

"We've worked hard." He saw a look of disbelief flicker across her pretty face. "It's true. You've worked just as hard as I have, and I couldn't have done it without you."

"It doesn't seem that way to me. It's been a joy. Having you for a husband has been a joy."

He kissed her then, a slow, passionate kiss. He felt her melt in his arms and marveled she still reacted to him like that.

He felt so blessed. The farm produced well and had from the very start. They had a nice, white clapboard farmhouse and a large barn. The small herds added extra income each year, and the farm animals provided plenty of food.

They heard a faint noise from the house and turned their heads to see Jonathan come running outside with David on his heels. The boys had let the door bang again. No matter how many times they were reminded, they went everywhere in such a rush and doors slammed behind them.

Jonathan, at almost nine years old, thought he could put in a full day's work on the farm, and he almost could. Seven-year-old David tried hard to do anything his older brother did. Thanks to Faith, they both were excellent students as well.

Little Martha made the tiniest speck in the yard, as she came out followed by Lena. Jacob smiled when he saw Marty, as he always did. She thought the sun rose and set with her pa. He'd never realized before how special a daughter could be. He wouldn't mind another one, and the way his wife always responded to him, it was quite likely.

"Do you remember our wedding ten years ago?" Jacob knew she did.

"Who could forget? We'd both just buried family, and Marshall and the council decided it'd be best if we married. I was so afraid of what we were doing, but from prayer and Lena's advice, I hoped for the best."

"Why did you agree? I always thought the arrangement gave me more than it did you."

"I really had nowhere to go after my aunt and uncle died, so that helped make the decision, but I looked into your eyes, and something drew me. I saw a warmth and openness there that I liked."

"Well, God certainly blessed me that day and set me on a path to fulfillment and peace. I feel as if I'm sheltered by love, His love and yours. He also showed me how stupid I'd been to try to keep away from you to protect you. I've learned to trust Him more, and He's always been faithful."

"He always is, but sometimes we fail to see that. And we had to go through almost two wildernesses, didn't we? The trip here reminds me of the Israelites wandering in the wilderness for forty years. Also just like they did, we made our own wilderness when we made things hard for ourselves."

"You mean I made things hard for us when I tried to pull away from you, thinking I was protecting you." He paused. "Do you know how much I love and appreciate you, Faith? I thank God for you many times a day. I never knew I could feel so much love, and, as remarkable as it is, it grows deeper all the time."

"I know. I feel like that, too."

"Well, let's take advantage of this day to ourselves. Let's go back to that secluded spot by the creek you like so much. We can eat our picnic and maybe take a nap."

The inviting look she gave him told him she knew very well they would do more than sleep. *Thank you, dear Lord, for all Thy many showers of blessings.*

As if He wanted to answer Jacob immediately, a warm shower of rain began to fall. Jacob picked Faith up high and spun her around as her laughter bubbled over.

For more information about
Janice Cole Hopkins
&
Through the Wilderness
please visit:

www.JaniceColeHopkins.com
wandrnlady@aol.com
@J_C_Hopkins
www.facebook.com/JaniceColeHopkins

For more information about
AMBASSADOR INTERNATIONAL
please visit:

www.ambassador-international.com
@AmbassadorIntl
www.facebook.com/AmbassadorIntl

If you enjoyed this book, please consider leaving us a review on
Amazon, Goodreads, or our website.

Also By Janice Cole Hopkins

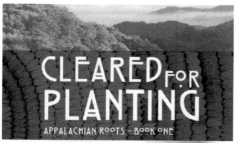

Emma has high hopes when her family moves to the North Carolina mountains. Her father appears to have finally quit drinking, and he plans to settle their family once and for all near the Linville River. Here Emma meets Edgar Moretz, an intelligent, passionate, and godly young man. Things are looking up for her, but when she is captured by a Cherokee raiding party, Emma's problems have just begun.

Years later, Clifton has finally finished his medical training and plans to spend some time at his family's mountain farm until he can decide his next step. He also hopes God will send him a special woman to become his wife. But when she arrives unexpectedly, he finds that the road to happiness is not always smooth.

After the death of their father, Ivy and Leah Morgan are suddenly thrust into unpleasant, arranged marriages by their mother. Ivy, however, has other plans. Having fallen in love with Luke Moretz, Ivy insists upon running away to Luke's farm in the Appalachian Mountains to be far from her home and her mother's demands.

Convincing her sister to come along, the Morgan girls leave with Luke. Along the way, feelings between Ivy and Luke become strained, as Ivy's true personality and distaste for the mountains begin to show. Luke must decide whether to follow his growing attraction to Leah or keep his promise to Ivy. Meanwhile, Leah can't help loving all the things about Luke that her sister seems to dislike.

Mixed emotions and the testing of relationships lead to dangerous and unfortunate circumstances that put any chance of future happiness at risk. Will this journey bring the sisters closer than ever or drive them further apart than they could have ever imagined?

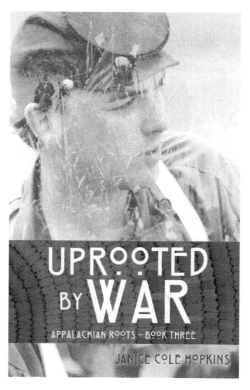

When brother must fight against brother, tragedy and terror become all-too-familiar visitors. The fate of a nation, and a family, hangs in the balance.

It's 1862, and the Civil War has arrived at last in Appalachia. Fearing that he will be drafted by the Confederacy, Luke Moretz leaves his farm and his wife, Leah, behind to join the Union. Although he loves the South, Luke can't abide slavery. However, Luke's brother-in-law and best friend, Lawrence, disagrees and will fight for the Confederacy. How can Luke keep his faith when faced with insurmountable obstacles and horrendous conditions amidst the turmoil of war?

Meanwhile, at their mountain farm, Leah is weighed down with the responsibility of now taking care of the family. Scavengers, raiders, and bushwhackers are always a threat in the Appalachians, but deserters and slave catchers pose new dangers. Hawk, the Cherokee brave who has long loved Emma, helps ease Leah's burdens, but nothing can soothe her heartache. Plagued by fears of a husband lost to war, she knows she must lean on God now more than ever, but hope begins to run scarce in these difficult times.

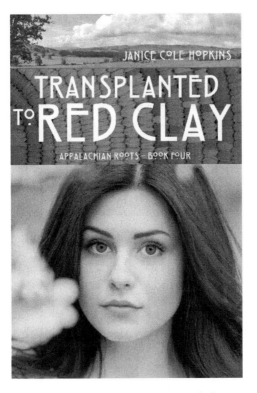

What could be more disorienting than an extended stay with unfamiliar relatives on a farm with no other teenagers? When her Aunt Ivy invites Rachel to come to the family's Stanly County farm, that's exactly the situation Rachel Moretz finds herself in. Although Rachel loves the mountain farm, she feels isolated there, and at sixteen she'd like to have some friends her age. She barely remembers her half-cousin, Patrick, though he seems to have intriguing memories of her. He soon becomes Rachel's best friend, helping her navigate many uncertainties. Rachel's trip down the mountain will bring unexpected friendships, problems, and dangers. She will have to rely on family for support as she faces unexpected trials, with a lesson of forgiveness thrown in for good measure. Through her circumstances, Rachel must come to realize that the best plan for her life is God's plan. In *Transplanted in Red Clay*, the final book in the Appalachian Roots series, the Moretz family's story comes full circle.